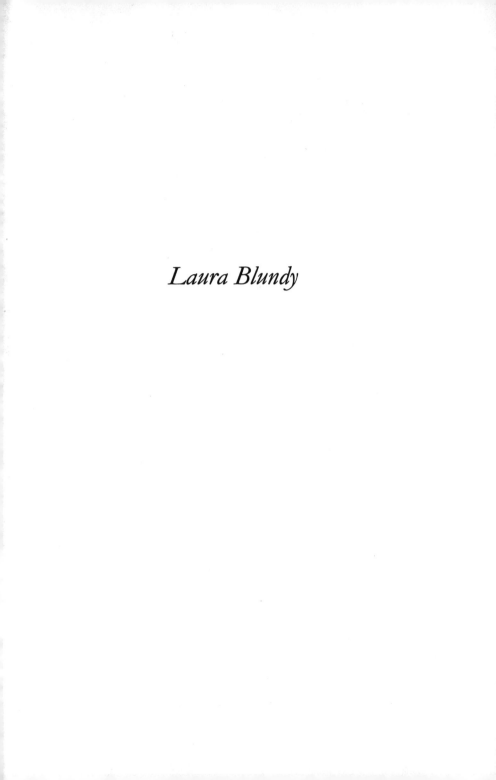

Laura Blundy

Also by Julie Myerson

Sleepwalking
The Touch
Me and the Fat Man

Laura Blundy

JULIE MYERSON

RIVERHEAD BOOKS

a member of Penguin Putnam Inc.

NEW YORK

2000

This is a work of fiction. Names, characters, places, and incidents either are the product of
the author's imagination or are used fictitiously, and any
resemblance to actual persons living or dead, business establishments, events, or locales is
entirely coincidental.

Riverhead Books
a member of
Penguin Putnam Inc.
375 Hudson Street
New York, NY 10014

Copyright © 2000 by Julie Myerson
Previously published in England by Fourth Estate Limited
First American edition published by Riverhead Books, 2000
All rights reserved. This book, or parts thereof, may not
be reproduced in any form without permission.
Published simultaneously in Canada

Library of Congress Cataloging-in-Publication Data

Myerson, Julie
Laura Blundy / Julie Myerson.
p.   cm.
ISBN 1-57322-168-6
1. Married women – England – London – Fiction.   2. London (England) – Fiction.
I. Title
PR6063.Y48 L38   2000   00-038707
823'.914 – dc21

Printed in the United States of America

1   3   5   7   9   10   8   6   4   2

This book is printed on acid-free paper. ∞

For Chloë — writer, daughter, tomboy,
friend — with my love

Laura Blundy

Storm

I do it on a hot and stormy late-summer's afternoon, shortly after the evening post arrives and some time before the lamps are lit.

It's five o'clock and the air is yellow. Thunder shudders through the sky.

It is not done that quickly. Well, he is a big man – five eleven in his stockinged feet – and I am not a hefty woman. It takes several goes. But I have surprise on my side. He never expects it – he can't believe it. Neither can I. In the end I use my crutches as well. I don't stop till he's down and twitching, till he's stopped shouting and screaming, till he's down.

The room flashes. Rain falls – delicate as needles then thick and hard.

I stand there for a few moments, electrified by what I've done. Funny that the dog-weight's still in my hand. I thought I put it down. The crutch is squeezed so tight under my arm that it hurts. Blood runs fast from his head. The air's hot – sweet and sticky. I need the WC. It is bad timing, that I should be coming on the rag just now.

I should go but I can't. Can't take my eyes off him. He should be dead but his nerves don't know it yet. Is that why his eyes are rolling around and his limbs are moving? Not much but a little.

I put the weight down on the table. Carefully so it's still within reach.

Ewan, I say, leaning on my crutch and bending slightly towards him, Are you all right?

I don't expect him to be at all all right, but what else can I say? How do I speak to him?

Ewan? Ewan? Are you?

He doesn't answer. He doesn't even moan. The little movements have stopped and he's the stillest and silentest I've ever known him. He makes my own voice sound too loud.

I should really light the gas but don't want to. The room's so gloomy, drained of colour by the storm, but I think I'd rather not see it any better just now. His body on the kitchen floor – our kitchen floor – the blood running.

Yes, I am glad of the darkness. Look at me shaking, I'm so tired. My brain is tired, so tired.

I can't believe how much blood is coming out. I think I can smell it. That and something else that is not blood.

It's a terrible sight. No one should have to see this. It wouldn't bother him of course, but I'm not like him. I'm not used to seeing inside people. None of this is what I expected. I wish I'd thought to fling something over his face. I could get something. When I get the energy to think.

The storm's still going – banging fit to crack the sky open. Very lucky actually for it drowned out his cries as he fell. But that sobbing now, is it him or is it me? I hope it's me. Hard to say what I'm doing or not doing and that's the truth – one act so tangled in with another.

I am shocked and choked and squiffy. What I will do is I will wipe my fingers on his mother's best linen tablecloth,

2

ha ha, and sit on the settle a moment and think of what to do next.

Peace. I am sitting here in the thick perfect dark, thinking how good it is to be in a silent room. Just the sound of my own breathing.

So many shadows in this room – his mother made it, with her small black cigarettes and her chipping away at everyone's character. It was a bad place while she was here and it is almost as bad with her gone. Bad dead people leave their history behind them. I expect they have their reasons.

Trying to relax, I see with horror that my skirt is entirely splashed with his blood – and then my crutch, the tip of one of my crutches is clotted with his hair and whatnot.

Clutching the mantel and then the table for support, I get myself round the room holding on to the furniture and douse the wooden tip in the big, deep sink, the one where Verity normally does the turnips. Pump the tap. There – a bright slither of his hair going down with a shred of skin attached.

It's gone so quiet – the storm must be moving off now. Now and then a judder of light, a distant crumpy roll of thunder.

The door is open to the pantry, where we struggled. Tins were knocked off, earthenware cracked, a jar of mustard and a half side of ham fell on the floor. Won't be eaten now. Muck and grit embedded in the meat. We fought in there – well, I say fought but he was on his hands and knees. Then he crawled back in here and I had to set on him again.

It is most odd and strange to see him, my husband, on the floor. Like a child or a dog. Hey, Ewan, what's the world look like from down there? I am sorry, my love, I am sorry for the manner of your going, but at least now you can't hurt him. I had to stop you. Some things you don't know how hard you will fight for. And I couldn't have you hurt him, I just couldn't.

Well, I think you know that now.

His name is Billy, but I didn't tell him that.

Don't try to stop me, is what I said, Nothing and nobody will stop me. I'm sorry. I'm going now. I won't be back, Ewan.

He still held on to his newspaper though his face was white. He liked the evening paper. He read it all over from start to finish, then went back to the beginning again to see what he'd missed.

Did you hear me, Ewan?

Where? he said, half smiling as if it was a joke, Where are you going?

To be with someone, I said. Which was very brave of me, to say that – to say someone. I did not think I would do it, but the words came to me – they burst right out of my head.

Ewan folded the paper but he still held on to it.

Oh, he said, crisp and calm as a Sunday school teacher, Who?

A person, I said.

He got the point. The look on his face said it all.

You don't know him, I added, He's someone I met.

Ewan stood up. He came towards me so I moved gently away.

Him?

I nodded.

Laura! he said, You – what are you saying?

I said nothing. My eyes filled with tears. I had told myself not to cry, but now my eyes would not listen. Ewan took heart.

Laura, he said, This is ridiculous. You've gone mad. Despite everything, you know I love you. No one could love you more than I do –

Really, Ewan, I hissed through my tears, Despite everything! Really! Is that supposed to cheer me up?

Slowly and carefully, as if it was made of glass, he put down the paper. Folded his arms.

You can't go, he said. He said it stiffly and without effort. He said it as if it had been decided by someone else.

I said nothing. I watched the shadows creeping into the room – over his head, around the door, around his face. He licked his lips. He was nervous. Look at him, I thought. I've made him nervous.

I won't let you go, he said, You know I won't.

How will you stop me? I asked him gently.

Noting with satisfaction that his hands were shaking, I took a small step away from him. Then a bigger one. More shadows, then a glint of late sun slid into the room, illuminated the wall and dissolved in front of us as if it had never intended to be there at all. Sorry.

Sorry, I said, But it is not what you think.

Oh? said Ewan, And what do I think?

I love him, I said, But for a different reason.

Ewan tilted his head – but rather stiffly – and laughed.

It is, I said and I hesitated, It is to do with my baby.

It's him? Ewan looked shocked, The man who – ?

No, I said quickly, No, of course not.

Who is he?

I'm not saying.

I take it you do mean a man? It is some bloody man we are talking about? One of your workhouse dossers?

No, I said, Not exactly, Ewan. He is working on the new sewers. He is rebuilding the city, you know, making it –

I bit my lip. I had said too much.

Ewan burst out laughing again.

Oh! he said, The sewers, eh? And what's his name, my darling?

I'm not saying. Don't try to make me. There's no point. Someone I've been looking for, who is important to me, that's all.

Ewan pretended to put his head in his hands but it was not from despair. He was just thinking.

I'm sorry, Laura, he said, But let me make something clear. You can't just spring this on me, you can't just run off with some little sewer squit, no way, my love. What I mean is – and he gritted his teeth – you're my bloody wife.

Bloody wife? It sounded like a foreign language, like the one the grey-faced pedlars talk on Saffron Hill.

And I said, Well, I know that, Ewan, of course I do –

Do you want to go back where you came from? he said.

I shrugged.

Laura –

I watched his face. I watched him check the fury in it. He was clever enough to know it would do no good.

Please, he said then without raising his voice – and I know he thought he sounded mild and reasonable – Please, darling, think about what you're doing –

I have thought about it, I said quietly, I have thought of nothing else for a long time.

Ewan sighed, ran his hands through his bright hair. So red. When I first met him I found its brightness unnerving. Now I had learned not to look at it if I could help it.

6

He said: Remember how you were when we met, Laura, when you came to me –

I never came to you, I said quickly.

In the hospital, he insisted, When you were brought in there – I liked you – from the first –

I let my hands fall to my sides.

I was very sad and confused, I said truthfully, I had no choice.

Immediately I regretted my honesty. It was Ewan's fatal talent, wasn't it, squeezing little truths out of you, till the emptiness you were left with took your breath away.

He took strength from my admission.

Exactly, he said.

I mean –

You are not a – how shall I put it? – a level person, Laura, he said, That's why I'm not angrier about this. You are a strange woman – gritty but with a big imagination, much bigger than is good for you –

I tried to interrupt him but he continued.

You have no sense of embarrassment or disgust. You fly into states and you don't know what you're doing –

I don't want any more of your pills, I told him quickly and firmly, I am doing fine without them. For weeks they have gone out with the refuse, so there you are –

Ewan smiled.

I don't believe you, he said.

I shrugged again, but I did not like that he was taking me away from the main point.

I have kept you out of trouble, he said, Haven't I made your life smooth? – Remember, I have seen all of you, Laura. Don't delude yourself. You can't hide from me –

Then let me go, I said, If you know so much, then let me go and so much the better for you – !

7

That's not what I meant, he said and I did not like his eyes when he looked at me.

I was silent. I heard faraway thunder, the first spatter of rain on the dark window.

Ewan stared at the rain as if it would tell him something.

What's his name and who does he work for?

I did not answer.

Who is he? Tell me, Laura. I can easily find it out –

It's nothing to do with you who he is, I screamed at him suddenly.

Ewan did not flinch. Carefully, wearily, as if he knew I was unpredictable and not to be trusted, he replaced his arms back on those of the chair. He let out a breath.

I don't know why you married me, he said slowly.

Neither do I, I replied as lightly as I could.

I loved you, he said, accusing me.

I said nothing.

D'you hear me?

He was sweating. I could see a trickle coming from his sideburn. I tried not to think of it.

Oh, come on, he said. He was trying to smile but his eyes were choked and angry. Again he tried to take my hand but I pulled away smartly.

He cleared his throat.

You'll take nothing, he said, You'll go with nothing –

Fine, I said.

None of your clothes. How will you manage without your fine things?

As I managed before, I said.

Ewan smiled at me.

In the workhouse?

I won't go back in there, I said.

What sort of life will your sewer man provide for you?

I shook my head.

Love isn't like that, Ewan, I said.

Oh, he said, Love is it now? You silly girl, you sound like a bloody Essex kitchen-maid, a bubble-head, can't you hear yourself?

I smiled again – I did not mean to but I could not help it. Thinking of Billy made my heart go hot.

I know you, Ewan said – but there was no trace of love in his voice, only possession and superiority – I know you like no one else –

No, Ewan, I said, but he ignored me. He reached for me, made as if to gather me in his hands as if I was a thing of his. And that's when I knew I would hurt him.

Shut up, I said sharply.

I know all the –

I don't want to hear it –

You go back to your crawlers and dossers if you want, but I'll find you easily and when I do, I won't hurt you – you know that, Laura, don't you, I would never hurt you, but by God I swear I'll hurt him –

Shut up, I said.

If he means so much to you, whoever he is, I'll hurt him so badly he won't want to know you, my darling – let alone (and Ewan laughed again) build a new bloody London –

No! I cried.

It won't be hard to do. Think of who I am and who he is. You think about it, he said.

On the mantel was a very heavy spaniel made of bronze and marble – or at least I think it was marble, a dull, mottled stone, pinkish in colour. It was a gun dog or a hunting dog. It had its ears pricked and something – a dead, fetched thing – was hanging out of its eager mouth. A patient had given it to Ewan as a mark of gratitude. It seemed very funny and unfortunate therefore that I now chose it as the thing to lob into his skull.

Two seconds – maybe three – as he realised. He just had time to shout: Laura, no!

But he certainly didn't have time to duck away before I crashed it into his head.

Laura, no!

It was a great weapon. It was so heavy that it wrenched your arms from their sockets just lifting it. I remember we'd laughed about it at the time, such a leaden, useless thing, in its shot silk presentation bag.

Ewan didn't like ornaments. Most of the unnecessary things in the house were mine. Peacock feathers with their blunt, unseeing eyes, swollen glass beads and trinkets bought at the market. But the dog, well, neither of us liked it much. So ugly, fit for nothing – but now for something.

At the first blow I felt a soft smashing, a caving-in of bone and brain. A slosh of blood came straight out, hit the wall beneath the dado which had just been done in a creamy colour. Jam and cream. I breathed in and the air filled my head and made me giddy.

I laughed or maybe I cried out.

Outside, the storm was going on and getting louder. Rain was falling very hard and heavy, hitting all the lead parapets and guttering. And every time the thunder crashed, the sky lit up.

Ewan was very brave, truly. Apart from that first attempt to discourage me, he did not scream at all.

He just stared at me with his head gushing and then – as if nothing had happened – brought up some more words, except this time they made no sense at all. Laura-no-Laura-no-Laura-no — they spewed out all cock-a-snip, like gibberish.

I did not mean to laugh but I couldn't help it. My head had gone into a different place where good and bad did not exist and there was only this and that. And he looked so funny, falling backwards off his chair — the shock widening his face and a bloody black hole taking the place of his mouth.

Somehow, he got himself up and dragged himself towards the pantry — perhaps hoping to lock himself in there. But I was too quick for him. I dashed across and swung the door back on its hinges and lobbed the bronze animal at him again. Easier this time. I got his face — felt the bone that held his nose in place crunch like sugar.

There was a clatter of enamel dishes, jars falling off the shelves, the earthenware beer smashing. That was when I saw the ham skid, pinkly glossy in the half-light.

Ewan was on the floor and he was crying like a baby animal. It was a snouty, fumbling noise.

I hit him hard with my crutch.

I knew from the very start where Billy lived and how. It was easy to know that he shared some cramped and dingy rooms at Shanklin Court with his skinny, makeshift wife and four babbies.

I knew the wife was named Cally, short for Caroline, and that her and the child Pinny slept in the one wide single bed by the window with the ex-babby Lulu. I knew that Baby Dora lay fretfully next to them in a rickety banana crate cot.

I knew that Billy shared a bed in the next room with Arthur, the only male child since the other died. I knew that was the sleeping arrangement most of the time but if he and Cally fancied a bit of a shag, then they shuffled the babbies around to suit themselves.

I knew what it was to live by the river, for hadn't I spent so many years doing the exact same thing myself? Though I was brought up by my dear father in a good and comfortable home with one servant and glorious views over the Thames and a great deal of books and maps, I had found myself at the age of fifteen on the streets and been drawn to the river for no reason other than that it seemed familiar.

And right until I married Ewan, I lived along its edges in the muck and dull damp, in cottages, rooms, on the steps of the workhouse with the meanest of the crawlers – even, once, under a tarpaulin dragged up on the shingle by the whiting factory near Nash's Yard.

Even when I was imprisoned at Tatum Fields, I was never far from the river's familiar stink. The place was close enough that the laundry rooms were constantly foul and slick with damp and more often than not ankle-deep in thick brown water.

In the Tatum laundry it was a constant battle against damp. You could fumigate the clothes all right, but sometimes you were better leaving them crawling with lice for, once they were soaked with stale water, it was hard to dry them. We had horses for airing – airing? what a joke! – so in the end would resort to flat-ironing them damp and giving them back with the sulphurous steam and odours still coming off them.

I say all this because when you live by the river, it is a certain style of life, a constant consideration. You are well acquainted with how the moisture clings to your face and hair regardless of the season, how the buildings lean so close in together that they coax the alley below into permanent shadow. How in winter there is flooding and in summer there is the big stink and then of course the cholera that floats into your chest, borne on the wind from all that filthy air.

They said that the structure that Billy was working on would save us from all that, though it has to be said that even B. himself did not exactly see how. They said that when it was finished you would not recognise London – and it would be goodbye to turds floating on the river and there would be salmon to catch again off London Bridge in its startled blue waters.

Well, I did not know about that, but meanwhile it was so damp and cessy at Billy's place that the whole family had to walk on bricks to reach the privy in the yard, for there was so much waste and overflow slopping about your ankles. This was not helped by his downstairs neighbour, the red-faced and rambunctious Mrs Reeves who, not being communally-minded, never bothered to so much as replace the candle in the shared convenience, so that Billy's littl'uns – having managed to teeter across the bricks – frequently ended by falling in the privy.

I know also that the said Mrs R. scrubbed the doorstep with ochre and then had a great old moan if any of the kiddies trampled it through. And that her own, solitary, female child sat forlornly on countless other doorsteps while her mother entirely forgot her in her hurry to go around poking her fingers into everybody else's pies.

I knew that Billy loved all his kids with a big, sweeping passion, but that he still had a sudden temper and could not stop himself knocking them about. I knew they had bruises in various stages of ripeness all over their small sweet faces. And that he was full of shame about this fact.

But he had a lot to put up with. I knew that Arthur was born with a potato for a brain and that he mostly just slumped in his chair or had to be tied in for his limbs went all jerky otherwise.

I knew that he had unexpected skills all the same – that he smiled at three weeks old and at two years could roll a ha'penny into an empty jar from three feet and that he could tell when the big girl Pinny had rounded the corner of the next street just by sniffing at the moist and tetchy air.

I understood that last January he fell down the backstairs and lost his speech for a while. And that these days he was mostly tied to the bed or the chair while his mother did a wash or fetched water for the copper. And that this was the reason for the soreness of his wrists and ankles, since he always worked hard to undo his bonds.

I knew more about Billy's children for I had made it my business to find out. I knew that his favourite boy Jack died one night of a chill on his chest and that he was only three years old and loved horses so much that he'd wait at the window for hours just to watch the night soil man go past. And that he had his own little rag thing – a wisp of a toy bought off a pedlar on Lambeth Walk – that he called hoss. And his favourite thing at night was to suck his thumb and stick a piece of hoss up his nose at the same time.

I knew that Lulu, the ex-babby, was a frantic and con-sumed little person – three years old now, the same age as Jack when they lost him and bearing this burden stoically. I knew that all she wanted in the world was to be the same as the others – as big and free and lively. I knew she spoke her first words at one year old but no one noticed. And that she could clap along merrily to a tune and was dry at night, but liked to cry and throw tantrums and was generally thought to be a delicate and peevish child.

But the fact about Billy's family that caused me the greatest and jealousest pain was this: that he had a particular and unfathomably deep and gentle love for the oldest — the one that was not even his.

This was the girl Pinny who, if he hit the babbies, would not speak to him, and this was what made him sorry and kept him in check. She was pure woman in the making, that one. She had the pull over him and could wrap him around her little finger. She knew all the delicate things you were supposed to take years learning and even then, in company, were best off hesitating to admit you knew.

I also knew that, though he would have maintained that he was quite satisfied with his life, Billy often lay alone and restlessly sad in the sour dawn light, tasting the four o'clock tang of bacon smoke from Shanklin Court and knowing there was no more sleep to be had.

I knew he lay there waiting, knowing that in another ten minutes the dog stealer would go, banging the back gate after him. And that soon after the church clock would strike the five, then the quarter, then the half. And I knew that, once he considered it all pretty barren and hopeless, he'd rouse himself and settle on the sill for a sullen, thoughtful smoke of the dib he'd left from the night before.

All the babbies still asleep, thank God.

And early wind would carry the foul smells of the tide turning at the foot of the lane which led to the cottages. Flood odour, too, was always very marked down there — doused paper, brick, flesh. And soon men would come from every door, stopping a moment in doorways to light their fags, before passing fast out of sight.

And I knew that my Billy would watch the sky flush

crimson and maybe notice the sound of Lainy Sampson's canary starting up, spiking the general birdsong. Then he'd hear the Dalley infant add its shrill twopenn'worth and he'd know that was it: morning.

I had never been to Billy's or met a single one of them except in my dreams. I just knew all of this, I just did.

Well, Ewan is dead, certainly. He is bleeding from lots of places and he does not move.

There is a dull pain in my stomach. I am ever so dry-mouthed and would kill for a soda. When you are thirsty that is all there is, no other sensation matters. All I want is to feel the sharp bubbles dancing on my tongue.

A great deal of dust has been dislodged in the fight – proof that Verity has, just as I thought, been doing a very half-hearted job for weeks. Big burbles of fluff are set in motion by my skirts as I travel swiftly across the rug to the door and leave the room.

Something, a dicky, cobwebby feeling around the back of my neck, makes me lock it. I pocket the big clunky key and climb the stairs one at a time, convinced that the most pressing thing to do is change my clothes. I am always changing my clothes – in my new life, since I had clothes, I have done it a lot – but now it is essential. The smell of him is on me and I must get it off.

In the dressing-room glass I see that I am splashed with his blood as he must once have been splashed with mine. Spots of it across my forehead and even in my hair. I find a pocket handkerchief to spit on and get most of it off. Stuff it in the big pine drawer, beneath his own ties and leather tabs and cedary man-things.

After going to the WC and finding I am indeed on the rag, I make my way slowly down the stairs, crutches thudding once on each worn-out step. In the hall, I pause, listen, but there is only the humdrum ticking that I would expect. I take my cloak and am about to leave when a sudden worry gets me. Shouldn't I close the shutters in the kitchen where he lies?

So I unlock the door again and go across in the half-darkness. The window-pane is black, flecked with rain, they haven't lit the gas yet. That's what I'm worrying over, the moment when the man comes to light the lamps.

I don't want him found today.

I do it and start back. I thought I gave his body a wide berth, but I can't have, for there is a sudden, bubbly sigh and a hand grabs my ankle. I scream and in the panic I drop both crutches – my hands fly to the mantel for support.

I thought, after how many times I hit him, he would be dead. I was so certain of it. How can his fingers still be moving? How can his brain still be making plans?

I am screaming and clinging to the mantel, standing here on my one leg which is captured and I am unable even to give him a swift kick. I must not lose my balance, I must not fall. How he moans – again and again, moaning, clawing at me. Blindly, I feel around for the poker – the one which was there when Verity left it this morning.

Got it.

Holding my breath, one hand still on the mantel, I use it to feel for the outline of his face and then I shift it across, lean hard on it and dig it in like a gardener does.

A definite juicy crunch, like going into raw potato. Another sigh, a rushy liquid sound. I am faintly surprised to feel my face wet with tears. As the seconds fall away, so do his fingers and my ankle is released. He does not move again.

Now the silence in the room is deathly and the taste in my mouth is ashes. I lower myself to the floor and crawl as fast as I can back towards my crutches.

Men are very hard indeed to manage. Even if you offer your whole self up on a plate to one of them, still he will dawdle and prevaricate and find a reason to say that what you are offering is not quite right.

So I go to Billy. I tell him that Ewan is out of the picture and now we must skedaddle as fast as possible to France.

He stares at me and scratches his head and then his groin. He looks extremely bothered, yet does not ask me any questions. Then he kisses me long and deep and I feel him shiver into life down there. Then he says that his family needs him.

I am your family, I tell him stoutly. And I kiss him again.

He draws back. Looks at me.

No, he says, You know what I mean –

He does not know what I mean but I do not enlighten him.

You are mine, I tell him, I love you and we must be together –

Christ, Laura, he says, Don't look at me like that –

Why not?

You're putting me off with your strange face – I love you too –

But – ?

But what?

You tell me, Billy. Sounds like there's a but coming –

He bends his head. Poor lad. He is a noodle, stumbling around for reasons. I could eat him whole, but I won't.

I don't know, he says, I don't know what to say. I mean, I thought –

What? What did you think?

That we'd got ourselves clear on this. I thought you understood. About me and Cally, the kids –

Oh, I say rather sharply, Forgive me, Billy, of course, I had forgot –

He looks at me warily, checking. His look says it all.

Do you understand what I have done? I ask him.

Silence from him.

Do you?

It is only now, as I say it, that I realise how tired I am. My eyes are dry and hard in their sockets, my teeth sinking so far down in my head. I am wiped out with it.

Billy says nothing. Stares at me. He has the neatest face of anyone I've ever known, especially when he's worried or confused. Wide, roguish eyes. Cheekbones and dimples that make everyone else's faces look dreary and flat. He is glorious, a perfect specimen. I am so gone on him.

So I tell him the whole thing – what I have just done, though I never meant to, and what it means for us. Yes, for us, Billy. I spell it out, in case he still does not understand. He is a young boy, after all, twenty-three is no great age. So I tell it slowly. I am careful to leave nothing out. I even tell him the bad bit at the end with the ankle and the kitchen poker. But a happy ending, nevertheless.

I feel suddenly lifted by the thought.

I did it for you, I tell him, pressing my deed on him, freshly done. For now the thing feels oddly like a gift – something carried a long time scrunched in the palm of my hand, and then released into the world, unravelling.

Maybe I expect him to be angry now. Or at least, let's say I wouldn't blame him, for the lad has a good heart and would not willingly hurt anyone. (I hesitate to say 'a fly' for actually I believe we would all kill a fly, would we not?)

But no, not anger. That's not it at all. He seems instead almost to struggle for breath. I wait.

Well?

He says nothing.

Speak to me, Bill –

Laura! he gasps, Please. Tell me it's not true!

Now I burst into tears.

I thought I was your family, Billy, I say again, bitterly this time. All I want in the world – I am sobbing now – All I want is to belong to you –

He does not hold me or kiss me. He says nothing.

Here it is, though. Here is his face containing all the grief and shock and pain I have been waiting for.

Street

My name is Laura Blundy and Ewan was the man who took off my leg.

The cab ran me down on the Wednesday. It was at ten o'clock, in the street. I had spent the night dossing on the steps, I believe, but I forget where I was going or what I was going to do.

At first I did not know how serious it was. I had pain, but not as much as you would think. I remember my blood all over the cobbles. I think I peed myself and remember feeling upset about it. I remember knowing where I was, but not really feeling myself to be there.

I saw and heard things. I know that someone shouted at the cab to stop, but it did not. I remember hooves ringing on the stone and some birds scattering.

My head was on the ground. I held on to my blanket – the faded wool scrap that I never let out of my sight. The closest thing was a pigeon pecking at the dirt and also, not so far away, an old bloke was sat perched on a crooked stool at the side of the road mending umbrellas. He was dressed as a clown – a high hat and pink on his cheeks. The brollies I remember thinking were all dead tatty.

I think it was him that ran to get someone. Actually I'm sure it was for I remember his work all lying there in a pile with no one tending to it. All in tatters and disregarded.

Well, anyway, I was taken to the hospital.

Late that night, I don't know how late, a surgeon was brought to my bed.

Quite a young man. Bright red hair, a carrot-nob. Even his beard was little dots of hotness exploding through the skin.

Are you a gypsy? I whispered to his eager face, Such amazing hair, look at you!

He laughed.

Goodness, he said, I reckon I should ask the same of you.

Why?

Well, yours is so black –

Well, I said, All I can say is I've only seen hawkers with hair your colour.

Come off it, he said.

I mean it!

Shh, he said, If the nurses see us chatting like this I'll be out of a job –

What? I teased him, Are the nurses in charge of you then? I didn't know the doctors were answerable to the nurses –

He laughed.

I'm not a doctor, he said, I'm a surgeon.

I gasped.

You're not going to cut me?

Well, I very much hope not.

He felt me up. Felt my face, my pulse, my legs and arms which'd had the clothes ripped off them with a nurse's little sharp knife. His touch was nervy, as if something was wound up inside him and making him jumpy. Funny thing was it made me jumpy too and, straightaway, I began to cry.

What is it now? he asked me gently.

I don't know.

Are you in pain?

Some pain, yes.

He smiled and I liked his smile. It was quick and unadorned like the ones you see on happy children.

I can give you something, he said then.

What sort of something?

Something good – something that will make a difference –

Hmm, what is it? I asked him.

You'll like it. It's just a little pill but it will make all the difference. I am a master of pills and potions.

But what is it? I demanded to know, though I was intrigued, I don't trust you. It might be anything.

You can trust me, he said.

How do I know that?

You're very wary, he observed.

Of course I am, I cried.

It's not poison, he said solemnly.

What then?

A pain lessener, a muscle undoer. It'll make you sleep and you need to sleep for I can tell you the pain will not get better as the night goes on, but worse –

Oh, but I don't want to go to sleep, I said quickly.

Why not? he said.

I am quite used to pain, I told him.

He looked at me so hard then that a single gingery lock of hair flopped down.

Why don't you want to go to sleep?

I don't especially like it, I said.

He looked at me.

But you must sleep. When do you sleep?

As little as I can, I told him, It is too dark. I always wake in a panic – I mean it –

He touched my arm.

I have to examine you now, he said.

I shrugged.

With one hand pressing on my thigh, he put something cold on the wound. The truth was it had gone past hurting to the point where I could hardly feel it. I closed my eyes. The pus stank. It did not hurt but I began to sob again.

There now, he said and then he leaned in close and sly and quickly pressed something over my mouth.

Instantly, the pain flew up out of my body and the world went black. When I woke I felt displaced, as if I'd lost something. I began to vomit.

He apologised and I guess someone ran for a rag and a bowl for the next thing I knew I was staring at the cracked white porcelain. Sweat breaking out all over my head.

Sorry, he said, That was too much.

What?

I gave you too much. Chloroform. My fault. Forgive me. It's hard to judge sometimes.

Did I sleep?

For a moment or two, yes – but it didn't suit you. I only meant to give you the smallest whiff –

It was good, I said, I'll have some more.

He smiled.

Not yet, he said, You can't have it yet. Later.

I was beginning to like him, this doctor, and I told him so.

Ah, sadly that's the medicine talking, he said, Pain relief – all kind of effects – I have other things – pills and tinctures to change your mood entirely –

How d'you mean? I asked him.

Ah, well. Pills to make you balanced. Pills to make you happy –

I'd like one of those, I told him.

He laughed.

So does everyone, he said, They are very popular, my uplifting pills.

What I meant to say, I told him, Was that you're kind. Or you seem so to me.

All medical men try to be kind, he replied.

I mean you're – handsome.

I giggled. The words were tumbling out so fast now that I had no chance to see them before I spoke them.

Oh dear, he said, You see? That's the drug. Now I'm feeling mortified –

For me?

No, for me.

I asked him what he meant by that, but he wouldn't tell me.

Do you have pills to make people die? I asked him and he looked at me and when he saw I was serious, he blinked and said no.

Why? he said.

No reason really –

Have you ever wanted to die?

Well, I said, A long time ago I have.

Not any more?

I thought about it.

Not any more, no.

How old are you? he asked me then, bending over my leg because despite the lamp the shadows were thick in the room.

None of your business, I heard myself say.

Twenty-six? Twenty-seven?

Oh, for heaven's sake, I said dreamily.

How old then?

Much older than you think – a woman well into middle age and much too old for you.

I yawned as the pain floated up again. He kept his head down.

I don't believe you, he said.

My age? It's the truth.

No, I don't believe that you're too old for me.

Now he was messing with me. I smiled.

And how long have you lived like this? he asked me as he shot his cuffs back down and moved the lamp and glanced towards where my petticoat was all rucked up and wayward.

Like how?

You know, like this. Dossing around, without a roof over your head –

Oh, I am fine, I said, It is fine and sufficient for me. I don't go in the kip much, I make my own way. I am in work, you see, minding the babbies while the mothers go off and work –

He looked at me curiously.

But you weren't born to it –

I hesitated.

No. No I wasn't. Circumstances put me here a long time ago –

And you like children?

I thought about this.

Yes and no, sir, I said, I am used to the little squits.

He looked at me carefully then and, because I've never been modest or even cared to be, I met his stare. In fact I did a great job of keeping my two eyes on him and he looked away first.

26

Why are you suddenly calling me sir? he said turning back to his work on my leg.

I have just remembered you are a doctor.

I'm not a doctor –

Oh, a surgeon then.

He laughed. He was not good-looking. Too gingery and he had no eyelashes. And, though he was probably not much past thirty-five, he had the look of Mr Punch, all swarmy and hooky and sad. And yet I felt shy of him and I wondered why.

So anyway, will I die? I asked him as casual as I could.

He said nothing. Rolled down his sleeves.

No, he said, Of course you won't. It's not a nice fracture and I wouldn't wish it on anyone, but nine times out of ten, they mend perfectly well. You'll use those legs of yours again.

I stared at him. He stared back at me.

You're lovely, he said, Do you mind me saying that?

I closed my eyes.

Please don't call me sir, he said – and as he said it his voice trembled oddly like a little child's.

I shrugged and opened my eyes.

Is there anything you need? he said.

I asked if he could bring me some water. Or better still, a nice cold soda. He said he would do his very best.

That would have been the time to die – straight after an accident. Logical, forgivable. You could not possibly be made to take the blame. You would have to say it was all in God's plan.

But, though the wheels of a clarence cab are made of iron, and though a woman's bones are crushed like eggshell beneath them, still when God decides to pull you through, he pulls you through.

It is funny how the pious give thanks in the church and say it is amazing what you can survive. I say that's rubbish. I am always amazed at how hard it is to die.

But it was a bad wound all right. Slivers of bone pricking up through the skin – and a mass of pus and blood and a grey liverish substance that I couldn't look at. No one ought to have to look inside their own body. Skin is what makes us bearable – to ourselves and to the rest of the world.

On the way to the hospital everything was coming at me through a mesh of red: sky, clouds, chimneys, everything pulsing scarlet. I put my hand down once and felt myself and it came up wet. I did not do it again.

It was very interesting to lie in a bed again. I had not done it in such a long time. The pallet at the prison scarcely counted as a bed for it was not supposed to give you any repose. This one though had a mattress and took me back to the soft bed of my childhood – the little high-up feather bed by the window where my father let me have the candle to go to sleep and only blew it out for me when he came up.

That bed smelled of soft soap flakes and the piles of books I liked to keep by it and read under the sheets in summer when the sun flooded in at bedtime. My father approved of books – pushed them on me even – but he would not have approved of my ruining my eyes. I don't think my eyes are ruined. And the rest of me? Hard to say, I don't know.

The hospital bed did not smell of soap flakes, but of dust and pee and perspiration. They gave me broth to drink, only I gagged on the third mouthful, puked it up over the bodice of my only good dress – or to tell the truth, my only dress. But this time the sick was no more than water – so little substance that it glittered as it caught the light.

Will you look at that! I exclaimed.

And the nurse burst out laughing, loud and snorty like a horse. She had good strong teeth, but she was not getting married in a hurry, that one.

I was thirty-eight, getting on for thirty-nine, but my hair I am glad to say was mostly black and the teeth I had left still had their whiteness and though my waist measured a little more now than the curved gap of two men's hands, I still had a lot of my young girl's punch.

And I did used to be a girl with punch. It is lucky my father died before he knew of my condition for it would have broken his heart.

All that education, he'd have said and, though he wouldn't have thrown me out, I know that, still he'd have pressed me to get rid of it. He had ambitions for me. He did not even want me to take over his shop. He said I was beautiful, a real bobby-dazzler. He wanted me to travel and see the world as he had not managed to do.

In his shop at number 318 Westbury Street, he sat me on a high stool behind the black oak counter and gave me weights and measures to play with to keep me quiet. I loved the solid cold brass in my palm. Stacking the weights in order of size. Filling the brass pan with as much rice as would make it tip.

One day my father stacked four weights on the one side and put a bag of sugar in the pan. It see-sawed up and down and then it came slowly to rest, floating.

See that, Lols? he said, That's what you weighed when I held you for the first time –

And he laughed and kissed the top of my head and told me I was his best and dearest girl. He loved me even though my coming into the world had killed my mother. I always thought, weighing it up, that it was an especially heartbreaking deal, to gain a daughter only in order to lose a wife, but he never held it against me – quite the reverse.

He was father and mother to me. He protected me. He hid the bad things and celebrated the good. That's why I never knew the business had gone so bad until it was too late. After my father died and I discovered my aunt had left everything to the Catholics, I found myself on the streets.

And, after losing my own child, many years of minding those of others. I did well for I was fit – fit and tough. I was not really a crawler. I could walk all day, all weathers, with a new, red-faced infant slung on my back. I could take two if necessary.

And then the accident. It takes strength and spirit, running after the bigger blighters, and my immediate concern was that this disaster would put me out of work. Then I would certainly starve. Minders were always in demand, but how would I earn a crust if I couldn't carry the babbies around with me any more?

Will I mend all right? I asked the doctor with the red hair and all he could say was, Probably.

He told me his name was Ewan. Ewan Lockhart.

When you meet the people who will be your fate, don't you always wish you'd looked and listened harder? Trawled for the clues which might have helped you manage them later?

I liked Ewan, but I barely thought anything of him. He was just the surgeon. I did not know that one day I would be sitting with him in a strange room with his hands well up my skirt and my boot undone and me puffing half-heartedly on a cigarette as he took me on a tour of the bits of myself that he intended to make a habit of visiting.

The future flies in our faces. Out of the window is the Channel – grey and flat – which I'm told leads to France. I have no idea of France, just as I have no idea of the future.

But I am an optimistic person. I have my father to thank for that. That is why I said yes straightaway to a trip to the coast with Ewan.

You are an ignoramus, he told me fondly, as his two-day beard bristled along the inside of my thigh, You are absolutely wonderful actually. Why do you never wear any stockings? Let's get married, go on, then you can meet my mother.

I knew about his mother. She was called Eve. She was half-foreign and had come originally from a hot place where lemons grew on trees. Maybe it was this that had made her sour and bad-tempered, for she had married a Scot and come to live in the cold and the damp and never ceased to complain about it. She said that was it: lovestruck and she was never warm again, though her husband meanwhile – Ewan's father – burned up ironically with a fever and died.

She lived in Ewan's house, somewhere near the top and ate raw liver and ginger to ward off the cold and rattled a tin of barley sugar when she wanted someone to come and do something for her. Her view was of chimneys and spires. Twice a day she could hear the children running and shouting at the Ragged School. The rest of the time, silence.

She sat all day in a stiff chair and waited for him, her son, to climb the stairs and see her. When he did – he always did – she went to great lengths to explain to him that he was stupid and worthless. He believed her.

I blew smoke out, dabbed a fleck of tobacco off my tongue.

She'll hate me, I said, You know she will. She'll say who is this cripple? And by the way, I never ever wore stockings even when I had both my legs.

Why not?

I can't afford them. And I like to feel the air.

Then Ewan said quietly: You'll be a lady. You'll be my wife. We'll marry first. Secretly.

Oh. That'll please her.

Didn't you hear what I said? Ewan cried – for he was thinking I had not understood his generous proposal.

What?

I'm asking you to marry me.

I can't save you from your frigging mother, I told him, for by then I was quite used to being cruel to Ewan.

Laura, he said, Mind your language! And that's not what this is about, not at all.

Ewan had lived with his mother all his life and never introduced a woman to her and now it was too late. I suspected I had been picked as his blunt instrument, his mother-bludgeon.

I stroked his hair.

She'll say: oh dear, what I had in mind for my son wasn't this, but a nice two-legged woman –

So? he said, smiling, I'll tell her it was I removed your leg.

Oh, I said bleakly, That'll go down well.

By the Saturday, my calf was turning black, oozing a yellow-ish pus that smelled of bad sweetness, like rotting peonies in the market after the rain has squidged them to a pulp.

My tongue had fur. I could hear the dry sound of my saliva, taste the roughness of my teeth.

Now Ewan was bothered.

He talked over my head to the nurses. He frowned. He gripped my wrist and checked his watch and I heard him say something about a compound laceration.

What's a compound laceration? I asked him.

He touched my cheek.

Nothing, he said, Don't you bother yourself.

My pulse was small and my leg hot. They laid it on a pillow and dosed me with tincture. I closed my eyes and held my blanket against my breast. I could not look at where the splinters of bone stuck out. It was bitterly aggravating, having my skirts hoiked up all the time. I wished I had a nightdress, decent drawers. He saw my bare legs.

I was very conscious of this, very aware of him looking at them. The throbbing, darkening one and the normal one. I especially wished he did not have to see the coarse hairs on the inside of my thighs or the silvery zigzags that came when I had the child in me.

I am ugly, I told him as the hours ticked by – and he looked at me strangely, as if he knew something I did not.

I am going to give you a pill, he said and I did not argue.

I did not argue but I puked so much I must have brought it up. So he ordered that they stop giving me the tincture and stick to boiled water. He jotted some notes for the nurse and I remember how he turned to blink his pale eyes at me once or twice.

By that night I seemed to improve. I was given some sips of red wine which I kept down.

But then something awful happened. The nurse tried to take my blanket from me. I think she thought it was just some old rag.

Oh no, I cried so loudly that it made her jump, Give that back immediately, it's mine –

What is it? – you could see her turning her nose up at the grubby piece of cloth.

It's mine, I said again, It is my best thing and I won't give it up. It was my child's blanket.

Well, it is a health hazard, she said, It wants fumigating.

Never, I replied, Over my dead body. It is the cleanest, sweetest thing in this place.

The nurse said nothing.

I won't be parted from it, I said again.

The nurse shrugged.

It may be over your dead body, she said.

I did not listen. I pretended not to hear. I held the blanket to my face and breathed it in.

Later I asked the nurses did they know what street it was, where I was run down?

Oh, it was Union Street, they said, At the junction with Bird Lane, why don't you remember?

Of course I remember, I said, I just wanted to check that's all.

But I had no memory of it at all. None. All I had was a wobbly dream in my head of an old man mending brollies but even that was fading fast.

Am I improving? I asked them, for I hadn't seen Ewan for several hours and I wondered whether he would not come again.

We believe so, they said – but I noticed that they all immediately looked at each other, not at me. As if the answer had been plucked at random from the air and might fly back up again at any moment without warning.

But by the Sunday more matter was oozing from the leg and the fever was really high, burning me up.

I slept a bit, drifting in and out of a place where crowds of faceless folk I'd never seen in my life were gathered. And then later on, some I'd seen and knew shouldn't be there.

My elbows and arms were fizzy with not being used. The light was strange. I couldn't tell if it was morning or the different yellow of just before they light the lamps.

Then something changed. There was a click somewhere in my head and I felt a strange, floating lightness.

Oh, good, I heard myself saying.

Immediately the nurse – the one who'd tried to nab my blanket – came rushing over, panting, pinning her hair, great sweat stains under her arms.

What? she cried, What did you say? What is it?

Oh, it's all right, I told her, making sure the blanket was safe in my arms, Really – it's just that the pain has all of a sudden upped and gone –

But she didn't look very happy at all. Not one bit. She clamped her teeth down on her lip.

I am to fetch the doctor, she said and turned on her heel.

Ewan came and pushed up my skirts again for a better look. I was getting used to it, though this time I noticed that the edges of my petticoat were all stained with brown stuff and I flushed despite myself.

Much better, I told him when he asked what I was feeling, Quite recovered in fact. I don't feel a single thing –

But he didn't look at all pleased either. He wiped his hands on his coat, but he did not look at me. Next to his hair his skin was very pale and I noticed some tiny freckles on the bridge of his nose that I had not seen before.

He coughed.

You must lose it, I'm afraid, he said.

What? I said. I tried to look in his eye but he refused my glances.

The leg. It's to come off. I'm sorry.

Lose my leg? I cried, feeling the flip of shock in my stomach.

Yes, quickly, I'm afraid, he said, The quicker the better. Speed could make all the difference. We'll do it tomorrow.

But, I began to shout, I'm better! Mr Lockhart, look at me. Are you mad? I really don't understand – what's made you say this? I feel so much better, the pain is gone!

He waited till I'd stopped.

Sometimes that's how it goes, he said, Sometimes, when it feels – when you feel relief – that's when the limb is dying –

Dying? I said, beginning to cry.

The leg has lost feeling, he explained, That's what you're experiencing. But if we don't operate, the infection will travel in your blood and –

Is it morning or night? I asked him through my tears.

Morning, he said, taking out his pocket watch, It's almost eleven. Why?

He had seemed to be leaving, but he changed his mind. He sat himself down on the edge of the bed and took my hand in his. I was still weeping.

It's all right, he said, I'm sorry. I'm not good at this.

You're sorry?

Yes, I'm sorry.

I don't want to have it taken off, I said.

I know. I know you don't.

I want to die, I said.

You won't die, he said, as if he imagined that would reassure me, I will do my utmost to see you survive –

But –

I felt the uneven throb of my fingers in his. With his free hand, he reached up and touched my hair. It was a bold action, but he did not do it easily. Despite all my terror and shock, I noted with some guilty satisfaction that it was he who flinched, not I.

Night

Billy said he didn't believe in spirits.

The dead don't come back, he told me scornfully, Why would they bother with you in death when they never did in life, tell me that?

I knew, even though he didn't say it, that he was thinking of his own mother – the nameless, faceless one that had handed him in to the hospital with just a piece of paper and the shirt on his back.

What he didn't know was that I had put my very own small child in that place also. It certainly squeezed my heart to hear him say these things and keep such a large thing back from him. But these were delicate days – the days when we were just getting to know and trust each other – days when each conversation was measured and separate and intent, carefully spaced and properly relished.

He told me that among the kids there was always much talk of ghouls and spirits. But that was just the unloved talking, he said.

I asked him what he meant and he smiled.

We were sad little blighters, weren't we? he said, What we liked was a good mystery, a bit of flim-flamming around. Don't you see that the less you have in your life, the more you'll go for it, the more you'll believe in anything and everything –?

I thought of my father. I saw him in the entrance to his shop with his wise, sober face and brown apron, and the alabaster lady with sword and scales standing above him.

He bought the lady at a shop in Lewisham and got her hoisted up there over the door by two of the lads, which took an hour and a good bit of cursing.

He told me she was a symbol for justice and order, as well as the careful weighing up of materials wet and dry. But I didn't know about that. I thought she had a nasty frown. I used to shudder when I saw her. I thought one day she would come to life and hack my dear father's head off.

I did not want mysteries, I told Billy, When I was a girl I know I wanted to be safe and looked after and to be perfectly alert to what would happen next and to understand how things were –

Billy smiled.

Well, I reckon you were loved, then, weren't you? he said, You were lucky. If you grow up in a safe place, then you'd have to be a twot to want to lose it –

He cocked his head and looked at me with his small-bird eyes. There was something sharp about Billy – sharper than any knife Ewan had ever wielded. You knew he would slice straight through you if for one moment you dared take your eyes off.

All right, I said, remembering how we had come to the subject in the first place, But how do you explain what you saw?

For he had begun by telling me that, several times now, he'd glimpsed a woman standing in his room at dead of night.

Ah, well, he said, I do not actually think it was the spirit of a dead person, you see, but of a person who is still living –

I stared at him, looking all so pleased with himself there, and demanded to know what he meant by that.

His reply scared me. He said several times he'd woken in the stillest part of the night to feel a silent commotion in the air around him and then had realised a presence at the end of the bed.

It was her, he said, This girl, this woman.

But – (I didn't know what to say, had no idea how he meant me to reply to this) – I mean, were you afraid?

I was bloody petrified, he said.

Billy, I said, I can't believe it –

Arthur was asleep, he said, And in the next room too – Cally, the babbies, the whole family kipping and snoring away.

He said he seemed to wake because something had roused him. Not a sound but a sensation that the air in the room had been disturbed. Or rearranged.

I knew it was done by her, he said, It was her. I knew I wasn't dreaming.

What's she look like? I asked him.

He paused and the pause contained a flicker of fear.

Different every time, but –

I waited.

Always dressed the same way and – he paused – A lot like you, Laura.

Heat lifted the hairs on my scalp.

Me? I repeated stupidly, But –

She's never that close up, he added quickly, Or at least I don't know – hard to tell, since the lines are all fuzzy. She's not clear at all. But her hair is black as yours and done in a knot like that and, yes, the same small, neat figure and she has on a greenish wool jacket like yours and is always gesturing madly and moving her arms around in the way you —

It's not me, I told him and I meant it. But I was secretly pleased he had said my figure was neat.

What's more — and you won't like this — once or twice she has been leaned over on crutches like yours, he said.

My heart swooped and I took a quick breath and turned away from him.

But what was funny, he added, Was it began before I knew you — you know, before the river and that —

Billy, I said tightly, Please don't start — I mean, I don't want you to think —

I don't think anything, he said, letting his hands — which were still rough and chalky with lime — drop to his lap, As I said, I don't believe in all that folderol.

But I knew that wouldn't do and I told him so. I asked him how he could possibly say that — what did he think? He must think something.

Women don't just walk around at dead of night, I said, So come on, Billy, what is it?

He kept his attention on me, calm and level.

You tell me, he said.

I averted my eyes and said nothing.

She is frantic to tell me something, he said, That's all I know. I think it's why she comes back, why she keeps on coming, like she's looking for something —

Now you're being fanciful, I accused him, Listen to yourself, Billy.

He shrugged but his face stayed serious.

I think she's looking for me, he said.

I laughed.

Well, there you go, I said, If it was me, what would I be doing looking for you. I know where you are, Billy. I know you.

Oh well, you do now.

Come on, Billy, I'd know if it was me.

Would you?

I sighed. I was getting cross with him.

How many times? I asked him.

How many times what?

Has she come to you?

Oh, a few, he said carefully, But it's hard to say exactly. Sometimes I dream she is there.

Well then. How do you know it isn't all a dream?

He smiled, shook his head.

You want to know how I know? Because she goes in the next room and wakes the babby. Each time, I see her go through and bend down to the cot and do something to our Dora – pinch her or scratch her maybe, I don't know what – and Dodo wakes bawling her head off and that wakes Cally and so on. She leaves the whole family in an uproar –

But that's – I begin, but I have to stop. Because I can't say what it is. I have no words for it, since I can't look babies in the eye, not really, not any more.

Yeah, Billy says slowly, never removing his gaze from mine, It's unnatural, isn't it?

I made myself into Billy's friend, his woman friend.

Ewan did not mind that I came and went in the daytime so much. As long as I was there for him on his return, it didn't bother him. He said he was glad to see I was getting out so much. I wouldn't have lied. If he'd asked me, I think I'd have said I had a friend, which would've been the truth.

He would never have suspected me of running after men – what, with my crutches and my stump of a leg? A fine joke that would have been.

I began to notice that, apart from the child Pinny who shadowed him all day, B. did not seek the company of others much and was not a chatty type. Even his bricklaying mates said they did not really know him, that he was a rum one, that he kept himself to himself, that he was a closed book to them. All those things they say when you are not one of them.

But slowly, as I got to know him and put myself in his company, gobbets of his world spilled out. He could not help it – it's the sort of thing none of us can help – it's how it happens. If you like a person and you spend time with them, then however hard they try to hold it in, their history comes loose and rubs off.

At first I was stupid. I was way too frank. I asked so many direct questions – which wasn't at all the best way to get things out of him.

But soon I learned. I saw that the less I said the better. The quieter, the more withdrawn I made myself be, the more he felt moved to tell me things. Unwittingly, he began to describe himself. After all, there was no rush. And slowly, I began to get to the essence of him – the Billyness of his life. It is grand to see a man relax and unravel, let out the information of himself without being fly to what he is doing.

He let me know that, when he and Cally was wed, Pinny – his eldest – was already in the world, a little sucky, fretful baby.

Not mine though, he was quick to say, Cal was in service for six month down in Blackheath and there she became friendly with the house painter. A couple of month later, she told him she was up the poke and he left without a word, didn't he?

I was surprised to hear this and I said so.

So you got wed anyway? I said.

He shrugged.

But – even though it was not your child? I persisted.

What could I do? Cally was my only friend. We were together since the hospital, weren't we? She was my sweetheart.

So, while he was still apprenticed down at Willings, he became the father of Pinny – Pinny, now nine years old and growing fast, so fast that her feet were now longer, he assured me proudly, than her mother's.

The picture he gave me of her early days turned my stomach though: this babby that he loved already, with her two red fat cheeks shiny and moist with sweat and milk, all the grit and dust and fluff of their meagre lodgings sticking to her.

But how could you bear it? I cried, How could you live with another man's child?

She was Pinny, he said bluntly, as if he couldn't see what I was saying, Cally never pretended otherwise and so I began the thing with the full facts in mind. It was well and good. She was just a little thing then, a babby. Goodness, Laura, how could I possibly blame her?

Later he explained that it was not the fact that Cally got banged up with Pin – no, he did not consider that her fault at all, since the man had plainly misled her. But the day to day of it tore him up. He was not ready for the sight of his wife doing all those mother things: the feeding, bending, touching and tending to a small, hungry, sobby thing.

It made me pretty bloody choked, he said, More than I

ever thought it would. Brought it back. Even though all my life I had given it barely a thought —

My cheeks burned and I took his hand. Tears were standing in my eyes, I couldn't help it.

I'm sure your mammy loved you, I told him, I'm sure she could not help what she did —

But he just laughed, brushed me off, turned away.

Oh, I don't care if she had affection for me or not, he said coldly, It's not that, Laura, you've got it quite wrong. Don't you see? It's just that I'd rather forget. I never expected to have to, you know —

What? I said.

See it all — have it all going on in front of me, though I know it would've happened soon whatever —

We were silent then, each thinking our own thoughts.

Pinny is my joy, he said abruptly, as if he reckoned there was a battle to be fought which maybe there was, She is the delight of my heart.

I thought about this. They were airy words, but I could see that they were also the truth.

Then he added: I've not told anyone all of this before and already I'm regretting it —

Why? I asked him, upset to hear it.

It's not you. It's — he hesitated — It's just that it makes me feel like a right berk —

Why, Billy? I said.

He shrugged and looked away.

Makes it all seem bigger than it is.

But you're quite wrong, it is a big thing! I cried.

But that wasn't the way to treat Billy. He shook his head, at a loss. For a moment I thought he was going to walk away from me.

Billy, I said quickly, I won't tell a soul.

I did not think you could miss what you never had, he said. He said it so forlornly that I wanted to take him in my arms there and then.

You were born to someone, I told him, despite myself, I don't care what you say. Someone held you and gazed at you when you came into this world –

Oh, bull's wool, he said, You don't know. Maybe they was just glad to get me out and walk away –

Billy! I gasped, Don't say such an ugly thing –

He bit his lip.

And anyway, he said, shoving the fact once again before my nose, Cal is a good wife to me –

I'm sure she is, I said.

I'd never do anything to hurt her.

Of course you wouldn't.

And I believed him then – as I no doubt believed myself – but I confess I didn't enjoy thinking of that family of his. The six of them, all ages and sizes and degrees of love. It cut me up to think of the intimacy of that room – the darkness they all slept in together – the snuffling babe in the banana crate cot, cooing away, patting the air with her fingers.

I did not like to think of his supposed relations with Cally either – the dead-of-night ache, the tip of him all swolled up as he gave it to her. Gave her babbies and babbies – they had four of them now in that pair of damp rooms, five if you counted the dead one which I knew Billy certainly did.

I had seen them, the men who went with the women along the edge of the river in front of Millbank. I knew what they did. I had seen them stand up rigid in the mud and stench and take as long as it took. Pinned like flapping butterflies against the green weedy wall till all the moving

46

and groaning stopped. As Ewan had sometimes tried to pin me in our marital bed.

Cally is my wife, Billy told me, as if it needed saying again, I've known her all my life. She is full of gratitude – that I am a father to Pinny –

Oh, it must be something wonderful to love your wife, I remarked, but the irony rolled straight back off him.

Well, we are old chums, he replied and I could feel him sliding back into his old formality, We are used to each other, I suppose.

D'you know, I have never managed to be used to anyone, I told him truthfully, Not since my dear father and he was taken from me.

And he looked at me properly for the first time in what seemed like ages.

Laura, he said, I'm very sorry for you, I really am.

He said it like he meant it but it made me blush.

Your Pinny sounds an unusual girl, I told him because I thought it would please him.

Sure enough his face bloomed.

She's a funny thing, he said, I'd be glad if you could meet her sometime. I would not have thought I could feel so much for a little snotty child –

Oh but I would have. The heart is full of surprises, not all of them convenient ones. I didn't say that to him, of course. It would not have been the right thing – and anyway I was much too taken up with thinking how delicious his face looked when he was thinking all these kind thoughts.

On the Monday morning, they woke me, washed me, brought in leeches and brandy. And the chaplain.

Go away, I told him, Just go will you? If I decide to die then I swear you will be the first to be informed –

47

The weather matched my mood: sky black and vague and swolled up with rain clouds just waiting to chuck.

It was not Ewan who bled me, but another older man with grubby longish nails and an unpleasant attitude. When the leeches ran out, I hoped he had finished and I told him so. But he just laughed and plucked the animals one by one from the floor (where they had thudded, sated) and squeezed them out over a bucket like so many dish rags.

Little economies, my love, he said.

He never stopped chuckling to himself and when I shut my eyes and put my hands over my ears, unable to bear either the look of him or the rattle of my blood on the metal, he laughed all the more happily.

The ward was busy. There were three young girls laying-in, all knocked up by the same employer, and quite a few older women with legs or arms waiting to come off.

And then there was this small child who belonged to nobody and who no one had a clue what he was in for. I'd noticed him earlier, bucketing along and knocking into walls and doors, aimless and unattended to and quite squiffy with drink.

Though I was awfully weak, I called out to him and demanded to know his age.

I'm four, he informed me with a little sob.

Four? – this was hard to believe for I was well familiar with four-year-olds – Really, love? Are you sure? You're very small for four.

Mmm, he said in his little man's voice, Yes I am, aren't I? But if I hold my hands up to the light they grow ever so much bigger, look!

And he held out his little, spidery hands which would not keep still at all but trembled uncertainly around his face. He was no more than a baby really, a little, wavering blob of meat and gristle, his voice lushed by the brandy which had been doled out to both of us.

And where's your mam? I asked him – checking – and at the mention of that little word he began to cry in earnest, a funny, bleaty sound that made him stand still on the spot, since making it seemed to take up all his sparse energy.

Come here, little lad, I said.

He stumbled over eagerly and I pulled him on my lap. I saw how violet his eyelids were, fat and droopy as flowers. He trembled with tiredness.

Where's my mam? he asked me earnestly, I want her. Do you know where she is?

I'm sure he had a fever. He had the runniest eyes and blood in his nose and there was something coming from his ear as well.

Has she died? he asked me, looking into my face as if his mam might issue from it at any moment.

Never mind her, you're here with Laura now, I said and I watched with pleasure as he toppled into sleep, lodged in the comfy crook of my arm.

Here I was with a child again. It was a miracle, a small miracle. I wondered if I could trust myself. Carefully, I sniffed at him and was amazed at his closeness and hotness – the soft snag of his breath, the hardly-thereness of his skin. I thought of my own child and half confused him with this one – a deliberate act probably and one that was certain to give me pain, but I could not resist. Here I was on the slope of his deliciousness and sliding fast.

I shivered and shut my eyes. And then the heaviness closed over me too and I think I slept. I dreamed of the river and the bridge – of the dark shadows where the water left scallops of pale brown froth as the tide turned. Froth and scum. And when I woke the little blighter had snuffed it in my arms.

Dead to the world and pale blue.

At first, if you had ignored the gruesome colour, you would just have imagined him to be deep asleep. For children do that, don't they? Any parent will tell you that once they're down there in that secret, dreamy place, it can be hard to get them up again in a hurry. But then I shifted on the bed and suddenly I knew it was a problem that his little body didn't move with mine.

I decided to scream.

The nurse made a dreadful fuss of trying to take him off me. His fingers were so effectively knitted into my hair that they had to be unpicked, one by one. And, in dying, the little terror had done a puddle in my lap – a dark stain, already getting colder.

Ewan took my leg off later that same day. I hardly knew what time it was, the booze and the bleeding had so frayed my edges.

In the old days, there wasn't any theatre – they just covered the bed with an oilcloth and did it there and then. But this got too distressing for them who was waiting to lose them. Even with the curtains round, you could clearly hear the saw snagging away at the bone. And sometimes girls toppled off beds and hurt theirselves in their struggle for a better look.

Oh yes, I'd heard all the stories.

Like the surgeon who whipped round with the knife forgetting his friend was spectating right behind him. Severed his vein on the spot. How then, in his panic and confusion, he managed to jam the knife down on two of his holder's fingers. And how the latter died four days later of his septic wound.

My father, who sold and sharpened all manner of implements in his shop and was very keen on the codes of safety for them, would have been appalled.

Ewan, they said, had a very low death rate. He was famous for his ability to take off a limb in under a minute. I was lucky he had chosen me, they said – not realising that I had chosen him.

Now it had all changed. Now the operating theatre was set up in the airy loft space over the church – a well-scrubbed and painted room where you could smell the rosemary and the garlic from the herb garret adjacent. It was the most fragrant place I had ever been in and yet – since it was where I endured my worst agonies – I have never been able to abide those smells to this day.

Some days they said you also heard the hymns they were singing down below – God's creaky music, seeping up, blending strangely with the cries of pain. I'd not heard it but I reckoned it must be a muffled sound for the floor was a double one, with a filling of sawdust put in between. I am sure the congregation did not want blood oozing through the rafters and dripping on them.

When Ewan heard about what had happened with the child, he was most concerned for me.

Are you all right? he asked me, and when I said I was, he added, You must not blame yourself, you know. He was very poorly indeed and besides that was supposed to be confined in his own bed –

Oh, I told him, Please don't worry about me. I am a minder and am quite used to the funny things infants do –

He looked at me and I could not read his look.

Well, there is nothing you could have done, he said, I hope you know that – ?

I smiled.

I ought to add that Ewan had been taking a very bold interest in me. Every time he passed through the ward, he thought of a new and convincing reason to stop by my bed. Checking my pulse, my temperature – finding new and important pieces of information to tell me, apologising when little kids took it into their heads to die on my lap.

Is there someone who could be with you? he had asked me earlier, just before I was bled.

No, I said plainly, There is no one at all.

What, seriously? No family? No friends?

If it was you, I asked him rather boldly, Who would you have?

He flushed. All this involvement and he did not seem to want it flung back at him.

It is not me, he said soberly.

But if it was, I insisted, determined not to be so easily put off, Well then, who? Would you have your wife?

I said it gently, quietly – as if I had simply assumed that a man like him was married. In fact, I knew very well he had no wife, for his cuffs were unlaundered and there had been a smudge of something high up on his cheek for days which any home-sharing female would have been swift to point out to him.

I'm not married, he said.

Really?

'Fraid not, he said.

Afraid?

Well, he went on, blushing even deeper, As a matter of fact I live with my mother –

What? I said abruptly, surprised, And is she blind?

He stared at me.

She is actually. More or less, he said, Why? How could you possibly know that?

I smiled. You haven't looked in a glass recently, I said.

What?

You need to wipe your face.

Immediately, he pulled out his kerchief. Oh dear, he said, Now I am embarrassed.

It was the second time he'd confessed to such a thing in my presence and now it occurred to me to ask him why.

Well, it's you, he said quietly after a moment's thought.

Me.

Yes, you. The way you are. You know it. You know what you're doing.

What on earth am I doing? I said.

He hesitated. Looked around him. He was in an odd state.

We shouldn't be having this conversation, he said, Not now. I am sorry. Please – forgive me.

I will always forgive you, I said, and I meant it then.

Maybe for lack of something to do – or maybe in order to touch me – he took my pulse then. His fingers were very hot and dry and hard. And the hairs on his knuckles were the shiny, sparse type – and red-blond in colour, as you would expect.

Where will you be cutting me? I asked him later.

Why? he said, taken aback.

I would like to know.

Most prefer not to.

I'm not like most, I told him.

I'll go in just above the knee, he said, There's too much damage to enable me to start any lower.

And he looked closely at me to see how I took this.

Oh, I said. And smiled at him.

You mustn't be afraid, he said softly and, though I knew he was only trying to be nice, I replied that I wasn't, for what was the point? Far worse things had happened to me and what would happen would happen and there was nothing I could do to change it.

Ewan didn't seem to know what to do with himself then. He was immensely agitated, I could see that, and I guessed it was because of me. He looked around him and when he saw the nurse was far away, he pulled out a stool and flipped his coat-tails and sat down next to my bed. Head in his hands. Eyes on the floor. Furiously awkward and shy.

Why, what is it, Mr Lockhart? I asked him.

When he looked up his eyes were dark and tired. It was at that moment that I discovered his first name and for ever after I connected it to those eyes: hollow and shadowy.

You can call me Ewan, he said, Not mister, not sir, but Ewan. Please do it.

What is it, Ewan?

I smiled. Ewan was a funny name – not really like a name at all but an action: a flick of the wrist, a nod of the head.

I don't know, he said, I don't know what it is.

He looked at me a moment longer and then he got up and left the women's ward with his head down and his boots scuffing the dirty floor.

He did not stop at any other bed or enquire after any other patients. Not even old Mrs Witty or June Fellows – even though both of them were having limbs removed the very same day as me.

River

It is night and we are by the river, sat on the hards by the temporary railway line where Billy's great works are going on.

The smells of clean mud and oil almost overpower the normal stink of Thames – except that every now and then the wind brings the smell of boiled bones from the soap works which are generally more noxious than all the rest put together.

I don't know why we came here except that B. knows it so well and it is deserted at night. Rightly so, for all over the area are danger signs. A young lad was fooling around and fell in the main drainage a week ago. Billy said he drowned in a cesspool, his cries unheard for miles around.

Behind us is the Baptist Chapel whose windows are all forlorn and broken and patched. I don't know but I reckon it will be knocked down soon. All along this shore, everything is being demolished and changed and built up again. They are taking land back from the river and building brick tunnels underneath which will carry the waste away. B. tells me it is a good thing, that London will have a proper sewerage system and lives will be saved.

At first he was crying with all the shock, but I held him for a while and now he seems to have perked up a bit and be all right. Well, not all right, but smoking, thinking, talking – his old self again.

Actually he is rather cross. He thinks I am taking the whole thing too lightly, thinks I am pretending to myself it did not happen. But he has got me all wrong. Women are supposed to be the gentle sex, but that's a joke. Boys are the burned sugared apples – brittle on the outside and mushy within. Girls are spun candy – a cloud of pink fluff, with a hard sharp stick rammed down the middle.

I feel my hard sharpness every minute of every day. But Billy only sees the pillowy sweetness. He is that type. He has never read books as I have, hasn't learned about the underneath of people. He doesn't know that what you see is not what there is – that there are layers and fascinating layers put there to confuse you. So he is trying to sort out our predicament in a manly and straightforward way.

He says we have to go to the house immediately.

We have to go and see if he is really murdered, he says.

I frown. I am relieved to hear him say the word 'we', but I don't like the language he is using. So brutal. It makes me feel horrible inside and I tell him so.

He leans up on his elbow and puffs at his meagre little cigarette and looks at me. Despite the full moon which lights up the sky and the area around us, I can't see what's in his look. It could be love. I would like it to be love. But his face has gone thin and mean with the worry of it all, so it's probably not love this time.

If you did it, Laura, he says, If you did this thing as you have told me, then what you have done is brutal. You can't have it both ways, you know. If you have caused him, your husband, to die, then that is murder and you must face it.

I shudder and feel for my crutches which are behind me on the cold grey stones.

And they will hang me, I say.

And I notice he does not bother to deny it.

Won't they? I say, and am about to fly into a rage at him for forgetting why I did it, who I did it for, but he puts his arm around me.

Shh, he says.

He puts his cheek to mine, settles his body against me. I feel the keen muscles in his arms – the muscles of a brickie he has. I sigh. He is my love.

You want me hanged?

I love you more than my life, I am nuts upon you, but –

Yes? But what?

I don't understand you at all, he says, I think you're barmy. So many things you have done are beyond belief –

And beyond forgiveness? I say, Are they?

I don't understand you, he says again.

I am quiet and then I say: Try.

He says nothing.

I have lost so much, I tell him, I have lost even more than you know. Now I will not let myself lose any more.

He hears this and, though he maybe doesn't mean it, he moves a little away from me. I ache at the absence.

When I first met you, he says, I thought you were just so bloody good and sweet – you were the sweetest thing with your wet clothes and your sad and squitty little face –

And now?

Well, now I know different, don't I?

I never said I was good, I tell him, It was you – you were always going to try and see those things in me –

He shivers. Well, now you sometimes frighten me, he says.

I look at him.

Oh, Billy, I say, Really? Do I? Is that what you think?

I don't think, he says, I try not to, Laura. If I think about what you've done to me and my life, then I'll probably go barmy myself —

I look away. I know he means it and yet he does not know what I know. He thinks we have just collided in a haphazard way. Well, it would be nice to think that.

He blows smoke out, frowning furiously.

I dig in my crutches and pull myself up on the shingle. He turns and watches and does not offer to help. He seems to take a malign pleasure in watching me struggle to stand.

I ignore his face.

So let's go, I tell him. I tuck the sticks under my arms and touch the crown of his head where his hair sticks up. I do it partly because I know it will vex him. It is the straightest, shiniest hair, even when it is dirty — though I must say it has been cut very badly this time.

It was on this exact same patch of shingle just by Nash's that I first came into Billy's life.

What he was doing was having a smoke on the frozen hards, next to where the boats were pulled up and in chains. Not far away, there was the racket of the demolition — and Billy was still covered in it all, the black slicks of mud and lime dust, fingers chapped and caked, hair stiff with it.

It was much too cold to want to be sitting, but there were some wood beams stacked up and he used them to shield himself from the wind and light his cigarette. It was heading for low tide and soon some great big pieces of metal would be sunk down in the river's bed when it got shallow enough. There is a name for them that B. has told me, but I forget it.

So, January. Four o'clock. The shot tower all lit up by

the red sun, the river's edges gone askew in the icy light. The machinery was loud and the stink pretty fierce but not as bad as summer and anyway I don't remember it.

When he'd finished his cigarette, he shoved his hands down deep in his pockets and paced the hards, spots of hotness floating before his eyes. I don't know why, but it especially pleases me to think of him there, all innocently smelling the meaty inside of his shirt, feeling the shingle shift beneath his boots – and about to find me floating there, my left hand bobbing just beneath the surface of the water.

Yes, a hand!

What was the first thing you thought? I asked him.

That it was a freezing bugger of an afternoon, he said, And I didn't know how you'd survived in that water –

No, I said, When you saw my hand – the hand – what did you think it was?

I was so glad, in that lovers' way, to go over every inch of our first meeting, to hear all his reactions and the background to all that he saw and did.

He shrugged.

Well, I had no idea, Laura, he said, I did not know what to make of it at all – just a light-coloured thing bobbing around in the water –

But did it look like a fish? Or a dead gull? – I asked him, for there are always enough dead things floating on that mucky tide between the whelking boats and the brick structure which was becoming the new sewers.

Maybe, he said, But then I saw part of, well, your curled-up fingers. And then the rest of you, attached to them.

Billy gave a shout – more of a cry of panic – and lunged forwards. At the same time he heard the tap of my boot heel on the hull of a smack.

You were floating, he said, Just hanging there in about five feet of water, with your skirts all blown up –

Bunker heard the shout, came running.

Help me! said Billy, so shocked, he couldn't get the words out. Help me! he said.

I thought you were dead, he said, It was awful. A dead woman with white fingers and your hair all streaming out. You were coming out of your dress –

I loved this bit.

What do you mean coming out? I always asked him.

Your dress, he said, The hooks were coming undone and it was slipping –

Slipping? What, right off?

Um – off your shoulders, yes.

Could you see my –?

Not really. Well, part of them, yes, he said, Though I did not look of course –

I hope you did not, I said as primly as I could.

But Bunker was unfussed. He grabbed you straightaway and yelled to me that you were alive. I was quite glad. Though I didn't know you, it already seemed –

What? I said, What did it seem?

It seemed to matter, Billy said, It seemed to matter that you were not dead. And then Bunker said he could feel a pulse in your neck. That he felt you stir, that your body was warm.

For a moment, Billy had thought he would faint, but now he heard the sounds around him again: dredgers, whelk-men, mewing of gulls, grind of machinery from the main drainage.

We laid you on the ground, on the bank. You were so dreadfully light.

And wet, I suppose, was I wet – ?

Oh yes, and streaked with muck and your hair all streaming like a mermaid –

Come off it –

All right, but a fish. Yes, half-fish, half-woman.

I stank of muck, Billy, you know I did –

Not that I noticed, you didn't –

You are a romantic fool. But what was Bunker doing – ?

Oh, Bunker had run off to fetch someone, I think. Certainly, he came back with a blanket.

Mmm, I do remember that – the blanket.

Its warmth and roughness. The tremor of young, eager
Bunker's boots crashing away again over the shingle. The
intriguing sensation of Billy touching my pulse, the feel of
him feeling the elastic little bone on the blue inside of my
wrist. Him rubbing gingerly at my shoulder blades. My heart
jumping against the flat of his hand.

Did I say anything?

No, your eyes stayed closed. I was afraid – I mean, you
were alive, but you were out cold –

I lay stranded in the cold, half-drowned, with my head
on his thigh. A young man's thigh, smelling of lime and
brick. I could tell it was a young man by the lean trembliness
of him, the unsettled, unfinished feel of his flesh. Yes,
I swear I could even feel the line of the nerves running through his trousers which were wool and stiff with
staleness and the damp of weather. And looking up from
underneath I could see the whiskers on his jutting chin
which was barely shaved.

I felt my insides bunch up – I wanted to vomit. The
stench of the river was on my sleeves, my tongue, in my
hair. Though I'd barely opened my eyes, I knew that the
sky was red now, a smoky dusk settling on the shot tower

— black birds circling and cawing. The jagged mechanicals of the diggers fading.

And what then?

Well, Bunker came back with Ed — Remember, Ed Almond? They wrapped a dust sheet around you to get you warm and the foreman sent young Kemp over with a tot of brandy.

Good of him.

Yes. I took a nip of it myself —

You did?

I had to. I was, well, I expect I was shocked.

What? At finding me?

At finding you, yes.

And that was it. We both of us knew the rest of the story. We knew this: that we had found each other. That I had drifted into Billy's life and the truth was no amount of brandy would ever save us from the shock of it. A chain of moments and events stretched beyond us now, into the future and even then, without looking, it was untouchable, resolute, irreversible.

And Billy knew certain things, too.

He knew that I had lost the lower part of one leg. That my soaking wet skirt was flat on one side where it should be.

And he knew other things — stuff he would probably rather not have known. He knew that when I opened my eyes to him, he would see the woman who had stood over him in his room night after night. Waiting. Watching over him.

You haunted me, he said, Somehow you came to me, admit it, Laura —

No, I said quickly, Don't be a fool, Billy, how could I possibly?

How could I have seen you otherwise? You're saying I'm losing my mind?

Come off it, Billy, I said.

Do you know what I did, he told me then, Afterwards? When they had taken you away? No, I can't say – it's, well, I'm too embarrassed to say it –

What?

You'll be shocked. It'll put you off me –

Don't be a bloody idiot.

Laura, Billy said, I nipped back behind the kettle shed and I – well – I – you know –

Billy, what?

For God's sake, Laura. What do men do? When they're – you know?

I thought about it and a picture flew light as a bird into my mind.

You didn't! I don't believe it –

There, what did I tell you? Now you hate me –

But –

Don't deny it, I can see it in your eyes!

I don't hate you at all, I said, pulling my hair over my face to protect me from his eyes, Quite the opposite in fact. I find it –

What? – he stared at me with his dark steady eyes, What, Laura, tell me!

A compliment, I told him, I find it a compliment. There! Will that do? Is that enough for you?

And I looked away.

Laura – he laid his hand on my thigh, the stump one which had no knee, and then he sat back and pulled his shirt collar up around his jaw as if he wished he hadn't told me.

I don't know why, he said, Don't ask me why.

I'm not asking.

It was what I had to do.

Fair enough.

Please, Laura, don't mind —

Billy, believe me, I don't.

And I didn't. I didn't mind at all what he had told me. But how could I ever tell him that I was entranced by the idea that, having pulled me from that dark water, he was left so full up to bursting for me that he had to do that, there and then on that very spot?

For ever after I imagined him standing there, between the new-built sewers and the shed, his furtive spurt rattling on the mud — and tears of the deepest, most unshakeable love sprang to my eyes.

I can't go in, I tell Billy as we stand outside, I cannot, I'm not joking. Please, I mean it, don't make me.

Come on.

No, Billy —

My heart is moving around crazily in my chest. The house is in total darkness. Not a glimmer of light anywhere — not that I should be surprised as that is precisely how I left it. Verity will not come in for two days and nor will anyone else I am pretty certain. We are a sporadic, friendless household, Ewan and me. There is a separate door for tradesmen and they will go away I imagine when they get no answer to the sing-song of the bell.

Billy grabs my shoulder.

Do you think I want a part of this? he hisses in my ear, This — this abominable thing that you did? Right now? Think about it, Laura. It is not mine, it is not my pie. Do you think I actually want this?

No, I say slowly, I do not.

Well then, he goes — but seems to lose track of his anger.

He is in there, I say — not knowing really why I say it, such an obvious thing.

Yes, Laura, he says, This is what is happening now, please come out of your sleep and help me –

I say nothing, but his tone does the trick. My heart stills and – carefully, carefully – I undo the clasp of my purse and take out my key. It is the heaviest, solidest key I have ever held in my life, for I feel it will take me into a nightmare.

You married him, Billy goes on, his face showing up all big and ugly now in the lamplight, He is nothing to me, the poor git. I owe you nothing. You attacked him, Laura – for God's sake, you hurt him. As I have said, it is your lookout.

Thank you, Billy, I say, Thank you very much –

My cheeks are burning and frantic as I get myself up the four steep steps to the front door.

Go away, I tell him, Leave me alone then. I can do it. I have done the rest as you say –

But he throws his cigarette in the gutter and follows me up the steps. Two at a time. When he reaches the top, I feel his breath on my face, sweet and smoky. Then his fingers. All over me.

Sorry, he says, I'm sorry, love – forgive me. I don't know what I'm saying –

I shake him off.

Laura, he says, This is such a – I am so shocked by it.

I'm sorry for you, I tell him.

But I love you.

I kiss his fingers as I fumble with the key.

Could we go to France? I ask him, taking advantage of his sudden penitence, Only I'd so love to go there, you see. On a boat, just you and me running off together – oh, please say we can, Billy!

Look, Laura, he says more soberly, The thing is –

I wait.

The thing is, we have to get you out of this before we can make any plans one way or the other.

I sigh. Plans. Yes.

You are right, Billy, I say, I'm being dreary, I know I am. Come on, I'm sorry. It will be easy. He was so dead, I am sure, when I left him – I felt the poker go right into his brain through the front of his face –

Christ, says Billy, biting on his fingernail, Stoppit –

I mean, I think it must've killed him, even if the rest didn't –

All right, stop, shut up, says Billy, Please, Laura. That's enough, my darling –

I swallow. I realise how much I don't want my Billy to hate me.

Poor Ewan, I say – and I think I do mean it – It wasn't his fault, marrying me. He was just lonely, he just wanted a wife, didn't he, as anyone would? And he was so optimistic, wasn't he? Such a child, really. Anyone could have made such a mistake –

But Billy isn't listening.

For Chrissake, he says, Hurry up – as I fumble at the lock I have unlocked without any problem every day for the past year – get on with it, woman. What if someone sees me going in with you?

No one will see a thing, I tell him.

And he does not know how true it is. How can he? But he is a good egg, my Billy, a good one, my boy.

So they put the blindfold on and took me in the light, garretty room where at least one pair of rough, strong hands helped me up on the table.

And I kept myself steady and I did not struggle and I kept on thinking how cold the room was – or was it just that I had taken no food for days and lost a great quantity of blood?

Well, the chill seemed to make me confused, so that I was suddenly unable to recall where I was in time. Only the sound of water being poured from a jug brought me back – that and the blunt sound of it being set down. Oh, and a great many men talking and a small dog yapping.

A dog yapping? Was it possible? Well, I swear I heard it and could even guess its size from the forlorn spiky quality to its bark. Meanwhile, the dark bulk of the blindfold pressed horribly hard on me. It smelled wet, of salt – but whether from my own tears or those of others I could not tell.

I smelled my own fright.

I smelled Ewan, too, long before I heard his voice. There was that distinctive pepperiness, a pale, red-haired odour. For better or worse, every aspect of his person had become familiar to me.

I felt the grip of his hand briefly on mine, which made me jump. Then I felt ashamed, for I knew he had intended it as comfort.

And then he said something – a quick, officious thing I did not catch – and the room immediately stilled and there was a creaking of so many men's bones as they all leaned forward to watch Ewan saw into mine.

A loud man's voice shouted that too many heads were in the way and I heard Ewan telling him to shut it and I suppose he did.

I felt Ewan's hand place a damp pad over my face. I slid upwards again as I did before and there was a buzzing in my ears and a kind of downwards loosening in my heart. But – even as it was occurring to me that escape was still possible – hands came from nowhere and gripped all parts of me. Head, arms, legs. Especially legs.

First, the sudden warmth of his hand on my thigh. Then the peeling back of my petticoats and the feel of him holding down my leg, pulling the flesh taut.

Me waiting, rigid. A trance of waiting.

Good girl, he said under his breath – and I think that the sun came out, for light changed the texture of the fabric over my eyes just as the blade went in.

I believe I blacked out as he severed the muscle and then woke some seconds later to the crunch as the membranes succumbed and separated. And then I was awake as his two hands touched the raw inside of me – the shock of the hot meaty smell – and I heard the faraway sound of my own voice yelling and screaming to God for mercy before they shoved something in my mouth to bite on.

Here, bite, be still.

Then I heard Ewan shouting near my face and something heavy was kicked across the floor. I felt it slam into the table and, clawing the blindfold from my face, I found the strength to push myself almost to sit and I looked down and saw the blood box, its sawdust now a mulch of black gruel.

My poor heart was bursting with the effort of spurting all that blood and now I began to faint in earnest.

So I never felt Ewan as he jammed the sharp knife between his teeth (a bit of bravado that certainly was, to impress the students) and grabbed the jag-toothed saw and started working it through my marrow.

Waking ten minutes later in a bubble of pain, I heard the crowd chatting excitedly. And, dragging the blindfold once again from my head, I saw my leg – the one I'd been acquainted with all my life and that had served me so well ever since I took my first, toddling steps on it – laying there all alone in the box.

The toes were pointing perfectly upwards and it looked alive, but it wasn't and neither was it any longer mine.

Billy told me that in China they build their shacks on stilts.

He said he'd read in the newspaper that they are so used to their rivers swelling that they make their dwellings to accommodate the floods. But we both knew this would never work in Lambeth, where the mud's so plentiful that anything heavier than a gull's foot sinks in a trice.

The mud and muck. I've heard it said that bones and jewels and junk and all sorts are buried down there. At low tide, some say, you may be lucky and find treasure. But these are fancy stories – from those who have not lived on its edges.

But Billy who works there sees what comes up and it's always something you'd rather not: a dead dog, the skull of a stillborn baby, a fat new turd, an old shoe with the foot maybe still in it.

Billy was just an ordinary brickie, that's all, but he wanted so very strongly in his heart to be an engineer. So he never shirked and he took a keen interest and pride in his work, in the excavation of the silty river bed and the simple laying of bricks.

I think Billy had a vision of it all in his head, that was his trick. There were plans, he told me with excitement, plans that they were working to – and though when I looked all I saw was foul mud and pulleys and sticking-up struts, Billy assured me that in there was the makings of a whole new London. It would be a jolly and sanitary place, he said, where ordinary poor people lived long enough to have their dreams come true.

In this way, he was every bit as meticulous and important as Ewan or so I believe. It may be that my husband had saved a load of lives by relieving folk of their limbs – but the sewers that Billy was building would save a great many more if it truly meant that we did not have to breathe in those infesting germs any more.

That way, babies wouldn't die at ten days old of the cholera. And folk would not have to save up for the night-soil man to come around, while slopping around in six inches of their own you-know-what. That way, Billy would be the hero of his own story every bit as much as Ewan was – well, wouldn't he? Naturally, this thought gave me great, jumping bumps of pleasure and I told him so.

Come down, he said, beaming at me, Come down then and I'll show you it all, give you a tour.

I went.

But I did not like the sewers – oh God, I so didn't like them. The long passages of curved brick were the spit of the insides of Tatum Fields. Bricked in, bricked up – a chink of light stretching into darkness. If you had to go in them, there would not be space for a person to stand up – you would have to bend your head in just the same way. I would not go in them. Inside was scurrying rats and black sticky air and the drip-drip of drainage, just as in Tatum Fields.

When Billy first took me down there, I began to cry, I could not help it. A mask such as I'd had to wear in the prison seemed to come down over my face and there was the sound of moaning in my ears and the smell of sulphur, the devil's smell. I thought they were going to march me down and take my clothes from me again and put them in the oven till they were done. I thought they would shave me and read me the rules and lock me away in silence with only the beating of my heart for company.

As we stood looking into the tunnel that Billy was building, I began to struggle for breath. He grabbed my shoulder as I bent over to touch the ground.

I cannot – I gasped, Get me away from here –

Billy was so bewildered, for of course he did not then know a thing about my past and could not see what had caused it.

Laura, he said, My darling, my love, what is it?

I can't, I sobbed, I can't go near them tunnels, I told him, but I could not bring myself to explain why.

Not tunnels, he said, Sewers.

I can't go to them, I said, Don't make me –

He was unsettled. He didn't know at all what to say. He tried to cheer me up. When he saw I was breathing again, he patted my arm.

They are built to last, he told me proudly, Portland cement – do you know what that is?

I shook my head.

It is what we lay the bricks together with. It is a new thing. Do you know what its special, magical property is?

I shook my head again.

It resists water, he said, The more you soak it, the stronger it gets.

That's very interesting, I said, but my breath was coming back.

Oh well, he said, One day it will be a famous fact.

Billy, I said, wiping my eyes on his sleeve, You are pretty clever, aren't you? I mean, I really am mighty proud of you –

He laughed and took my hand.

71

Look at you, he said, You've mucked up my coat —

I made a face and apologised for the snail's trail of snot on his sleeve, but he told me he did not mind at all. He told me he loved me, every mucky bit of me, and I could leave whatever juices on him I liked. To prove it, he pressed his lips on the part of the sleeve where the dampness was.

Then he looked around to check there were no men watching and pushed me up behind the wood slats where they piled up all the mountains of soil and infill and there he kissed me hard. Or at least that's how it felt — tight and hard and hot — but maybe it's just that I was soft.

For I was shaking and sad. I had begun to think that maybe the sewer system was God's own warning — to remind me of where I had come from and where I would surely go back again if I did not behave myself.

Silence. Tunnels in the silvery darkness. Brick and the terrible drip-drip of silence and darkness.

They gave me a cell of my very own — no one mooning at me or tearing their hair or trying to read the Bible to me. All there was in the cell with the low brick ceiling and the high barred window was the liquid chewing sound of rats and the smell of carbolic that they had washed me in. Carbolic and sulphur and in the corner a bucket but I could not see into it.

When they took me in, I am glad to say they did not handle me too roughly. Though it was in the rules that they had to cut off my hair they did it most gently and then tucked a piece of it in my apron pocket to keep. Then they handed me a thick veil that smelled badly.

Put it on, they said. They explained I was to wear it at all times and not take it off.

But, I said, groping around in a panic and feeling only my head that now felt light and silky and fragile as a baby's, I can't see –

There's nothing to see, they said, This is it. This is the punishment – darkness and solitude – the best way to contemplate the errors of the soul –

I tried to answer back to them that I had done no crime, it was not yet proven, but already their steps had receded and only the loudness of the silence buzzed in my ears.

I was in darkness. My number was on a metal disc that hung from my waist. All I could do in the dark was finger its hard roundness and wait.

Later someone came who had a rough voice and said I was to speak to no one. I would get meat and potatoes and be sent out in the yard for one hour each day but must keep the veil on at all times.

Brick

The blissfully sudden passing of Ewan's mother had caused a ton of problems between him and me.

He cannot have been surprised when she finally went – he just cannot've for she was incredibly old and worn – and yet he grieved for her bitterly. Maybe it was that he was so used to being trampled by her that he had forgot what it was to raise his head and look around him. Certainly, he had been most upset to come home one day and find her cold and wide-eyed in her chair and me not doing anything about it.

Laura! Oh my God. Where are you? Come here please immediately, this minute!

It was hardly my fault.

I had been standing by the long tall window on the back stairs, looking out at the dull winter sky, admiring its whiteness, its comforting blankness. It made the whole world out there seem calm and inevitable and I liked that – how I wished that it could always feel that way.

I can't believe you didn't find her, Ewan said when he had shut both her eyes and poured himself a brandy without offering me one and called the undertaker, Didn't you think to check on her? What were you doing, Laura? What was so important for heaven's sake that you did not put your head around the door once during the morning?

I was arranging flowers, I said truthfully, for these were the days before Billy – days when I tried to be a proper lady who ran a house and lolloped about giving Verity orders and kept her hands busy and always wore a dab of cologne behind each ear.

I tried desperately to remember whether she had called out at all during the day. Mostly I did go to her when she rattled a tin or banged with her stick or called, though I will admit I liked to linger a little and find things to do which would keep her waiting, for she was a poisonous woman who found fault with everything that was done for her anyway.

Flowers? said Ewan.

Yes, I said, Isn't it surprising? Despite the frost I found narcissi in the garden, round in the overgrown area behind the pond. You know I am trying to walk around with my peg on most days, like you said I should? Well, I was so flabbergasted to find them and I could not resist cutting some and I was just putting them in a jug –

Isn't that a job for Verity? he interrupted, scowling and suspicious as if I was a small child who had just confessed to wetting myself on the Persian rug.

Verity doesn't do it right, I said firmly, She is lazy and always cutting corners. She doesn't put in enough water for a start and then the stalks all dry out and then they die –

Die. He looked at me and I looked back at him. We looked at each other.

Ewan turned and walked from the room.

What is it? I called after him, but he did not return and even when I listened hard I could not hear him rattling around the house.

*

There was a funeral that Ewan attended. I did not. I felt I had plenty of solid reasons and I was also ceasing to care what my husband thought of my behaviour.

You act as if I killed her, I told him bitterly, I don't feel I'm at all welcome actually.

Don't be silly, he said unreassuringly, You're my wife –

Thanks, Ewan, I said, I think I'll stay away. I think you'll be better able to express your natural grief without me around to watch you do it.

The truth was I could not trust myself to attend. I was so pleased at her death that I might not have been able to prevent myself dancing a one-legged jig at her graveside.

Peggy, she had maliciously called me and when I had informed her that my name was Laura, she laughed and said it was a pet name on account of my peg leg.

I won't wear a peg, I told her, Whatever your wonderful son says –

Oh but you should, she said with a put-on shudder, You give me the willies walking around without one. I don't like to think of what it's like –

What what's like?

She grimaced in that stiff, ugly way she had.

You know, Peggy. Up there. Under your skirts.

I'll show you if you like, I said, for my one big advantage was that I had never been at all proud or modest.

I began to lift them but she shrieked. She said no thanks. And then she told on me. She did. She made a point of mentioning it to Ewan.

What's this about you frightening my mother? For heaven's sake, Laura, can't you consider her nerves? Can you at least be kind – ?

I protested. I told him the truth of what went on between us, but he did not believe me.

Or at least he acted as if he did not. In fact, I think he had engineered this war between Eve and me. Bringing me into the home had given him just what he most wanted – a little peace from her and a weapon to use with me.

Lucky Ewan. Clever Ewan. At last and finally he was king of his household. At last, instead of one woman who nagged at him, here were two who both sought and desired his good opinion. You could see why the situation suited him. You could see why he was dismayed when she went.

But if I had thought that he and I would have a better time with her gone, then I had been wrong.

In fact, with her going, a new distance grew between us. A distance, or a chill. It was as if the surface of Ewan, which had always been cold, was now entirely frozen over and I was a lone skater, skidding and sliding and barely leaving a mark.

What was most surprising about this new mood – and certainly most difficult for me – was that it turned Ewan's mind to making a small Lockhart, a subject I had so far skilfully managed to avoid. Or if not to avoid entirely, at least to tamper most effectively with.

But one night I caught him, still in his operating coat, with his head in his hands. Feeling quite genuinely sorry for him and trying to be wifely and affectionate, I poked my slender lady's fingers in his warm, bright hair – always soft and shiny that hair – and I felt the tense, grainy curve of his scalp.

He looked up at me.

He said nothing, but caught both my hands in his and pressed them to his lips.

I closed my eyes but I could feel straightaway from the

eager roughness of his face that he had not even bothered to shave. His coat stank of blood and pus like the worst sort of charnel house, but I tried to stay tender and not pull away.

I rubbed his head. I thought I smelled a tang of drink on his breath.

Why, Laura? he kept asking, Why? Why?

I stopped and listened.

Why what? I said.

You know what. Every time we do it, you won't –

What?

He looked at me.

You know what, he said, and looked down again, You won't let me – you know – will you?

I knew what he meant. He meant that when we shagged at night in the dark in the big marital bed as we sometimes did, I never let him go quite the whole way. I always made sure none of it went in me.

He meant that sometimes I even had to take hold of him and pull him out forcibly which he did not like at all – well, what man would? – for I would not on any account let him spurt near my fanny. He was seeing that I would take any precaution not to bear his child.

He did not know why. Oh, he knew by then I had borne a child at fifteen and that the child was gone for I had told him so. He thought that situation merciful and wise and had gone out of his way to say so, believing it would ease my burden of grief and make me feel better.

He said quite forcefully that children should not be lumbered with children, for it was a sure way to see that both ended up in an early grave. That was what he thought. He did not ask for my opinion.

But he could not understand why I, a childless woman

of increasing years, should not want to bear her husband's child. It irked him considerably, it made him mad with me – and this night he had decided to change it. Now, he thought, he would take things into his own hands.

Even though I struggled, he began to push me to the bed.

I panicked.

You haven't even shaved, Ewan, I accused him gently, And look at you – your terrible clothes and that –

He ran his hands up from my wrists and over my breasts and then he kissed my little, flat belly.

You are always in a world of your own, Laura, I never know where you are –

I am here, I said stoutly, refusing to enter into his dangerous mood.

You are married now –

I know that, Ewan –

Married to me and I want to see you fit to burst with my son inside you –

Your son?

I stared at him.

He smiled sheepishly.

Our son, love, ours. Or daughter, I don't mind –

I pushed him away. I'd had enough of this.

Oh, but you don't even like children, Ewan, I reminded him, I am sure you don't. And neither do I.

He was silent a moment.

Well, I think I would like my own, he said at last and, with sudden angry determination, he picked me up and put me on the bed and threw off his stinking coat and began unbuttoning everything, his and mine.

I tried to sit up.

I don't want to, I said.

Shh, he pushed me down again.

You're drunk, Ewan –

He got on me and I saw with dismay that he was all ready for me. I had a sudden thought.

Ewan, let me up, I have to use the – you know, please you have to let me –

He sat up looking disappointed.

Be quick then, he said with a snarl that froze my heart, Or I'll come and haul you out –

In the cupboard next to the bath was the thing I wanted. Such a little thing – a wad of cotton on a long string with a button attached on the end – but so indispensable. It was what I used when I had my monthlies, but I had discovered other things to do with it too.

Hurry up! came his voice, the voice of my husband.

Coming, I said, hastily undoing my drawers.

We're going to do this! I heard him yell across the landing, for the state of arousal makes men clumsy and loud.

I put it in hastily, taking care to push it well up inside.

The button was swinging in a tell-tale way, so I positioned that carefully up between the crack of my two cheeks. There. Safe. He would never know a thing.

I went back in and looked at him, lying there and smiling fondly at me.

My darling, he said, Three sons, that's what we'll have – though I won't mind I suppose if the last is a girl –

Three is an awful lot, I told him as if I was really considering it, Think of my age, Ewan.

You're not old, he said and he held out his arms to me.

He kissed my cheek.

Don't cry, he said.

I am not crying.

What's this then?

Just thinking, that's all.

Yes thinking. Of my own child lying in my arms with his little faraway pucker of a mouth and his two small fists and kicking legs and the silence filling up my ears. Filling me up till I was tight and terrible with it.

Ewan's baby-maker was still sticking right out. It had gone into a totally different shape as if someone had turned it around and stuck it on the wrong way.

I tried not to blame him. I was sure he thought he was being kind. He pushed me down gently and began to put it in me. It was not an unpleasant feeling and I tried to kiss him back. But my heart was moving too fast. My skin was hotting up. I tried to breathe out my feelings of rage and replace them with ease and certainty and calm.

But anger is born in the brain. It starts in your head and edges slowly downwards, flavouring your whole body and leaving only its bitterest dregs in your gut and heart. By the time it has reached the bottom it has gone too far.

Can't forget. Won't forget.

He moved inside me a moment and then he froze – moved his hand down, frowned, groped, pulled.

What's this? he said quietly and I knew that his deft surgeon's fingers had clutched at the button.

It's nothing, I said quickly, putting my own hand down to get it but finding it blocked by his bigger one.

Laura, he said with a fury I had seldom seen in him, I can't believe you. You are a bloody liar and a bloody cheat and –

No! I cried as he pulled it out, and No! again as he did not let me pull away, as with a tremor and a grunt he emptied himself into me.

I felt him sag and relax. His forehead hit the bolster.

That'll teach you, he said roughly – and then a moment

or so later he kissed me tenderly on the neck and said he did not mean it.

He took my hand and squeezed it.

I love you, he said, This is natural between a man and his wife. I really love you, so what's your problem, my love?

I returned the squeeze, for my only thought was to get to the bathroom.

That's my girl, he said as I slithered away.

He thought I was happy, but I looked at him and my eyes stayed exactly the same. He should have seen. He should have known.

That was the beginning of my death and I suppose also the beginning of his. Once I'd tried to douse him out from inside of me and failed, I would find another way to wipe out what he'd done, to obliterate it.

My marriage and my life were sucked of meaning, drear and terrible and grey. I had tried long enough to live on this earth without him. Now it was time to go to my boy.

Billy's love affair with the river had begun when he was a little foundling lad of five years old and they were marched in a crocodile along past Millbank by their helper.

Though it was sunny, they had on stiff grey hospital clothes all of them and each small child held on to a thick rough piece of rope that Miss had the end of.

Billy said it must have been summer, for each child was bought a halfpenny ice, which they ate pressing their noses up against the railings at Cooper's Place and his own one melted and slid down his wrist.

I did not realise you had to gollop them down so fast, he said, I had never seen anything melt before –

He said that Miss W. showed them the gaslights – a bracelet of globes that stretched across the further bank.

And she promised that in the winter she would bring them back and they could watch the man make them flare up one by one.

And did she? I asked him, already sorely jealous that some other woman had been able to explain such wonders of the world to my Billy.

Oh yes, he assured me, She did and it was marvellous.

I badgered him then to tell me what Miss W. was like but he said he could not remember. Men! All the best information they let slip away, as if their heads was sieves that only catch the big, lump-like facts and never the sly, slippery details.

Was she young? I asked him and he shrugged and said he really did not know.

I bet she was, I said.

I imagined her young and slender with her hair piled up above her pretty neck. I saw her with shivery blue eyes and a faraway, daydreamy look. I imagined him listening to her voice as she described the lighting of the lamps along the water and wishing he could cuddle up to her hot and scenty woman-shape.

Well, did you like her then? I asked him.

He looked at me as if it was a most peculiar question.

I suppose so, he said, I suppose I must have done –

In what way?

What?

In what way did you like her? As if she was your mother? Was she motherly?

He gave me a sharp look.

I didn't know what mothers were, he said, How the hell was I to know if she was like one?

I did not know what to say then. I thought of the melted ice sliding down his wrist and it wrenched my heart to think of him out there in his grey clothes and not knowing what you did with a cold thing in all that easy summer warmth.

I woke up that morning, after Ewan had spilled himself into me, and my heart was fluttery with excitement.

I did not think about it, I did not have to. The idea was a delicate one, a feathery, trembly little thing which might dissolve if I looked it in the eye.

I had some boiled coffee and biscuits in the dining room early with Ewan while he read the paper. Yes, even though he had been working hard at getting me in the family way, he still turned away from me now and read the paper.

When the silence had gone on long enough, I stood up and told him I was going to the shops.

Oh? What for? he said.

He did not mean why was I going, but what exactly did I have in mind to buy? He was genuinely wanting to know, for one of his favourite things was to supply me with lists and suggestions. He was an ideal husband in that way, taking an interest in the running of the house just like a woman and picking up haddock, ham, suet and lard whenever he thought of it.

Oh, this and that, I replied, Some rashers of bacon and some greens perhaps.

Mmm, cabbage would be nice, he said and wrote me a list.

Goodbye, I told him, folding it carefully.

Goodbye, love, he replied, I will catch up with you later no doubt.

He was still in his dressing gown. It was his day of meetings and no cutting up people at all. Sometimes the surgeons all stood in a room and worked out what they should teach their students next. Or maybe, as I sometimes grimly supposed, they sat around a large, carbolic-scrubbed oak table and shared out the latest pile of limbs to experiment on.

I carried the breakfast things through to the kitchen and left them for Verity who would be in later. In the hall I paused and turned for the whole place seemed suddenly wobbly, the light far too vivid and strange.

There was sun coming in through the blue glass plate in the door and it fell on Ewan's good overcoat and made the weft of the wool stand up like the hairs on the hide of an animal. The look of it made me shudder, turned the ends of my fingers most fuzzy-feeling and unpleasant.

I put on my hat and got on a tram to the area where they were building the Embankment. Then, barely stopping to look about me, I walked down as far as I could, past Swan's Yard and the Iron Works and along the southern edge until I hit the loneliest, oldest wharf at the end of Melior Street I think it was. There was no street sign and the part beyond the wharf was ramshackle, but I knew it well from previous walks.

No one was around, only some urchins skinny as dogs who had finished bathing and come running up to dress. Their shrill, dirty bodies went haring past me as I loaded my pockets with tin cans and stones and anything else I could find. I scowled at them but they took no notice of me, poking along – except for one who turned around and spat very rudely I thought, though it may just have been that he had a piece of river to get out of his mouth.

Two bricks, I had thought, would do it, but there were no loose bricks to be found. So I just made do with the cans and the stones which were not all that large or heavy. Then I laid one crutch down on the flags and with the other eased myself to sit on the edge looking down at the thick, putrid, lapping brown water.

Staring at its heavy darkness made me dizzy and more than anything made me realise how much I wanted to be with my boy. To be back against his softness and mineness and without any other things pressing in.

When you love someone and you've lost them, I think all you want really is the peace and quiet to grieve for them, the space to think of them, the freedom to lavish your time on them if that's what you wish.

I wanted that. Yes, all I wanted really was him, him, him – in my head and my heart. I was greedy for it, for the thought of him. I felt I had not been allowed it for a long time.

I had a flask in my apron. I was not a drinker normally, but a little bending of the elbow always dulled the sparks in my brain and now I really hoped to make myself stupid with it.

Well, I was not a martyr or especially brave. I knew I did not want to feel it – the going under and being sucked down. There was a strong current, but still I did not want the moment when you had to choose between the air and the water going in your lungs, to tempt me to panic. I would give in, I thought. I was a poor cripple. I did not stand a chance in there.

And I was so keen to join my baby boy in heaven.

Along the wharfside here it was the lonely part. Brick walls stained by flooding, broken windows, rubbish piled up. A dead cat or rat, whichever, I did not look too hard. Rusty chains on the boats.

Not a soul, or so I thought, to see me fall.

Billy and me met in the public bar of the Red Cow in Queen Street.

86

It was a week to the day since he pulled me from the river and now I was feeling pretty glad to be alive. Simple as that, my fortunes and my thinking had all been turned around in just seven days!

And yes, it was all thanks to him, to this strange young man all covered with the smell of digging and cement. I only had to think of him to find my life flooded with brightness and meaning. How could I have ever wanted to die! It was in my head to live for ever now – and it was as if the river had offered up that strange possibility, by bringing me to him.

Ewan collected me at the police station, where I had been given a cup of tea and a change of clothes four sizes too large and smelling horribly of sweat.

When I mentioned this, one of the bobbies could not apologise enough. It wasn't true that I minded the smell, not in the least (the muck of others has never bothered me) but it had seemed the right thing to do, to make something of it.

And I thought, isn't it funny how you can complain about these things when you're a lady and it really seems to do you a favour and go down quite well – and yet any real and valid complaints from the crawlers and dossers would always be chucked straight back in their faces?

Ewan did not apologise at all, not to me at any rate. He arrived straight from the hospital, an odour clinging to him of paraffin and blood. He was white-lipped and furious because he did not understand what had happened. And fearfully embarrassed for the same reason. He imagined the officers might think that I his wife was going barmy, for that was his own true suspicion – a feeling enhanced by the fact that I seemed so radiantly happy in my lumpy old gown and borrowed shawl.

What's going on? he blurted, You were going shopping –

I fell in, I said, smiling.

Where? Where on earth were you?

Just walking along by the wharf –

But, Laura, I don't understand – fell in how?

Poor old Ewan. He really could not get it. He began to fuss and ask me what I'd done with my crutches.

I couldn't say, I told him, realising I had barely stood up since I arrived, I must've left them on the side –

What do you mean? What side?

The wharf. Where I fell in.

Why are you smiling? Ewan demanded as if I should never smile again.

Such a nice man saved me, I told him truthfully.

And I touched my cheek – my filthy, river-smeared cheek – at the memory of his wool-clad thigh. I remembered the quick, solid pulse of his leg, the feel of rightness and relief.

All I had to do now was wait. He had looked at me and he had felt me and I knew for absolute certain he would find me again. But it was wretched, waiting. Hurry up, I thought as Ewan collected my clothes in a paper bag and gave me his stiff, accusing arm, I don't know how long I can wait.

And sure enough three days later a bobby knocked on our front door and handed me a note.

From a well-wisher, he said.

It was sealed and I thanked him and shut the door before I opened it. Inside it was scrawled directions for the Red Cow and it was signed 'Bill'. Just Bill. I thought what a cheeky bloke he must be, to use the police to do his courting.

The Cow was a place I knew, a tavern down by the river, a leftover haunt from my life before Ewan. It did not seem extraordinary that he should ask to meet me there.

It was a chilly spring dusk. As usual, several light trades-men's carts and costers' barrows were lined up outside and pieces of paper and other rubbish blew about in the wind. A couple of foetid mattresses had been flung down in the alley and three stray cats were curled on them. One I reckon was pregnant for she was well bumped up and licking herself. Below the street, you could hear the lonely chop of the turning tide.

The bar was almost pitch black apart from the glow of a few cheroots. I saw him come in straightaway and was rather shocked to see that he was followed by a child – a chubby hatless little scrap of about three or four, with her face dirty and her frock torn.

He took off his cap and looked around him, squinting to accustom himself to the dark.

Hey, I said from my corner and he turned and stared at me.

I returned the stare and he reddened.

I thought you wouldn't come, I said.

It was not true. I had been surer of his coming than I'd ever been of anything in my life.

Of course I've come, he said and very lightly he touched the head of the child and turned her to face me, This is Lulu. Say how d'you do to the lady, Lulu.

The child didn't speak – maybe she couldn't yet, for I have forgot what age they get the habit – but just lowered her eyes in a sullen sort of way. There were smudges of street dirt all over her and when she came forward – pushed by him – I saw her little nails were bit down to the quick. And a long red scratch led very noticeably from her elbow to her wrist.

Hello, Lulu, I said.

She moved her mouth.

What you done to your arm then? I asked her.

The lass kept her mouth clamped crossly shut and stretched out her arm and looked it over solemnly as if she did not know there was anything the matter with it.

It was a cinder, she said stoutly.

I looked at Bill, who looked at her and laughed. Anyone would have noticed how his affection for the child lit up his face.

Oh well, she went and hurt herself, he said, There was a piece of cinder lodged in the soap, since Cally had used it earlier to scrub the floor and Lulu here would go running –

Cally?

He looked embarrassed.

My wife, he said and tried to look me in the eye when he said it which I thought was sweet so I smiled at him.

Then I tried to touch the little girl's head in a kind way but she pulled away smartish so I went off her a bit. Still, she was a sharp one. She did not take her beady eyes off me, but continued staring rudely all the while as if I had a cabbage stalk growing out of my head.

Couldn't she run along and play? I asked Bill and when he hesitated, I asked him what he was so scared of.

I'm not dangerous, I said with as serious a face as I could manage and he laughed, but it wasn't that funny because I was lying. I was dangerous. It took all my effort to stop myself reaching out and touching him there and then, so familiar and enticing he was to me.

I'm sorry, he said lamely.

Why? What're you sorry for?

He began to say something but Lulu took hold of his hand and pushed her face against him. Gently – so gently that it gave me gooseflesh – he persuaded her off him.

Go to the yard, love, he said, Go on and I will catch you up in a moment.

She went slowly, dawdling. She was the type to make the persons around her pay for their peace.

Yours? I asked him, when the child had finally gone.

He nodded.

How many d'you have?

They are four counting the babby, he said matter-of-factly, There was — well — I had another that is with us no longer —

I told him I was sorry to hear that and he looked down at his boots for a moment. There was a lovely, unimportant silence between us.

I don't know what to say to you, I said and it was the honest truth, I mean you. And all these children. And your wife who is so short of soap. Why did you want to see me? What's going on?

He knew what I meant because he frowned and puckered his face at the word wife. Or was it soap?

You tell me, he said and his voice was rough with emotion, I don't know why I'm here at all. You tell me what the frig is going on.

Look here, I said, laughing incredulously, You came to me. You asked me —

He shook his head.

You know that's not it, he said.

Silence again.

And you? he said.

What about me?

Well, he glanced up, You are nicely dressed and you have a ring on your finger.

I looked at it, the strange, hard circle that Ewan had taken such pleasure in sliding on to my finger a year before and I twiddled it around, showing off that it was loose. Then I let my hand dangle so it slipped off into my upturned palm and I passed it to him. Real gold, warmed by my blood.

He did not know what to do with it.

Why'd you do that? he said.

I shrugged.

Come on —

I wanted to, I said, I don't care for it if you want to know —

Don't be a twot —

I don't, I said, And I don't care whether you believe me either.

Have it back, he said, passing it to me as if it was contaminated, Don't fiddle-faddle around with me.

I married the surgeon who took off my leg, I said matter-of-factly and I made sure to see the expression on his face.

He winced again. And his eyes were so light and keen and full, that once I looked at them it was very hard to remove my own.

Why's that? he said.

Why's what?

Well, it doesn't seem like a regular thing to do, to get wed to your surgeon —

What's regular? I said.

He stared at me so hard that I felt pushed to explain myself.

Look here, maybe I loved him, I said stiffly.

Did you?

I sighed.

Let's start again, shall we? I said, suddenly not enjoying it all as much as I'd hoped, Who are you? What's your name?

You know my name.

All right, I'll tell you mine.

Bone

It is terrible. It is even worse than we thought. The silence and the thinking about it and the idea that he is in there.

Billy says we definitely need a drink, but I am worried he is just wanting to loaf around and take advantage of Ewan's apparently plentiful supplies. He has never been inside this house before, you see, and he is pretty impressed.

I never thought it would be so bloody big, he says, staring around the parlour which is one room I particularly hate, Nor everything so spanking new and shiny, I mean look at it all.

Much of the furniture is old, I say, because I wish he would not be so full of awe, Much of it belonged to Ewan's mother. She had it when she lived abroad and the style of it is so starchy and old-fashioned and I hate it if you really want to know –

But so much posh stuff, he says, ignoring me and going around and stroking the silk upholstery and heavy velvet curtains and lifting and examining things like they were his very own and seeming to forget completely what sad, awful reason we have come here for.

Billy, I tell him rather sharply, You are not being respectful. Have you forgotten? There is a dead man right here in this house.

I'm sorry, he says, But I do need a drink.

I fetch Ewan's brandy and pour him some. My hand is shaking so much I can barely pull the glass knob on the decanter and I am sure I get more on the table than in the glass.

And there we sit, in the dead quiet parlour with our drinks and our feet on the fender like two bad urchins who have collaborated in a dirty deed. The brandy burns my chest and the sensation reassures me – it is one I have always liked. No, we haven't yet looked in the room and in a short time we will.

Well, cheerio, says Billy dolefully and lifts his glass. I am about to be freshly annoyed with his crassness, but then it occurs to me that I am just strung up and so is he and he certainly doesn't mean anything by it.

I need to wash, I tell him, laying my crutches carefully against the fender and sniffing my armpits, Oh what I would give to draw a nice big hot bath and loll in it for half an hour –

Afterwards, he says, putting his arm around my shoulders and pressing me against him, You will need one afterwards, girl.

But as he says it, we both look at each other.

After what? The truth is, we've no idea what we are going to do, no idea at all. Ewan is lying there and the drink is just a way of putting it off, we both know that, though we haven't said it.

He stares at me.

Chrissakes, Laura, you've put me in such an awkward position –

If this was you, I remind him, I would stand by you and not complain.

And he can't argue. It is a fact, he knows it, it is absolutely true.

Oh, stop, he says wearily, What does it matter what you would do? This is me. And what we have here is another of your frigging disasters. Another of the ways in which you have messed and disordered my life, as well you know –

Oh well, I can't argue with that, I think, so I don't. Instead, I take his big lanky hand, feel its steady warmth as I wrap it around my littler one.

I love you, I tell him, but it comes out far more shaky than I mean it to.

He says nothing. He does not speak. Billy is good at that as all men are – at getting away with not saying anything at all. Instead, he is looking at the mantel with all the bits and pieces, the tallboy, the small occasional tables from India inlaid with mother-of-pearl. The silver, gone all murky and tarnished since Eve's departure. The stuffed squirrel with the falling-out eye.

This stuff is worth decent money, he says at last, Whose is it?

Ewan's, I say automatically.

No, whose is it now, I mean?

I think about this a moment, but no likely answer will slide into my head.

I don't know, I say, realising, Is it mine?

Billy stands up. Puts down his glass with resolve.

We have to deal with it, he says slowly.

It?

Him. If no one finds him, then nothing can be done. Don't you see? We're safe.

Oh, Billy! I cry, thinking automatically of my father's solid face and hands, his way of making the world seem manageable, I would so like to be safe.

He comes to me again.

I know, he says and pats my arm the way I've seen him pat the child Pinny's, I know.

Now I get up, take his hand. My stump aches but it is just the effect of nerves and I know the best thing to do is ignore it. And he is trembling now, full of energy for what we must do.

There is a dreary, staring silence in the room and I realise how much I loathe the place – yes, the whole place, it is so full of Ewan and his mother and their lives lived in cahoots with each other.

I never thought this would happen, I say, wishing I was a whole lot more lushed up.

Of course you didn't.

I used to wish and wish his mother would die, I tell him, And then when she did, I could not shake off the idea that I had somehow caused it –

Well, you hadn't, he says without much interest.

No, I say, But you see, the idea was there – I used to wake at night all hot with sweat –

Billy covers his eyes with his hands, rubs them, then looks at me again, his brow puckered. I must say he is not so good like that – I do much prefer him with his face smooth and gay.

Laura. This is what you should be sweating about –

This?

Him in there. The thing you have done.

I take a quick breath.

In a moment, I say, In a moment we will go in.

When he saw the blindfold had gone, Ewan was livid. I was never supposed to see my own leg lying there in the blood box.

He swore and cursed at the holders. Immediately I felt the darkness slip back over my eyes.

Next, he set to work with his sharp bone nippers. I was sobbing but the quantity of pain had also made me numb. I could not think, I could not scream. I lay back and hardly flinched as I felt him snap away at the shards of cartilage that had missed the saw.

I once asked him, a year or so later, what bones were like inside when you cut them open.

White as milk, he said after thinking a moment, And not dry as you might think, but waxy –

Like lilies? I suggested, thinking of the big star lilies I'd held on my wedding day – lavish-scented but angry blooms that stained my underwear with their wretched orange pollen as he undressed me later.

Ewan laughed.

Lilies? Not exactly, love, no. Why, how can a bone possibly resemble a flower or vice versa? You do have a strange and wonderful mind.

Well, maybe I did, but not as strange as his. In bed for instance, he liked to bring one of his knives in with us, not to hurt me with but just to pretend, loving the spasms it caused inside me when he played the hard cold around on my body.

Different people have different ideas about what's bad. To me that was not how the act should be – I'd something safer and sweeter and altogether more abandoned in mind. To me bone meant well-worn knife handles and rich folk's hair ornaments with pale, dull teeth. And love I think should not be mixed up with death.

Death? said Ewan when I told him so, This is pleasure, my love, not death. I can show you death if you wish and you will see that it is nothing at all like being jumped in bed –

Jumped or not, despite what Ewan said, I couldn't help thinking of the inside of living things when you snap them open – the keen white sap of a twig, or a bud nipped off while its pale, creamy furls are still shrunk tight.

Ewan said he loved me, but I don't think he could have because he had seen inside of me and he could not forget it.

Maybe that's what the knife was about – a reminder that he could go in again at any time if he chose to do so.

He used his tweezers to pull out the finer flakes of bone. I didn't hear them plink into the dish. Then he had to sit very still indeed for a moment or two.

Don't get the wrong idea. I'm not actually having a good look up her skirts.

Is that what he said to the crowd? And did it get him a big burst of laughter? And did he then add, more seriously:

Who can tell me what I'm looking for?

Arterial vessels, sir?

Hmm, and what should I do about them?

Again Ewan's hand was on me – his fingers on my bare hip, circling, caressing. I was half in and half out of the world that I knew and my leg was red-hot and alive. In my fever dreams, a thousand insects were diving frantically in and out of it.

I moaned a little, I couldn't stop myself, and then felt the sudden sweet wet of a flask of brandy pressed to my lips. But it seemed that I had unlearned the action of swallowing and the liquor trickled down my chin and into my dress.

No one had the answer to Ewan's second question. But

I know it. I know that he secured the vessels with ligatures and then, once the skin flap was tightly stitched over, dressed the stump with stinging-hot rags soaked in paraffin.

I know because he liked to tell me – over and over as he touched and looked at me. Till I cried out for him to stop.

First time I met Pinny, so-called delight of Billy's heart, she made her feelings about me perfectly clear.

Thanks a lot, Pinny!

Well, it was a hot, blowy day and I had been to a dress-maker on Kentchester Street, for Ewan was always going on at me to have new clothes made up. And I must say I was fed up because the patterns she had cut and tacked were much more fussy and awkward than I'd have wished and I found myself telling her what she could do with them.

I was a bit rude to her actually and she quickly took offence. I used some language then for I was getting fast to the end of my tether – and sure enough she asked me to leave.

This was exactly the outcome I desired.

And you, a surgeon's wife! she threw after me as I pulled up my skirts and grabbed my crutches and got myself pains-takingly down her front steps which by the way were covered in green splats of bird poop.

Goodness me, I retorted happily, Didn't you know? – they are the very worst, the wives of medical men!

I did not really care in the least what she thought of me, but I was pretty angry that she'd managed to get me in a state. Despite my well-off and decent times with my father, I had lived with the crawlers so long that I had lost sight of what was deemed sociable behaviour and was not in the least bit good at being a lady.

And I was heartily sick of standing on my one leg and being pinned and unpinned in that musty front room while her moaning offspring sat in the window and loudly sucked its fingers.

Outside, through her flimsy lace curtains, I could just make out the trees waving at me from the park and the creamiest blue summer sky which seemed to promise permanent light and heat. Light and heat. My spirits lifted and my heart burned to get out of there and my one leg did its best to comply.

No, despite my good upbringing, I did not make a very docile or satisfactory lady. To tell the truth, I was sick of the whole mediocre business of sitting in stuffy, swept-out houses and agreeing to tea and cake and pretending to be interested in this and that.

This was what Ewan could never understand – that I never asked for an easy life, that I never hankered after it, not at all. Whatever happened and however many fine things I had, still I badly craved my own type – the wobbleshops and the jolt and spark of the bright air and the brown dirt of the river.

So I left her rooms and was about to get on a tram straight home when I suddenly had the good idea of looking for him. I hobbled along the street towards where it sloped down and you could see the beginning of Millchamp's. Lots of traffic and people shouting. My wrists ached with the effort of the walk, but my heart was lifting all the time. The air smelled strongly of Billy Boy. I knew he must be somewhere around.

I loitered on the patch of wind-burned grass outside Fitch Cottages, with the sole intention of coming across him. No one paid any attention to me and he did not come.

But, after twenty minutes or so, just as I was preparing

to give up and go home, there he was striding briskly round the corner – so surprising that I couldn't quite believe in him, for he felt like a vision I'd dreamed up.

Hey, I said.

Hey, Laura!

He flushed bright red as people do who suddenly come upon their friends unexpectedly and in the wrong places.

I was very breathless and pink from all the exertion, and it suited me and I knew it. I was glad I had bothered to put my hair up properly and had on a decent light green wool jacket and a touch of powder to tone down my freckles.

I leaned on my crutches with my gloved hands and I fiddled shyly with a strand of hair that had come loose behind my ear. I saw him watch me do it and I was glad. Glad that he seemed hypnotised by my presence, that he could never take his eyes off the most mundane things that I did.

Why, what are you doing here? he asked me, still surprised, but smiling all the time.

Ah well, what does it look like? I said sweetly.

How do you always manage to find me?

He asked this question quite seriously and I was just wondering what the perfect answer might be when I noticed the person standing next to him.

She was a most dreary young girl, skinny and long-faced with grubby and patched clothes and no shoes on her feet. She had a small squishy nose and her hair was in rats' tails, yet her blue eyes were totally startling, yes, they really hit you. There was no child whatsoever in them. They knew stuff that very few other souls did.

I looked her over and she made me a little afraid. With eyes like that, I was not going to spare her.

Pinny, I said.

How do you know me? she asked me sharply and I did not like her tone which was suspicious and judgemental.

I laughed.

Well, you're so pretty, I lied, He has described you. I recognised you.

She wasn't fooled. She was staring at my crutches and then she looked straight at her father, who looked awkwardly back at me.

Laura is an old friend of mine, he told her bravely and she immediately shrank back.

I'm ever so pleased to meet you, I told her, I have heard a great deal about you and all of it good –

I extended my hand but she ignored it as if it was not there. Billy, meanwhile, seemed not to notice but just kept on looking at me very warmly.

I have been to the dressmaker's, I told him brightly, But I am so fed up with her and I'm afraid I let her have it. Now I will be in big trouble with Ewan –

I had tried to lean confidingly towards the child but now she was walking swiftly away from us. I turned to watch but Billy said, It's all right. Let her go –

What is it? I asked him, pretending that I cared, Is it my crutches? Is she afraid of them? Or my leg? I know I should wear my peg, but it rubs so I can hardly bear it –

Don't even think it, he said, Of course it's not you, it's her, she's in a glump.

I did not mean to frighten her, I said again.

Billy touched my arm and my heart jumped.

Please don't mind her, he said.

All right, I said, I won't then.

He hesitated and he kept on looking at me and he smiled.

It's good to see you, he said.

I want a fag, I told him, Do you have any dibs on you? Do you fancy sitting on the bench a moment?

There was a public seat by the cottages which normally had a number of mothers and children sprawled loudly all over it. Now by good luck it was empty so Bill helped me over there and I sat myself down which was a great relief.

I cannot touch you, Billy said, Though I would so like to. Oh, Laura. You know why.

I said nothing. Pinny was sitting on a fence some way off by the cottages, swinging her long bony legs and frowning to herself. Billy called her over and, after a bit of bickering with him, she came and sat on the other side of the bench – but as far off as she possibly could, frosting us out.

Billy made me a fag and I pulled off my gloves and he lit it for me. Pinny scowled. I put out my tongue at her and then pretended to blow a little smoke over into her face, but she made sure not to get the joke and then put on a great show of turning her head away.

Why don't you like me? I asked her straight, because in my opinion it's best not to beat about the bush with children.

Of course she likes you, Billy said straightaway and then he told her roughly to lighten up. It won't kill you to be civil, will it? he said.

I tried to make some conversation, even though the sight of the child was making my heart speed up and gallop to Doomsday.

She looks just exactly like you, Bill, I told him as I flicked my ash on the dry ground.

He frowned.

How can she? I told you she's not even mine –

Well, I don't know about that, I said jauntily, All I can tell you is she's the absolute spit.

And it was true, him and her were just two peas in a pod – the one sullen and the other sparkly, but nourished by the same sap all the same I'd swear. Whatever there was between them scared me to death.

Billy seemed to relax, then he laughed and looked at Pinny and the look he gave her pinched my heart.

Maybe you two have grown so alike through love, I suggested quietly even though it cost me something to say so.

Why? Can that happen? Billy asked me, for he was like-ably dense in these matters.

I don't know, I said, keeping my eyes steady, Can it?

Just then – and rather surprisingly – Pinny burst into tears.

Now Billy was really annoyed.

For God's sake, Pin, he said, What's going on with you? Whatever is it?

She carried on sobbing and put her arm up as if to cover her eyes.

If you don't tell me, he said, I will clout you –

I don't know, the child whispered through her sobs, It's just – I just would rather not –

Rather not what? he said.

But Pinny couldn't say.

I looked at Bill.

Oh, leave her be, I told him, for I did not really like whatever she might be going to say.

But the girl lifted her head suddenly and looked at me.

She is a bad lady, she told her father, That one, she is a wrong'un –

Pinny!

I can feel it, Pinny said, Right here —

And she touched her middle where the poor cheap fabric of her dress sagged and frayed.

Billy reached right out and belted her. He meant to hit her face but she ducked and I think he got her on the neck. It wasn't very hard, but it was enough to shut her up.

You are the one that is bad, he said, D'you hear me, girl? Such cheek from you, I can't understand it. I wonder what your mother would make of it —

You won't tell her, the child accused, quite rightly, and I saw there was a red, smarting mark on her neck.

I laughed, though I know I shouldn't have, but Bill jumped to it.

If you tell your ma a single word of all this, he told her, I'll beat you to your last breath, d'you understand?

The child kept her blue eyes on his. She held them on him like a weapon, as if the light from them could slice into his face.

Do you understand? Billy asked her again.

I understand, she said, but it was me she looked at as she said it.

Pinny, of course, was the whole trouble. She knew more than she should have. I was fly to her ways. It did her no good at all, to know what she knew.

He called her a dreamboat, Billy did. A dreamboat and a love. He said she was small for her age but sturdy and quick as a needle.

You're soft on her, I accused him and he laughed. Then he thought about it a moment and said yes, maybe he was but he certainly didn't know why.

What about your other kiddies? I said.

Oh, I love them too, he assured me, But Pinny's just so frigging special.

He said proudly that he would happily starve to put food in Pinny's stomach and had often been moved to share his only sausage with her. He said that half their goods was up the spank and once all the stuff like coke, rent, clothing club and burial insurance had been paid, Cally often couldn't scrape enough together for a meal.

We take it in turns to starve, he said, Her and me and Pin, because the babbies of course must be fed.

You don't get any sleep if you don't feed babbies, I observed wryly, for I of all people was entirely familiar with that equation. It is the first rule of the crawlers. You get as much food as you can into the mouth of the kid you are watching, especially if it's a young one, even if it means going without yourself.

With your belly empty, the lethargy sets in – but at least if you are curled on the workhouse steps, the kid can't wake you. Crawlers are always dozing – it is the only way they have to get out of the world. But they mostly doze with one eye open, on the lookout for trouble.

What I don't understand about you, Billy said, Is how come you minded all those babbies? I just can't see it –

I shrugged.

It was that or the workhouse – and I was better at it for not loving it, I told him, I was not soft, you see, Billy. No babby ever scared me.

He looked straight in my eyes.

Except perhaps for my own, I said.

There was a beat of silence between us. It was getting to be our natural silence, containing as it did everything we always did not say.

Anyway, he added, changing the subject back to his

beloved she-child, Pin never complains even if all she gets is bread and lard, which is often the case. And she makes do quite happily with Cally's old split boots, though her feet have growed so much since she was five so they are dead tight on her.

Oh but she is perfect, I remarked sourly, Quite clearly she is an angel!

And very helpful too, he added, Her arms are always full of something, bless her, whether the babby or the ex-babby, or else carrying my dinner to me at the works and never for one moment loitering or complaining on the way –

You and your wife must be very proud of her, I told him, but he still did not take the hint.

Oh, he went on. She is a great comfort to her mother, I know that – and to me also. And she's that clever – she is the cleverest girl in all the world. Even though we can't spare her to go to school, she'll spend hours patiently sitting with a candle and writing out her alphabet –

Enough! I said and I kissed him lavishly on the lips to shut him up. Gave him a modest amount of my tongue to show him there was something else in the world besides Pinny and so that he did not get the hump.

But all the same I couldn't stop thinking of him and his little girl and how the two of them would go off up to Saffron Hill and how she would craftily persuade him to get her a raspberry ice from the Italian cart.

It's not raspberry of course, he told me happily, It's that cochineal muck they put in to make it pink. Everyone knows that. But Pinny swears she can taste the real raspberries in it, even though I know she's never had such a thing in all her life –

When I married Ewan, I interrupted him, We had a cake made of nothing but vanilla sponge and cream and it was served up with raspberries in silver dishes hired for the occasion.

Oh, said Billy, but his face was crestfallen, as if it was a sad thing I was telling him.

And fine white sugar sprinkled on them and then great dollops of real cream —

He thought about this and suddenly seemed dreadfully downcast.

Why, Laura? he said, Why did you marry him? I don't understand it. Why in the world did he want to marry you?

Well, thanks, Billy, I said.

No, you know what I mean —

It made me a lady, I told him quietly, Look at me, it made me well off —

Did he love you? When he married you?

Well, he liked me, I said simply, He still likes me a bit. Why did you marry your wife?

That was quite different, he said soberly, We were already together — we were thrown together from the very beginning.

Yes exactly, I said, for I liked the sound of this, That's just how it was with Ewan and me. Thrown together, you see, by the accident.

Billy did not smile.

But you? he said, Why you?

Because I cast a spell on him, I said, He is a clot and I knew what I was doing. It's very easy indeed if you know how. He saw me and whumph!

Saw you and what?

I intended it, Billy, it is what women do. It is what your Pinny already is doing. Just look at her. Casting spells. Oh, she is subtle, you can't feel it. But she has bound herself tightly around your heart and she will not let go – take my word for it.

They took my leg, I told Billy, They took it away from me.

I know they did, love, he said gently, I know it.

We were in the bed together. His face was close to mine and his skin and hair were so bang next to my eyes that they looked like a whole world. He was relaxed and happy, wiping the milky spray of stuff from his chest.

No, you don't understand, I insisted, They really took it. They wouldn't let me see it. Afterwards.

Why would you want to see it? he asked me dreamily and he tried to take me close to him and arrange the stray wisps of hair that clung around my brow. I pulled away.

Because it was mine, I said, Don't you get it, Billy? This was my property, this leg – it belonged to me –

Billy laughed a little uncertainly.

What would you have done with it, Laura?

I would have buried it, I said, I would have put it in the ground. What else do you do with a dead thing?

I was lying there on the ward with my stump draining into a basin. I did not dare look at it, nor at the terrible sudden flatness where the sheet fell beyond it.

I asked the nurse where it was.

It?

My leg.

She wouldn't tell me. Pretty soon I made such a bawling fuss that she fetched Ewan – who must have been sleeping for he came rubbing the side of his face haphazardly and with his shirt rucked up and his cuff buttons undone.

It's my property, I told him firmly when he asked what the problem was.

He yawned. Scratched his neck.

Actually, he said, I'm not sure it is. It may in fact belong to the hospital now.

I stared at him.

What? I cried, But what would the hospital want with it?

Laura, he said, waking up now, You should be resting yourself, not making all this noise. What're you doing?

I want my leg, I said – and I was crying bitterly now – Where is it? It must be somewhere. I want it now.

Ewan looked at me a long time. I thought he would come over and take my hand, but he did not. Instead he stood there with a very careful face – as if poised on the edge of deciding something.

All right, he said, Do you want the truth?

Of course I do! I cried.

I mean, if I tell you the truth, will you calm down?

How can I know that? I said.

Well, I think one of the boys took it, he said, One of my students. So you see, I must take full responsibility. I'm sorry, Laura. It was a good one –

A good one!

So many are wasted or foul or decrepit before they come off –

But – I began.

They took it to have a look at, he said, If they can't have a look at the inside of things, then how will they learn?

I looked at him. Tears were creeping down my cheeks.

Are you all right? he asked me and he seemed suddenly weary.

It is a piece of me, I said, weeping, It is my leg.

He seemed to think about this.

Of course it is, he said, You're right. It is.

And now I have lost it, I told him.

He said nothing.

I am always losing things, I said, Or at least that is how it seems to me –

He smiled.

Laura – he said.

No, I said, I mean it. I have lost all manner of things. A person can only take so much loss –

You seem remarkably intact to me, he said.

Stop it, I said to him.

Stop what?

You're trying to compliment me, I told him, And I don't like it – I don't like it at all.

He smiled and, as if I'd invited him, he came over and sat on the bed and put his hand on my knee.

I'm not, he said.

You are. Stop it or I will call the nurse.

If you like I will call her, he said. But he kept his hand on my knee.

I paused, took in the hotness of his fingers.

No, I said.

No what?

No don't call her. What were you doing just now?

Sleeping, he said and he did not blush.

How is your mother? I asked him and he removed his hand from me as casually as he had put it on. He laughed.

She's the same as always, he said, Why?

And how is that?

He thought about it.

Dissatisfied, he said.

Why?

Now he put his hand up and touched my cheek. Very gently, as if it might dissolve under his fingers.

Goodness, he murmured, So many questions –

Why? I said again.

Well, he hesitated a moment, She doesn't think I'm a good boy.

And are you?

He smiled.

A good boy? Not really.

I sighed. The touch of his hands on me had given me a lump in the throat like tears welling up. He smiled again.

You are a rum girl, he said and his voice was light and tight as a little child's, You are rude and jumpy much like a dosser off the streets, and yet –

What?

And yet I am baffled –

Oh? I said and sniffed.

You have the bearing of an educated lady –

Well, I am one, I said, smiling, I am educated as you say –

But –

I mean I went to school. I read books. I learned music and French and – comment ça va?

I laughed, but he looked serious and puzzled.

It was a long time ago, I said.

And look at you now –

I shrugged. I knew he meant more than my clothes.

Yes, I said, Look at me now –

He took my hand and put it against his lips. It was the third thing like that he had done. He looked at me while he did it and I did not mind the feeling.

You make me want to rescue you, he said.

I turned away from him. I did not want rescuing. I did not want anything. I did not really even want my leg.

Bed

After that first meeting in the Red Cow, Billy and I agreed that another was necessary very soon. As soon, in fact, as we could possibly sort it out.

But without the kiddy, I told him bluntly, Will that be possible, d'you think, to get away without her?

At first I thought he hadn't heard me, for he did not reply but just sat back on the bench and took out his pouch and slowly made himself a fag. Then he looked up at me with his lazy eyes.

I can, he said, But why?

I felt myself blush.

What d'you mean why?

I mean, love, what are we up to? What'll we do? Will it be a drink or what?

Steady on, I told him, amazed that he could be such an innocent, Can't we just take it a step at a time? See what comes?

He smiled, but more to himself than me.

Easy enough to say, he said, licking the paper.

He was right. It was easy to say. But mostly we made sure we did not say.

It was tricky. We could not meet at my house of course and naturally we could not meet at his. But I knew a woman in Dacca Street, a factory seamstress who was out for the best part of the day and happy to loan her bed for thruppence so long as we left it clean and tidy and replenished the candles as and when.

Oh, we won't need candles, I told her quite openly, for I'd made no secret of what I intended to do.

Who is he? she asked me, This man who merits such elaborate plans and excitement? He must be someone special, to get you in such a stew –

Do I look in a stew? I asked her, surprised that my feelings weren't more shut away from view.

Well, you're normally such a calm lady, aren't you? she observed and delved in her apron pockets and held up a glass that showed me how my cheeks were all pink and my eyes shining bright. She was right. I looked like a person with a fever, hectic and burning.

Slow down, girl, she said, Or you'll come before you've gone – and then she laughed a lot at her own dirty joke.

Women that sew for a living are the very worst. As if all that exacting work and neatness drives them mad so they have to let off steam somehow and they do it by bunnying on about men, men and more men.

Make sure you bring a blanket to lay on, Elsie said as we parted, I don't want to come back to mess on the sheets.

I don't know how Billy and I got ourselves up the rickety stairs that first time. I guess his heart was thumping and bumping at the exact same rate as mine.

I went up first, being the woman, but naturally he had to help me. I had on my woollen skirt, the brown one with the dark stripe and my green jacket and his arm was around me, hoisting the weight of me up over each step.

Right at the start he had offered to carry me up there but I had insisted I was fine to do it myself just leaning on his arm. But the stairs were much steeper than the ones in Ewan's and my house and halfway up he saw what a sweat I was in and he said he would do it anyway, without my say-so and whether or not I minded.

Aren't I heavy? I demanded to know as he swept my skirts up in one arm and held me purposefully, his breath shivery on my cheek.

Don't be bloody stupid, he said, You're nothing – a lightweight. A bit of fluff that floats and dances on the frigging wind –

Yeah, yeah, I laughed, Enough with the fancy ideas –

At the top he put me down and I handed him the key and leaned on my crutch to get my breath. It wasn't the climb but the man – his sudden touch and closeness – that had knocked it right out of me.

A crack of light came from under the door, but the stairwell was in darkness and it smelled of piss.

You all right? he asked me.

I'm fine, I lied.

Our faces were inches apart. This was my dream. This was all I had lived and died for. I wanted to cry I was so choked up with happiness.

When he slammed the door, the room shook. It was a cleanish, whitewashed place, very spare, making the most of a smallish space. Elsie was a neat and thrifty person so I was not at all surprised to find it so.

A thin iron bedstead was shoved against the wall with two covers on it – and beyond it stood a chair with its rattan fast unravelling. A stained petticoat hung on a hook by the door. (Why leave such a thing hanging up for all to see, I wondered?) There was no covering on the floor and at the window was tacked up a greasy blanket full of holes.

Billy went immediately over to lift it.

Don't, I said.

But we can't see each other.

What is there to see?

I want to see you, he insisted. And he fastened it back, despite what I said, so the light flooded in and the comfy darkness was all gone.

I had thought, when I said goodbye to my child, that it was all over for me then, that I'd had my quota of love. The child loved me and I loved the child and that was bound to be the best love I would ever know. What followed could only ever be blank and heartless by comparison.

I was fifteen when I lost him. Earning a penny an hour making party streamers whenever the work happened to come along. There I was, sat alone in an empty room and doing the work as best I could, trying to ignore the drag and prickle of the milk. Every day it was dwindling but still there was enough that by dusk I couldn't lift my arms for the heaviness and hurting.

Mondays between the hours of ten and twelve I could call and ask after him. The first weeks, just standing there outside the big oak door was enough to soak my bodice through, even though I stuffed half a dozen rags inside.

Just knowing that he was in there somewhere – my little love breathing and gurgling in that daunting place – was enough to make the milk spring out. It was lucky, then, that I had my shawl to pull around me and hide the stains, for sometimes I waited up to an hour before I was attended to.

Child Z, they called him, looking him up for me in the big ledger. They turned the pages so slowly that I wanted to scream. How many children could there be?

Child Z is thriving, they said at last. And then opened the big door again for me so I could leave.

Eventually the piecework dried up and I was turned out of my lodgings and found myself in a mouldy basement in the back of the cottages on Conro Street. There I managed to learn mush-faking from an old geezer who lived across the yard and took a shine to me.

Bad Laura, he called me. I did not like him. He was always coming by and backing me into a corner with his old man's body and his bad breath. I told him to leave me alone – and I meant it – but then one day he came over and generously gave me two of his cast-offs. He said that he was going to instruct me in the making of a pretty near perfect mushroom out of the few reasonable struts that was left.

As we worked he told me his life story, which was a dreary enough tale, much as you would expect and not that different from anyone else's around there.

Oh, goodness, you're so unusual, I lied, I mean, you've had so many experiences.

I love you, Laura, he confessed, blotting a tear from his filmy old eye, I think I am wholly smitten with you –

That's a load of old flannel, I told him, You're a sad old geezer with an even sadder mind –

That too, he agreed with an enthusiastic giggle, That too.

He loved me to criticise him, loved to hear himself put down. He'd been lonely in his life, so lonely that no one had ever chastised him. He'd never had his hopes and dreams made fun of by an affectionate friend, nor relished the rub and grit of family life.

Meanwhile, though, an excitement was growing in me. All the time I was thinking – this is easy, I could be good at this and work hard and make a decent living at it. And then an even bigger possibility exploded in the centre of the smaller one. That once I'd got some money together and my life in order, I could go and get my baby back.

I've come to claim Child Z, I'd tell them, pulling out with a flourish the little cambric shirt I'd been keeping all along for him. (Oh I know it, I know he'd have grown. But in my mind he'd shrunk and was somehow even smaller and daintier than the day I gave him up.)

And straightaway they'd bring him out to me and he'd cry 'Mummy!' and I'd touch his face and hold him in my arms and press my mouth and nose against the sweetest, softest, mustiest part of his little head.

And I'd whisper how much I loved him, how I'd never for one moment stopped loving him in all this time and was never going to leave him again – and it would be an exquisite agony to be so close to him again and relive all those sensations I thought I'd given up for good.

The room is in darkness, packed with shadows. The candle Billy is holding is smoking badly. Every time it flickers, the wall seems to move as well. I hate the feeling. I want to light the lamp and I say so, but Billy stops me and says a candle is enough.

We don't want light showing at the window, he says and I immediately take against his tone – as if I am a small child that wants to take its clothes off in the public street.

But the shutters are closed –

All the same –

Please, Laura – I know what I'm saying.

He sets the candle down on the long bench and together

we peer into the centre of the room where there is certainly a body on the floor.

A body where I left it. I left him there. It is the same place, yes, that's certain – no, he has not moved. It's not that I expected him to – I am sure I finished him when I drove the poker in – but a million years seem to have passed in the few hours since I hurried from this house. A million. All the crying and waiting. It is amazing to me that anything is the same – amazing that any of it can be as real as this, a body on the floor.

What's the time? I ask Billy.

No idea. Late. Why?

I can't look at him, I say.

You have to, Laura, Billy says, We have to move him.

So I put my eyes on Ewan, feast on the sight. He is real. More real than I am, that's for sure.

What is it? Billy says.

What do you mean?

You look so strange sometimes, you –

Yes of course I look strange, Billy, I am very upset –

No, he says, You looked – for a moment you looked –

He is staring at me with a rigid face.

What? I say, What? Tell me what it is, Billy. Stop scaring me –

You looked as if you weren't really here at all – as if you were off somewhere else –

What a thing to say, I tell him, Come off it, don't be so foolish.

No, he says, I've seen it before, you know, I mean it – it's how you sometimes look –

How? I ask him impatiently, How do I look for God's sake?

Unreal, he says then as if he's decided it finally for good. And his mouth is all ugly and slack as he says it.

I laugh.

No, love, I tell him, This is unreal – this – seeing him down there – like this –

I can't believe you did it, Billy says as he is saying all the time now, Look at him –

Now, despite the gloom, you can see there is so much blood over his face, neck and arms that you can't tell what happened to him or where the injuries are. Too much blood pooling over the eyes to see what his expression is.

There is a smell in the air – of blood and something else, a dreadful, acrid stink.

Jesus Christ, says Billy, and he moves back slightly, but I step forward for now I am not afraid.

He is turned slightly on his side with one arm underneath him and the other flung out as if reaching out for something. There is something strange about the flung-out arm and now I see what it is. It is too long. It has come out of the shoulder somehow. Did I do that? And one of his boots is nearby, but the other has gone right over by the table. How come?

There was a struggle, I say – and the sound of my own voice, biting into the room's thick silence, makes me jump.

You're telling me, says Billy and his voice just then is so heartbreakingly soft you could lay your head down on it. Every sound is made strange – even our breathing, the two of us, looking at him, sounds like someone else.

Suddenly I can't remember how long we've been here in this room and I panic.

Did we just have a conversation? I ask him.

What?

Just then, a moment ago, about me not really being here. Did you just say that?

No, says Billy.

Billy?

My voice is tight with fear and Billy stares at me.

Laura, stoppit, he says, Don't do this.

But did we? I whisper, I mean it. I'm not messing with you – it's – just now, in my head, I heard us saying things to each other.

Shut up, he says, Shut up about your head, I don't want to know – look what you've done. This is bad enough. Don't –

What time is it? I ask him.

Late. Almost dawn. I told you. Which is why we have to work something out.

Moments pass and then:

Look at his hair, says Billy, Look at the colour of it –

But you knew that, I remind him, You knew he had red hair.

I didn't –

But I know I've told you, a million times –

No, Laura, I don't think you have, he says and he takes another step backwards, away from Ewan and away from me.

I try to touch him or grab his coat-cuff but he moves and takes himself round to peer at Ewan from the other side.

Your kids would have had that hair, he remarks as if he doesn't at all want to let go of what he's seen, A load of little carrot-nobs you'd have had –

Look, Billy, I say firmly, Ewan and I are not having any

kids. Can you just get that into your stupid bonce? For heaven's sake, I am not even a –

Not a what? Billy asks me sharply as I stop myself.

I am not a maternal type –

No, he says with sudden passion, I know you're not, Laura.

So what are we going to do? I ask him, for I won't, I will not, be threatened by him.

I ask him this also because I know I am waiting for him to tell me how to behave. Frankly, if I could ask Ewan, I would. He was always the one to know what to do.

Why're you smiling? Billy asks me, pouncing immediately.

I'm not.

You were – just then. Grinning all over your face like a twot, girl.

Nerves, I tell him, It is nerves. Have you never seen a person smile out of nerves?

There is a silence and then:

How could you do this? he says quietly, I don't know what you were thinking of.

It felt like the only thing, I tell him.

But – I mean – I can't believe it. What was going on in your head? Jesus, Laura, I mean, what sort of a person are you?

I am a person who can only take so much, I tell him sadly, I am an ordinary woman who has been reduced to this. And anyway, don't ask me who I am if you can't take the answer.

Billy is shaking. I can feel it and I wish I couldn't.

None of this is fair on me, he says, Look at what you have made me cope with. Sometimes I would much rather not love you, you know, and I mean that.

That's sad, I say.

I know it is. And you have done it. What you have done is sad.

I'm sorry, I tell him, Really, I am sorry, my darling.

Which is true. I am sorry for everything, I really am. For though you might think the world is bottomless, endless, the reality is it can only contain so many people.

And you can run away all you like, or they can shut you away in darkness. But just when you thought you'd got away, someone has a great time shaking it all up – watching the trouble and the pain as the dirt settles and we, the wrong people, all find each other all over again.

The first umbrella I made still had tiny, slitzy holes in the cambric, but the old man praised what I had done to it and told me it didn't matter in the slightest.

Look here, he said, Just go and stand on London Bridge at crack of dawn in spitting rain and show the brolly to some fine gent on his way to Threadneedle Street –

He pestered me so much to do it, that soon I gave in and went off one morning as he suggested.

Ask the highest price you dare! he advised, so I did and I sold it easily.

Great! I was getting a taste for the job.

So I went to buy another skeleton off him, but this time he refused to take my money and said he would only part with it for a kiss.

Oh, I thought sadly, It always comes to this.

I'd rather you felt my bubbies, I said cheerily – for my lips were somehow still my own, but since I gave up my child my breasts had been two sullen and useless things, reminding me only of pain and loss. What did I care what anyone did with them?

So the old man played them like they were a musical instrument – careful and intent and with his dazed old eyes closed. He ran his trembly fingers over them, up and down and round abouts. He called them his charlies, his dears, his loves. He really was a right old mug.

And I hardly felt it. He was very gentle and tentative because he could not believe his good luck at being allowed to do it. After three minutes or so I said his time was up and he went to get me an umbrella.

Where did you get it? I asked him.

Aha! he said, because of course he wasn't going to tell me. I held it and tested the mechanism. It was a forlorn enough example but several struts were intact and it still had a passable handle.

The trouble was he was getting to see that I was better at the mush-faking than him. Quicker fingers I had, and much bigger advantages when it came to selling. When he suggested we join forces I said no thanks and though he called me ungrateful and tried to take my tools off me, I did not care. Because by then I'd figured out a way to make my business bloom.

All along the river if you walked long enough and looked hard enough, there were, among the bedsprings and jags of broken bottles, bits of brollies – the struts and ribs and mechanisms of stuff discarded by them who could afford to chuck away their belongings.

Sometimes I walked for many miles along the muddy shore till the buildings fell away and so did the foul smells and all there was left were purple fields and wide, dizzying grey skies. In summer in a hot, dry wind I collected till my cheeks burned. In winter I had to force myself to turn back before I was plunged into an icy dusk.

And sometimes if we'd had no rain and the brolly business was slow, I'd turn to the beer-making. Not having a pan of my own I had to improvise, so I had the bright idea instead of broiling the ginger, cloves, loaf sugar and lemons in the copper that the old man and Ma Blebs and the others stewed their dirty clothes in.

If you waited for the scum to float up, you could skim most of it off and who was going to spot if there was some crud and muck left in the sediment? And once the beer was cooled and bottled I could spike eighteen shillings in a day when the weather was hot.

Billy kept on finding things to say, so I asked him which he wanted to do first – talk or take off our clothes?

Pardon? he said.

Look, Elsie will be back at four, I told him, So we must be decent when the clock strikes the quarter – and I reckon we should be gone soon after.

Oh, he said, Take off our clothes then, I suppose.

You don't sound very sure –

Take off our clothes, he said.

And you a family man, I teased him as I sat on Elsie's mean little bed and began to unbutton, I'm surprised at you.

I'm surprised at myself, he agreed rather soberly, adding, But it's what we've come here for, isn't it?

Oh what, I said, For a surprise?

No, he said, To – to see each other and be together.

I don't know, I said, because I hadn't asked myself that question or any others for that matter. All I could think of as I undid the front of my blouse, was how slight he seemed and how we might be in for a shag but I just couldn't picture it.

I sat there and got to work on the lower-down buttons and hooks and whatnot. It was a long job. I had proper lady's clothes with many fastenings now, but it didn't seem like so long since I had wandered along the river's muddy edge with my two bare feet and no stockings and my one cheap pair of drawers flapping against my thighs.

What? he said suddenly and I looked up.

I didn't speak –

What're you thinking about?

Well, I told him, I was thinking about how it's only a few years that I've had these sort of clothes – good clothes, you know? And yet how strange that I am completely used to them already. I don't think I could ever go back to poor garments, not now, I just couldn't.

What about when you were a child? he said.

Oh, I smiled, Then I had the very best. My father saw to it. I was a very dressed-up little girl and rather spoilt too I think, quite disdainful of the poorer children on the street –

He looked at me and immediately I saw my tactlessness.

Not that yours are at all bad, I added, taking in his stained waistcoat and patched wool jacket probably got from a clobberer, I'm sorry, Billy, you must think me very stuck-up. I really had no intention of sounding superior –

He laughed and then his face went serious.

You nearly always wear the same clothes anyway, he remarked.

I looked at him.

Well, you do, don't you? he said matter-of-factly, I don't doubt that you've many fine things. But every time I see you, you're dressed just the same.

I am not! I cried.

Laura, he smiled, It's all right. Don't take offence but you know very well that you are –

I tried to shrug.

Well, they are clean enough, aren't they? I remarked, for they certainly were.

It doesn't matter, he said, Look – that green jacket for

instance. It's the very same you had on when I pulled you from the river –

My cheeks burned.

How could it be? I said, The coppers put my clothes in a paper bag, but I believe Ewan threw them away and he was right to do so for they were so stinky –

Maybe you have more of the same, then –?

Maybe, I said uncertainly.

Look, it hardly matters, he said, smiling. And, seeing that he too was unbuttoning, I realised how much I was looking forward to seeing him without a stitch of clothes on.

When I was halfway through taking off my petticoats, I asked him if he was afraid.

What d'you mean? he said.

Everyone is, I told him, So you must be too.

He dropped his hands to his sides.

I don't know what you're talking about, he said.

Billy, I said, laughing a little despite the seriousness of the situation, Aren't you afraid of my – of what you might see?

He smiled then and came over to me.

Mmm, he said, What might I see?

He had his jacket and shirt off and his nipples were small dark smudges on his chest and there wasn't much hair at all, just one or two little ones that barely counted.

I had thought he would be hairier, but I think I'd forgot how young he was, just a baby really and so perfectly formed and sweet and dear. I just wanted to take him in my arms and squeeze, stroke and hold him. In fact I wanted that more than anything in the world at that moment.

Why should I be afraid? he said, and his face was so honest and open I could have kissed it there and then, What is there to be afraid of, Laura?

Your mam must be well proud of you, I blurted out because I couldn't help it, I felt such a rush of straightforward affection for him.

What makes you want to do that? he said with such sudden gruffness that I wished I'd never spoken.

Do what?

Bring up my mam like that —

Well, I faltered, I thought —

I never had one, he said firmly.

What? I stared at him, But it's not true —

How do you know? he asked me, I was brought up in the hospital for foundlings —

I grabbed my own left hand with my right and pulled at the fingers, trying to hide my shock.

What? he said, You know it then?

I have heard of it, yes, I said.

He looked away from me towards Elsie's patched and frayed window where a little afternoon sun tried halfheartedly to poke its way in.

I'm sorry, I said.

He smiled. Oh no, he said, It was fine — they do their best and I never lacked anything. If you get in there you are a lucky one, for everyone wants to put their babies there. It is an efficient place — I was even fed at the breast —

I bit my lip.

No! I said.

He laughed.

Don't look so worried. It was all done very well and happily. They send you away to the country — I was there till I was three. I can't really recall her, this kind and wheezy woman with a big face. Seemed old but can't have been. Always lushed though. And a load of bouncing dogs.

Where in the country? I asked him.

Oh, I don't know, he said, I've never really thought about it. Essex maybe, somewhere near there –

Do you know who your mama was?

He frowned.

How would I?

She never came to claim you?

He shook his head.

Why should she? They generally don't – mostly, they don't want to, you know –

I was crying. I had not meant to be, but I was. Billy looked very surprised, as if he did not think his story was a cause for weeping. He touched a tear from my cheek and looked at it as it hung there on the end of his fingertip.

I'm so sorry, I whispered, I would never have thought it –

Oh, he said, staring at my tear as it dissolved between his finger and thumb, It's fine, it's not as bad as you think.

Really? Wouldn't you have thought it? Why not?

I don't know, I said, But I wouldn't. You seem so, you know –

He waited.

So nicely brought up, I told him.

He threw his head back then and laughed, though I noticed his mouth still turned down a little at the corners. I so badly wished I could cheer him up.

We are doing too much talking, he said, I thought we were supposed to be taking our clothes off?

Oh, I said.

Are you too upset? To do it now?

I brightened.

I will get it out, I told him, remembering that all my petticoat and stay laces were undone, Don't you think that's best? And then you can have a good look at it, in your own time. It's all right – it's only flesh after all – and you don't have to touch it if you don't want.

Billy stopped everything and looked at me. He seemed almost distraught.

Laura – he began.

Just to get it out of the way, I explained, trying to keep my voice even and bright.

Laura, he said, putting his arms around me for the first time ever, Please. It's all right, please stop –

I stopped. I closed my eyes and felt him. I experienced his heart thudding against my ear. I thought, if I die now, if this proves to be the high point of my whole life, I will be happy.

Then he spoke.

You don't have to do it. You don't have to get your kecks off, he said gently and I felt his hand on my hair, cupping my head.

But – I said.

Calm down, will you? You're rushing at things. We can just look at each other, can't we? I don't care if we haven't long – we will make another time. I just want to be with you for now. Really, that's what I came for.

It isn't much like a man, I said hotly, even though his arms were still around me.

He laughed.

You aren't much like a woman, he said.

What?

I did not understand him at all.

What I mean is, I don't feel like I normally do, he said.

Normally?

With other women.

Oh, I said, crestfallen, So you have other women? You mean as well as your wife?

He let go my head and sat back, his hands still on my arms. He looked troubled, his eyes never leaving mine.

Sometimes, he said, I have done. Now and then it happens. Not that often, if you want the truth.

I do, I cried, I do want the truth, Billy!

Well, I'm giving you it, aren't I? he said quietly, and now our fingers found each other and gripped on hard, I would not lie to you, Laura.

I'm too old for you, I said, I know it. That's what it is. You don't have to lie about that, you know —

No, said Billy, No, no, no! you've got it all wrong. It's — well — this time it's all different

He let go my hands and went and got the tatty chair and sat on it with his legs wide apart and pulled out his tobacco. He had a convenient way of rolling cigarettes so that his head was always down. Suddenly he put down the pouch and pushed the heels of his hands in his eyes as if he was trying hard not to cry.

Then he looked at me.

It's not you, he said at last.

I sat on the bed and watched him. Already my fingers were missing his — they felt loose, dismal and cold.

I have strange feelings about you, I told him and as I said it I let out a huge sigh. It felt like the first true thing I had said which was odd, since I cared very much and was trying very hard.

He smiled.

I have the same — about you, he said.

I laughed. I did not know what to say. He looked at me, I looked back at him and laughed again and he looked down again. Soon we were both laughing, but I made sure I kept my eyes on him. I felt steady, daring. After a moment, he said:

Let's see it then.

You don't want to.

Yes I do.

Silently I hoiked up my petticoat and opened my stays and untied my drawers. My fingers were trembling so much I turned the bow into a knot and had to prise at it with my nails to get it undone.

At last I slipped it down over my thighs to reveal my one long naked leg and the other, shortened into a stump, buckled and inert. The flesh dimpled and puckered where Ewan had stitched it and there were funny, luminous zig-zags where the skin had been pulled so taut.

You see? I said, kicking the good and shapely leg out towards him, curling the toes nicely, I once had quite a reasonable pair of gams –

Billy looked, but he stayed where he was. He struck a match and lit his cigarette, keeping his eyes on me all the while.

Why're you showing me? he said at last.

I tried to think of an answer.

I don't want it to be between us, I said, but I knew as I said it that it was a lie. The real answer was far more slippery than that. I had been alone with it all for so long – was that it? Did I want a companion for my losses?

Does it hurt? he said.

Not unless I wear my peg, I told him, Then I promise you it hurts like hell.

He looked pretty surprised.

But I thought you didn't have a peg? he said, I've never seen you with one –

Oh, Ewan makes me try with one – he says it will give me freedom and so on. But I don't like to do it, not often. It's so unwieldy and it gets so sore –

I'm not surprised, B. said, still staring.

I'm supposed to walk around the garden, I told him, Where no one can see me, not even our servant, can you imagine? But I can't be bothered. Maybe I don't want to be freer. Maybe I am happy to hobble around –

Are you? he said.

I thought about it.

Up to a point I think I am, yes.

He stared at me and shook his head. Blew smoke out. Just looking at him made my insides go hot and I realised I wanted him to touch me.

Feel it, I ordered him.

And, when he saw I was serious, he came over and knelt before me and ran his big brown hand over it, the pleated smoothness, the part of me that Ewan had sawed and stitched. The stump of me that no one ever saw.

I watched his face carefully.

Feels nice, he said and he lodged his cigarette between his teeth and placed both hands on it, on me, Feels like –

I waited and he smiled.

Feels like an arse, he said.

I laughed.

No, he said, Really –

Don't you want to touch the other one now? I asked him, for I was so liking the feel of his hands on me.

In time, he replied, But I'm enjoying this one for now.

And, keeping one hand on my stump, he moved up to sit beside me on the bed and with his other hand he touched my cheek, my nose, my tired, parched lips.

Then he pulled my face towards him and kissed me, very gently, so gently that I couldn't tell where he was doing it and yet at the same time I felt it all over, in every ordinary, undiscovered bit of me.

You're lovely, he said.

So are you.

No, you're lovelier –

No, you are –

No, you are –

And so it went on and we sat there doing so much kissing that my lips turned numb and I felt that everything was frozen, stilled and stopped. Thinking of this punched the air from my lungs and I could not stop myself. I gasped.

What is it? he asked me as I broke off from his mouth to stare around me wildly.

Nothing, I replied with a shiver. And moved my face hurriedly back to his.

Blood

Billy has so many plans and ideas that they light up his face. But he has also drunk a little too much so the shadows are beginning to crowd in and confuse both of us.

He says we have to get the body from the house.

He says we should even think about going out at dead of night and just laying Ewan as he is – all blooded and smashed up – in some gutter or alley in another part of town. The notable surgeon, set upon, at dusk. Blows, cries, pockets emptied. Done in by who knows? – well, it sounds likely and it's tempting.

But how would we ever get him there? I demand to know, Heave his bleeding body on to a tram or what? For heaven's sake, Billy, think of how it really is –

If we leave him here, Billy says slowly, suddenly keen on playing the grand detective, They will want to know what you were doing, Laura. You know it. You will be the first one they look at –

But – anyone could have got in –

He sighs.

There's no sign of someone forcing the door. Think about it, Laura. You are the only one apart from him that has a key –

We could make it look forced. We could smash the lock —

Billy shakes his head.

We'd never do it well enough. Believe me, Laura, they know about ruddy locks, they'd soon find us out.

But look how damaged he is, I tell Billy, All the bone of his head is gone, all the part that was round is squashed quite flat —

His skull, Billy breaks in dully as if he thinks that I, a surgeon's wife, don't know what to call it, His skull is smashed —

Yes, I say, I know it is his skull thanks very much, Billy. But what I mean is, no one would think a woman could do that — surely not? His skull is cracked open in at least two places and that light-coloured stuff that I'm sure is the brains, has all slid out. Look at me — would a cripple like me be capable of such a thing?

Billy appears to give this some thought.

I wish you had not done it, he says unhelpfully.

Billy, I say, gritting my teeth at him for he is driving me more or less up the wall with frustration, It is done, the thing is done. Will you please get that into your head —

You are a tiger, Billy continues, his voice weighed down as if in a trance, Look at you —

He kisses me, but he is quite drunk now and there is both horror and longing in the kiss.

From my lips, he tries to go back to Ewan's gin bottle but I stop him.

You've had enough, I say, because now I am feeling very upset and ratty. There is sweat damping the top of my stays. Here we are back in the parlour again, having not yet actually dared touch the body.

He will be very difficult to move, I say, Think about it. He's not – complete –

Billy laughs.

I like that! he says, Complete. It is certainly a nice way of putting it.

Well, it's true.

Complete! Ha!

Billy, come on. Be practical –

It's not a problem, Laura. He can be wrapped in something – he will have to be –

But his voice trails off.

Oh! I exclaim impatiently, My best plan would be just to leave the bugger here and run off like I said, Bill, just the two of us, to France. Think of it, the relief – I don't believe they would come after us there and besides –

Billy is silent and not as enthusiastic as I would have liked.

I mean, why can't we just go, I say again, A train to Folkestone and then catch the next boat and –

My kids, Billy says lamely, You have forgot my kids –

I make an exasperated noise and look at him.

I can't just leave them, he says.

Your bloody kids.

Yes my bloody kids and what of yours? he cries.

I glance at that bitter face of his and it grinds my insides up. He makes a little noise of pain and comes over to me and I take him in my arms and hold his head and bury my face in the hair that smells not like the river but like fresh air and blue skies.

Inside my arms he is crying.

He is crying but even so he tries his best to reach down and get my skirts up – he's so drunk. I slap him down.

For God's sake, Billy, I say and then I remember, Let me go – please – I have to go to the WC –

It's you, he whispers after me as I leave the room, It is you who has done all this, who has churned me up –

I think I hear him sobbing, but it could be the sounds that ring in my ears perpetually now: sobbing and sobbing like an infant left alone.

I leave the room and cross the hall where Ewan's hat and coat still hang in a totally unreal way – husk of a man, still there and not there. In the small cloakroom off the passage, I check my underthings. The blood that started when I killed him has stopped and all I have is a little dry brown stain now. I try to calculate what day it is, but in the state I am in I'm too confused to count back. I am sure it is due anyway, so I leave the rag there in case.

Back in the parlour, Billy is smoking, his feet on the fender, and doing a good imitation of someone thinking.

All right? he says and I am glad to see he looks recovered. The sobbing was not him then.

I nod and take his free hand and hold it firmly in mine. Feel him relax a little in my grip.

There is a problem with the street plan, I explain, A big problem which I have only just thought of – what about his overcoat and hat? He would have had them on, he'd never go out without them, and it would be pretty imposs- ible to get them on him now in his present state –

Of incompleteness? says Billy and laughs.

I nod, but I am serious.

So we have to run, I say, my heart racing, the panic piling up again, We have to get out of the country before they get a chance to come and find him –

No, Billy says slowly and I am so grateful to see the light is seeping back into his eyes, Stop, Laura, stop rushing.

Hold on. I have a plan. It's the only plan when you think about it – it's so obvious it's like something in one of your blinking books – well, listen to this –

Give me a clue, I say, glad to see he is at last getting into the spirit, What does it involve, this plan of yours?

Well, it involves the river, he says.

Everything involves the river –

Well –

In the end, my love, I tell him, It does.

Shh, be quiet, Laura. Just listen now.

And he puts his arms around my shoulders and kisses my ear till my arms go frozen up and down with the hairs wafting up. And with his breath so close that the shudders start up all over my body, he proceeds to tell me the nature of his plan.

Ewan caught up with me, appearing across the street as I made my way with some difficulty from the hospital.

It was raining hard and it was my first time out on the crutches they had given me and I was finding them incredibly unwieldy and difficult and annoying. It was very hard actually even to swing my weight on them and I was sweating and the world seemed suddenly at the wrong level, as if the whole of me had been lopped off in some vital place and not just my leg.

I walked a couple of steps in the pouring rain and then stopped, then walked again. I wanted to throw the crutches down, for it felt like it would be easier just to give up and hop like a child. But I could not have got very far like that and anyway I had strange tired creeping pains all over my body from lying down so long in a hospital bed.

The wet in my hair and clothes was making me cold and I only had on the thin shawl I was run down in.

All around me, things were happening on account of the weather. A bale had been flung accidentally off a cart and clods of straw were streaming past and stopping up the gutters. Part of the street was ankle-deep in water. Folk were shouting and a man was trying to unstop the gutter with a pan handle or something.

I wished I could just dissolve in that gutter, wished I could have disappeared from sight, whisked on the fast-running water like a thin strand of that straw.

Ewan had a big, black, man's umbrella which he held high above his head. He must've walked fast or even sprinted to catch me up for – though I made achingly slow progress – it seemed that one moment the street was deserted and the next there he suddenly was, rather redder in the face than he could afford to be with that colour hair – pulling on his overcoat with one hand while attempting to manage the umbrella with the other.

I stared at him with as much shock and guilt as if I had seduced him into coming after me, which of course was not the case. Despite what happened later, I was not on the grab, nor did I at that time – or indeed for a long time – mean him any harm.

I had no thought or intention of ever seeing him again. I did not want anything from him and certainly felt no particular involvement with him. And yes, of course I was sorry he had taken off my leg, but I saw it only as him doing his job and I bore no grudge and did not hold him to blame for any of my losses in any way.

But if I was anxious at seeing him, he seemed even more so at seeking me out. He waited agitatedly for a cab to pass and then, barely even noticing the commotion and flooding on the other side, he crossed over towards me, never taking his eyes off where I stood.

It's all right, don't look so worried, he said as he caught my arm, It's only me – look at you, you're soaking – I just wanted to –

What? I said and he looked at me so hard that I had no idea what to say. I had no words that would match his brimming, agitated face.

I don't mind the rain, I said quietly for I wasn't enjoying the big shadowy thing he was so intent on hovering over me.

Well, I never said goodbye, he said uncertainly, You never came to see me as you promised. You said you would and I wanted – aren't you cold, Laura, look at you –?

They told me to leave, I said.

Well, they shouldn't've, should they? Not in this downpour.

Well, I mimicked him, They did, you know. They said I was discharged. I didn't think they especially minded about the weather frankly –

He thought I'd made a joke and he smiled.

And I don't mind the rain, I said again.

For the next moment or two we said nothing, just adjusted our faces as our ears was drowned by the sound of the water pouring. Then:

So how are you managing? he asked me, indicating the crutches.

Badly, I said.

And have they fitted you with anything? he wanted to know.

What d'you mean? I said.

A prosthesis. You should be trying one. Sooner or later, and preferably sooner –

What, a peg? I said scornfully, Oh no thanks, no way, I'm not having one of those things –

Ewan smiled at me quite kindly then and, feeling rather annoyed, I tried to look away but found I couldn't. His eyes were so blue and staring.

What is it? I said, Why're you looking at me all the time in that way?

You're very direct, he observed, For such an agreeable woman. Where do you get the nerve, to be so direct, I mean?

I've nothing to lose, I told him truthfully. And I yawned.

Bored?

Not exactly.

Tired?

Maybe.

Then come with me, he said, taking my arm with noticeable care, We'll go to the best and pleasantest tavern we can find and drink something. Beer or anything you like. Would you? Would you like to?

If you like, I said.

You don't sound convinced.

I've nothing to lose, I said again.

Laura, he said and touched my shoulder as he steered me, I would like to make you feel better, not worse.

Oh, all right then, I said.

So here's the thing. I was fourteen. It was dark and late. I should never have gone with him. I entirely blame myself.

I wasn't hurt. I think I got off lightly. He had on such nice toff's clothes that when he touched my elbow and offered a lift in the hansom, of course I said yes.

Well, of course I did. It was late, cold and I was supposed to be in Dalston where my auntie was very poorly with a tumour in her breast.

Which aunt? Ewan asked me when I told him the story on the second day of our marriage, I never knew you had an aunt?

Yes you did, I told him, She was the one with the money. Well, some money. That she lent to my father's shop when he fell on hard times –

And then she died and –

Yes. Left it all to the Catholics.

Oh, said Ewan, That one. Your father's sister then?

Yes – and the tumour was in the left breast if you want to know.

She was dying then?

Yes, I said, As I just told you, Auntie was dying and she was expecting me and it did not seem a bad decision to go with the man, it was a kind offer made on the spur of the moment that any sensible person would take.

But once I was in that stuffy, soupy-smelling cab, the gentleman reached for my body and sat me on his lap facing him like an infant and commenced roughly pulling up my skirts.

I cried out as he put his fingers in for I had never felt anything like it and it hurt horribly.

Ewan gasped as he heard this, but I deduced it was a gasp of pleasure more than sympathy. He laced his fingers in between mine.

Did you struggle? he asked me eagerly.

Struggle? Are you joking? I said, Of course I did and shouted and kicked and threw as big a fit as I dared.

Ewan edged closer to me on the couch and began tonguing my ear. The moistness sent shivery air all over me but in a bad way.

And I cried till my brain hurt and my heart was almost jumping out of me with the fear that he would not stop till he had killed me. But the fingers stayed right in and when he pulled them out he said –

Mmm, said Ewan, pulling my hand speedily down to his trousers, Tell me, my darling, what he said –

He said: Tomorrow you won't know this happened.

That's what he said? Ewan froze in the middle of all this business, as if it was an effort to have to think.

Yes.

Odd thing to say, Ewan mused as he returned my hand to his lower parts, Why d'you think he said that?

Your guess is as good as mine, I said.

And –? said Ewan, breathing close to me.

And he released his – you know – into the space between my thighs. And his voice went low and strange as men's do when they're off in that world of theirs –

Ewan put his arms around me now and kissed my lips wetly even though I was talking. Then he climbed on me.

And the cab went on, the seat was sweaty and digging into the back of my legs – and though I felt the tip of him nosing at me, I kept on screaming and trying to keep my whole self shut –

Oh, my darling, Ewan whispered in a rhythm all intent and his own, Oh, my sweet, my love –

But no such luck and the next thing I knew there was wetness and muck all over and on the seat too. Is it over? I whispered to him, Did you do it? – and he said Of course I did, you silly bitch, and to shut up now and passed me a big silky kerchief to wipe myself.

But – hold on a minute, Ewan said, stopping again even though his own hand was up in my skirts at that very moment, You mean you didn't know?

What?

You couldn't tell if he'd, well –

Oh, Ewan, I said impatiently, I'd never had anything bigger than my own little pinkie inside of me – how could I possibly know how it was supposed to feel?

But, Laura –

And no, I know what you're saying. I guess it didn't go right in, not properly. It just went far enough in to –

Ewan was on top now, putting his own inside me – there was no question about this.

Put you in that condition?

Yes, Ewan, to burden me with a babby.

Ewan moved in and out.

Well, I continued, I wiped myself off with his expensive laundered kerchief and though I was still shaking all over, my teeth knocking together in my head, he said, Look, girl, we're almost at Dalston now –

Enough, murmured Ewan, who had got it together now, pumping madly and lost in another world that involved only our two lower parts, We don't need the rest –

But, I said, You see I could not speak for the tears coming so fast down my cheeks and into my mouth and all I could think of was to get out of that cab and when he set me down I ran and ran, almost getting kicked by the horse as I dashed across its path –

Shh, Ewan covered my mouth with his surgeon-husband's hand as he moved harder and faster inside me, That's enough – mmm.

My aunt was very deluded when I got there, I whispered – for I was intent on going on with the story even if only in the peace and quiet of my own head, It was the delusions she had that made her leave the money to the church and put me out on the street, for my father owed her everything. Anyway she was hardly there any more when I arrived and soon afterwards she sank into –

The brain, Ewan muttered, for he couldn't resist a good symptom, The disease had got into the brain –

And I stroked her hand and sat with her there, wishing all the while my skirts were not so sticky –

Sticky! moaned Ewan.

And when she died a few days later she was put in a fancy Catholic grave at Dalston and that was the end of it. They did not say any prayers for her once they had got her money. And no one ever took flowers to the grave, not even me.

But Ewan had long stopped listening.

Ahhh! he cried as, eyes shut, face contorted, he catapulted himself into his own private heaven.

Ewan glanced down and seemed to notice (as I had) that his cuffs were edged with blood – brownish, flecked – and a little darker in the places where the material had worn and frayed.

He seemed on the point of apologising for them, but instead he sighed and extended his big booted feet towards the fender where the fire licked and crackled. Steam came off them.

Dry yours? he said to me, but realised his error as he spoke and looked tremendously embarrassed as he apologised.

I pointed my one black boot as daintily as I could and enjoyed the kick from the strong ginger wine he had bought me, for I was realising with some annoyance that I was really very nervous of him.

Well, he said, when I did not speak, So here we are.

Why? I asked him, Why the hurry to come after me?

Just as I'd expected, he did not meet my eyes.

Because I like you, he said, Because I did not know

where you would go. Because I didn't want to never see you again –

I smiled at the plainness of this.

But why me? I said, remembering just in time to crick my littlest finger as I lifted the glass.

It's not – well, it's hard to say but – look, Laura, I don't normally get to know my patients –

Ewan was incredibly flustered, he really was. I was quite glad. I could see it had cost him dearly to follow me into the street.

And you don't know me, I told him as I drank up his discomfort.

No, he said, hesitating, Of course I don't, but –

You would like to?

He pulled his coat-cuffs down over his soiled shirt and examined his boots. I knew it was just a pretext not to look at me.

How well you put it, he said.

He smiled. And I smiled. And the heavy wine slid down and warmed all my thoughts – so much so that they seemed for a moment to merge madly into one another. For a second or two I felt dreadfully happy for no reason at all.

Well, really, sir – I began.

Ewan, he said quickly.

Ewan, I echoed, You've baffled me. I mean, you're very kind but I don't know where all of this has come from –

Ewan hardly got a chance to reply for in the tavern a man was shouting and a small white dog was going round licking up crumbs off the floor. When he got close up to me, he must've sniffed the raw wound of my stump for he became rather too horribly interested and proceeded to lick and snaffle at my skirts.

I tried to shoo him off and Ewan quickly got up, meaning

to drag him by the scruff of the neck, but the dog was having none of it and rushed at my skirts now all the harder. Just as Ewan made to grab him again with both his hands, I had the bright idea of using my crutch. I dealt the wretched creature such a whacking blow on the head that he whippered away, very adequately damaged and stunned.

I was rather pleased with myself. I drew my crutch to me. If it had been a pistol I'd no doubt have blown on the barrel like the man in the tuppenny picture book.

I expected Ewan to be equally impressed, but instead he faltered and looked around him as if he expected consequences. I must say he seemed a little shocked and surprised.

Oh dear God, he murmured, I'm so sorry, I really am —

It was not your fault, I said.

But he made a brief show of looking for someone to chastise, then stopped as if dismayed.

Laura, he said, My dear. You could've killed it.

And he watched my face.

Well, you're right, I said steadily, I suppose I could've. But I don't really have a soft spot for animals, you see —

He said nothing. He tried to smile, but he was having a hard job, look at him, he just could not do it.

And anyway, you're wrong, I continued, About me.

He turned back to me.

You would not like me, I told him frankly, If you knew me any better —

Look here, only I can be the judge of that, he said.

And, though the words were claiming to be bold, he spoke them with such extreme diffidence and awkwardness that, if I hadn't already known him to be a famed limb-cutter and all that, I'd have suspected him of being a useless type of man with no experience of ladies at all.

What do you think I am like, then? I persisted, checking surreptitiously that the dog was not returning.

Well, Laura, he said, with some passion that showed he was warming to the game, You're funny. You say funny things sometimes – or I don't mean funny, but clever, yes, clever things. I like your mind. I like the way you cut straight through all the rubbish and you get to the pith, the truth –

The truth? Do I?

This was extremely interesting, this thought – the idea that Ewan perceived me to be an essentially truthful person.

In a manner of speaking, he said, Yes, I would say you do. And I'm intrigued by the way you have invented yourself – reinvented yourself perhaps, through great hardship, it seems to me. I sense that you are a person who has suffered somewhat – I don't mean your leg, I mean before that – and come through. And now, whoever you were before, you've chosen to be this rather beguiling Laura person –

I blushed hotly.

I have not ever invented or made things up! I cried, feeling terribly offended and rather frightened that he should get me so right.

No no, he said, not realising how near he'd been, You don't get it – you're misunderstanding me –

And anyway, I cut in, seeing a means of distracting him, Now I am forced to be someone else, aren't I? Now I'm one-legged Laura –

Well, that doesn't matter, he said.

What?

The way you are now. Your new state. It does not mar you at all in my opinion.

Oh well, thanks.

No, he said, I mean it.

Easy for you to say, I told him swiftly.

Maybe so, he said, But all the same I mean it. I do, you know.

You tell me then, I said, With my crutch and my stumpy leg, solve this. How will I – someone such as me – go about finding a husband?

He flinched but you could barely see it, he was trying so hard to stay level and calm. With a blank face, he drank down the last of his beer.

Like this, I said, Who will want me? Who? Not that dog over there, no, not even him –

Laura, he said – and stopped.

Who will want to be with me?

He swallowed.

You never married? he asked me at last. I knew he had been wanting to ask it for a long time.

I sighed.

It is a long story.

I'd like to hear it, he said, If you'd like to tell it.

No, you wouldn't and anyway I would not like to. It is full of ugly, inconsistent things that you would not like and that anyway medical men are best kept clear of –

He began to laugh. I knew he would.

You are so strange, he said, So amusing. I have never met an amusing woman –

I frowned.

What I mean is, he said quickly, as if thinking I would get the hump, You're surprising. You're not tame. All women I know these days are pretty tame and not at all clever.

Are you? I said, ignoring this last bit, Are you married?

I live with my mother, he said miserably and clouds fell on his face as if he'd just been reminded of a great burden, You know I do.

Oh yes, I said, making a show of remembering, So I do, forgive me.

He seemed so ill at ease then that I actually felt sorry for him and changed the subject. I asked him why, though he'd removed my leg and I'd seen it with my own eyes lying in the box, I could still feel it as if it was joined to me.

Sometimes I'd swing the wrong foot off the bed – the foot that had gone – and I'd find myself sitting, bump, on the floor. Sometimes the ache in the leg that'd gone was so bad I found myself rubbing frantically at the air to displace it.

Ewan's face went light again and he looked very interested when I told him all this.

Aren't you surprised? I said.

Well, I have not come across it, he said, Because patients do not generally tell me. But I have read and heard that it's a common enough phenomenon.

Fancy words, I told him.

But he seemed to be thinking.

Is it there now? he asked me shyly.

I nodded.

What? – now he did seem mildly surprised – Right now, you mean it's as if – you have the sensation of both legs?

I shut my eyes a moment, checking. Wiggled both sets of toes.

Oh yes, I said, I would say so. Just about.

Keep your eyes shut, he commanded, then, Do you feel this?

I did not. But I opened my eyes – and laughed, for he had placed a hand on the sunken part of my skirt where my old knee would have been.

Of course I don't, I said.

Then it's perfectly all right for me to keep my hand there, isn't it? he said. His face was triumphant – pleased and afraid and slightly savage all at once. I'm afraid to say it suited him, this new, wild face.

I said nothing – tried to take in this unusual form of flirting. I felt the light pressure of his hand dragging on my skirt. It was everything and it was nothing but it was very hard to ignore.

And so began our strange courtship.

I had a baby once, I told Billy.

He looked at me doubtfully.

But, Laura, you don't even like babies, he said.

I lost my baby, I told him, The loss went on me very hard. But you're quite wrong, I do like babies, mostly – well, I do and I don't – can you blame me?

I did not tell him anything more at that time. I did not like to. I knew his own history – knew how it wrapped itself so eerily around mine – but I was afraid of how he might take it, the idea that I was one of the very mothers whose type had caused him so much loneliness and pain.

In fact I had intended to stay smooth and wise and never get on to the delicate subject of my baby, but love squeezes the truth out of you at the strangest times and in the strangest ways, whether you want it to or not. A good and well-meaning man pulls you out of yourself, just as surely as he puts his own self in.

Well, we had just done it, the shagging part, on Elsie's bed and I was by the window, leaning on one crutch and trying to get a rather damp dib (damp on account of its having been found in the pocket of Bill's overalls) to light. I had on nothing but this thin, worn shirt for I loved to take his clothes. I liked how the cheap cloth slowly gave up his smell as my own skin warmed it.

He was lying on the bed, watching me. Smoking also I think. We were a couple of enthusiastic smokers, we were.

Baby, he'd called me and that's what made me say it. The words just fell from my mouth in a sad little heap:

I had a baby once.

You lost your baby?

Mmm, I said and looked away out the window where the street was still light and sunny and yet smelled dank and oppressive – of the river's solid mass.

Poor love, what did it die of?

I don't know, I said.

Come here, he said, but I stayed where I was.

I can see your bum, he told me, The shirt does not cover it at all, I can see it peeking out –

Still I said nothing, but I tried to cover myself.

So sweet – it is all white and plump, he said, And I can see the hair between your legs as well –

Stop it, I said, You are teasing me.

Come here, he said, I want to touch it, it's making me want to feel you, darling, oh let me –

No, I said, for thinking of my baby had got me all sad.

We were silent, both thinking – or at least I was. After a moment or two, Billy said:

Mine are all alive but one. And his presence is so strong that sometimes I have to pinch myself to check he's – that he's really gone.

Is it Jack? I said, for he had mentioned the child to me some time ago.

Yes, said Billy, Little Jack.

And he gave an upset little laugh.

I have his tooth here as a matter of fact, he said, diving

like an eager child across the bed to where his clothes lay in a scrumped-up pile on Elsie's dusty floor, D'you want to see it? Look, Laura –

And he held up a fragment of something so small and colourless and see-through I could not make it out from where I was.

His tooth? I said.

Yes, look – it has the speck of blood still in –

I believe you, Billy, I said, I won't actually come over and look if you don't mind.

It's his, Billy continued, oblivious, I took it off him. As he lay there – after – what I mean is, it was nearly out and would have come in a day or so – Jack would've got a coin for it. Was that wicked of me, d'you think, to go an' pull it myself?

I don't know, Bill, I said, How can I say?

He did not seem like a corpse. It did not feel like taking from the dead –

I'm sure it was all right then, I said, hoping to shut him up.

There was a bit of blood in the gum, he went on, But not much. Just, you know, where it was fixed – though his heart had stopped pumping it around him –

I wanted to tell him to stop, but I could not.

Have a look at it, he said again, I don't mind. Shall I bring it over?

I know what an infant's tooth looks like, thanks very much, Bill, I said.

Just a little stub, hardly anything – you can see through it if you hold it up to the light, look. It's always with me, I keep it on me all the bloody time, you know –

I said nothing.

All the bloody time, he said again, then, Hey, Laura, baby, you're crying.

I am not.

You mustn't cry, love, all the crying for Jack has been done and I didn't mean to –

He started to get off the bed to come to me, but I turned away.

It's not that, Billy, I said, I am not crying from sympathy so don't flatter yourself or me. I am crying for myself and that's the end of it. I am upset for things I can't forgive myself for –

He waited and when I didn't speak, he said, What? Something you did?

Yes, I said, That's right. Did.

I can't believe you've done anything, he said, Not knowingly, not you. Stop blaming yourself.

He meant well enough. He only meant to be nice. But I could hear from his voice that he was afraid to take me seriously. I could tell that he did not think there was anything, that he had already forgotten about my dead baby and wanted to go back to the subject of his own.

I said nothing, turned back to watch the stupid street. Children were dashing by all the time. Many of them were ragged and hatless and no doubt covered in sores. Some had long hair and thin, sloping bodies like his girl Pinny. A small crowd were playing at tipcat and nearby an apple seller stood on the corner shifting from leg to leg and shouting to them when they got in her way.

I am a bad person, I said softly, so softly that he might not have heard.

How did your baby die? he asked me very carefully.

It was my fault –

It was not! It cannot have been –

You don't know, Billy, you know nothing about this. I am responsible. I took – certain actions of mine –

But – maybe you acted for the best? Billy suggested, for he always loaded his own goodness on to the actions of others.

Well, I must say it didn't feel like it.

Billy sighed. He had stopped looking at my backside. He had stopped looking at me at all and was staring at the stained and peeling wallpaper by the side of Elsie's bed.

And I am sorry, I said, About little Jack.

Billy's hands went straightaway to his groin which they always did when he was bothered or thinking. He pushed absent-mindedly at his whatnot, moved it back and forth distractedly with his hands.

Sometimes, he said, I go to the cemetery, you know. Nearly always at dusk, just as the light is going –

What, to see the grave?

No, he said laughing, It is worse than that. I go for the company –

He was laughing as he spoke the words but I could tell from the stillness of his eyes that he was serious.

What? I said with a creeping dread, Living people?

No, he said softly and carefully, No, Laura, dead.

He smiled and as he did so, my heart turned over with a kind of recognition. I wanted to cry out but I didn't.

Funny sort of company, I said.

No, he said again, Really. You go there. You stand still among the graves and look around you –

Maybe I do. Maybe I already have, I whispered, but he did not hear.

Rows and rows of stones, he said, Frigging crowds of them.

And Jack? I asked him, Does he have a stone?

Oh yes, he said, Of course he does – though we had to

do a collection down the street for it, for we had never got him burial insurance – but I would not have let him go in an unmarked grave and nor would Cally for that matter.

I was silent.

And even though he was four, Billy said, He still fitted under the driver's seat – so it was a bargain, you see, he saved us money by staying small and being lodged under there, the little sod –

Bless him! I cried, before I could stop myself.

Yes, Billy looked me full in the face as if he was trying to find out something, but he did not know what, Yes, bless him.

He pushed crossly at his eyes to stop the tears.

I have not spoke of this for a long time, he said, You must understand that, Laura – it is very strange for me to hear you speak his name and that –

And that was when I felt I had to tell him.

Billy, I said softly, The dead – you were wrong, what you said that time – they do come back, you know –

He seemed not to hear.

I'd have liked pink granite for him, he said, The stone, you know? I'd have liked one of them spangly rose-coloured ones –

They come back, I said, And they don't give up. They keep on looking till they find their own –

Ah well, said Billy, It's a pretty enough idea. If God decides to –

It is not to do with God, I said quickly.

But one day, said Billy, whose mind would not stay pinned in one place for long, I will make him a beautiful grave. A peaceful place for my boy to rest. I promised myself I would do that – I promised it the day he died, Laura –

And he carried on talking, but I had stopped listening.

I picked up my one crutch and got myself over to him. Moving through the sullen air of that room to where he lay crying and going on about the dead, it would have been easy to take advantage. But I reckoned he knew I was coming by the pock-pock on the wooden floor.

And, sitting myself down on the narrow bed, I reached over and took the sweetest part of him – soft and sad and damp now – in my hand and lifted it, felt its smallness and its slightness.

And I passed my thumb over the stickiness of the head, pressed down for a second on the oozy slit, watched as he shut his eyes and trembled. I think I told him I loved him, but I don't know if he heard. Anyway, when I'd done so, I kissed the thing and laid it carefully back on the warm soft place where it belonged.

Blanket

It was the sunniest day.

It was late in May. I was nearly seventeen. Birds were shouting their songs into the sky that was the loudest blue and all the trees were fluffed up with pink and white. It was a day that lifted your wary heart right up out of itself and set it spinning into the beyond.

I made my way up Oareboro Road and into the top of Sail Street where the railway arches were turned into temporary stables for the cabbies and you could smell the manure and hear the lazy chomping of the big animals. There I slowed my steps, for I always loved passing that place – I liked the energy of it, tempered as it was with calm and contentment.

Everything was sharp to me that day, everything especially sensible and sweet. I remember things, many things, for no reason other than they were a part of that day. Later, it seemed wrong that I had remembered so much – as if I knew all along what was going to happen. As if it was no surprise, what was told to me that day by those men.

But I know I was happy then, dazzled by the cleanness and the brightness all around me. I know that one house had a blue and white pottery Virgin Mary over the door, which seemed a strange thing to have set against all the grimy brick and dark slate. And I am sure that many of the shabbiest dwellings still had carefully-tended pots of flowers and well-washed curtains. It was an optimistic neighbourhood where people looked out for each other and there was an overwhelming feeling of calm. I envied it.

Later, in a side street, I noticed other things – that a man was laying long earthenware pipes on a cart and a woman was shouting and a child crying. Just crying bitterly with her two fists jammed in her eyes for no reason that a passing stranger could make out. A passing stranger who was no one other than myself, me on my way to the hospital. With that unreal lightness in my head that I always got when going to ask after my baby.

I knew something was wrong when they did not go to the ledger straightaway. I knew when the man pulled out some papers and went to get someone and said I was to wait please, thanks very much.

I knew from the fact that he was polite to me yet did not look at my face and that there was some general sounds from the room behind, of drawers being slid in and out – and the fact that more than once the inner door opened as if someone was going to be coming out and then quickly shut again as if that someone had thought better of it.

If I hadn't been frightened and getting a cold sweat on me, I'd have been very fed up. Maybe I'd have got up and asked them to hurry. Or else left and said I'd come back later. But I didn't. I waited until my head hurt with the anxiety of it. Presently the first man came back, emerging from the unlit room behind with another, older, behind him as if the one was shielding the other.

Madam, he said and still he could not look in my face, You are the mother of Child Z?

I nodded.

I have to tell you then that he – the child – is no longer with us –

I stared at him. My stomach seemed to fall and a rush of hotness swallowed up my heart.

Shaking all over, I began to ask what he meant – to ask where in hell's name my baby was, but before I could get the words out the second man came forward and placed a cold hand on my wrist. He said that what his colleague had meant to say was that he was afraid that my child had died.

What?

I smiled because I could not understand and because it seemed the only thing to do. I smiled and then the smile went and there was a big blackness in my head and a taste of sick in the back of my throat.

What? I cried, You mean he's poorly –!

Madam, they said, We are sorry, but he passed away. He is – gone.

I hesitated, trying to hold on to the idea in my mind. But I found I did not believe it, I could not. My baby boy had been so vague to me for so long – no more really than a sweet, hazy warmth in my memory – that his death seemed just flimsy, no more real or solid than his birth or his life.

A fever came on very suddenly, said the man, though I had not yet thought to ask for any explanation, He was perfectly fine on the Monday and but took bad on the Tuesday, and that night he – well – I'm sorry –

He coughed.

Will you be wanting his things –?

What things? I said.

Well, there is something – a small wool blanket that was left with him when he was –

Blanket? I said. Blanket?

In my head that was spinning round the word made no

sense whatever for it was a lumpy word from another world. Blanket. I held it in my mouth like I had been given someone else's food by mistake.

The one he came wrapped in. We signed for it, along with the child. Your own one I imagine it was, Madam?

I stood there and I could hear the nervousness of his mouth juices drying up. My legs shook. This was it then, the baby, gone. No more nothing. No future. No more boy.

Then I felt a sudden dragging in my stomach – a terrible, stretching pain – as if he was coming out all over again.

Oh God! I cried, Oh my God!

A chair was pulled out and I was helped to sit. It occurred to me that in all these months of Mondays I had never once sat in this room, always been standing, and it looked quite different from so much lower down, unlit and edged with shadows.

Did he –? I began.

The two men were polite, I'll give them that. They stood and patiently waited for my question, even though there were now other people in the room to be dealt with – other people with living infants to ask after.

Could you tell me – did he die alone please, sir?

One of them – I know he was the one on my left – smiled faintly as if relieved to have a question that was simple enough to answer.

Your boy would have received the very best care, he said.

Not a single small soul is neglected here, the other one said.

I tried to think. I was panting now with the effort of it.

And please, sir, where is he laid? I said.

In the public grave in Goad's Place –

Is it — it's a decent place?

You should go and see for yourself, madam, they said, one or the other of them.

I replied that I would.

They asked me, was I all right? They asked me to write my name on a piece of paper to show I had received the news. They said they would get me the blanket now.

And after several minutes more of waiting, a scrap of worsted wool was brought to me, barely big enough to wrap a small baby in. Its edges were all frayed and stiff and it was stained and marked in many places. It was a colourless thing, but a few years before it had been pinkish. I remembered it very well.

I put it to my face. It smelled of something. I wanted to die.

Well, we are heading for the river and taking him with us.

It isn't yet dawn, though the far-off sky has been threatening for the past twenty minutes to turn a dirty mauve. It will be light soon and there isn't a lot of time.

He is not easy to carry so it is a good job we have him in three separate parts. Billy takes the two most cumbersome — trying not to stagger under the weight of the heaviest that is slung in a leather bag over his shoulder. I have the head and, though it is the neatest, I am surprised to find how weighty it is given its small size.

What is it that weighs so much? I ask Billy, The brains or the skull? It is the brains, I suppose —

Oh, Laura, please, Billy says.

But, my love, I was only wondering —

Please, he says, Shut up. Can we just get there and save the wondering for later —

Later! I think that later we will be free — free of this

whole bad episode, this awful burden, free of what we have done.

For that is certain. It is 'we' now. He has done it too. We are tangled together for ever he and I, whatever he may say. Though I do not mean it to, this idea – the idea that I am in solid, permanent company – cheers me considerably.

I look at him, at his dear, frowning face. The worry on it and the hard graft that he is having to do today. Yes, I think, we are a couple, him and me.

You didn't mind me talking back there in the house, I remind him gently, In fact I would say you badly needed me to talk or I guess you would have fainted clean away in a heap on the floor –

That was in the house, B. says gruffly.

Ah, I say, I get it –

Well, I don't think you do, Laura, not at all, he says, But please shut up anyway –

Hey, look out how you speak to me, I chide him for I am getting fed up of his superior attitude, I am not one of your family to be yelled and sworn at –

No, he says, You are a lady, aren't you?

But I don't like his tone as he says it, not the way he grunts and slings a look up at the sky.

On the corner of Fair Street, a man is standing in a dim doorway in open shirt and bare feet and smoking, I don't know why. His face is shabby and unshaven and he does not nod but looks straight at us, probably because of my crutches. He has I think just relieved himself, for there is a steaming puddle by his feet which is only just beginning to settle into the dips between the cobbles.

We pass him swiftly. Neither of us flinches.

I try to hum a little under my breath for it is important

to look normal. Trouble is, I can't think of any songs at all and especially no gay ones. I am afraid that worry of this night has wiped them all from my head and my brain has become a blank space with no music, nothing at all.

I don't think I will ever sing not ever again, I remark to Billy, but he does not say anything in reply.

Not that I was such a great singer in the first place, I add, answering myself, since no one else is going to, But it used to buck me up, a little ditty here and there –

Billy laughs, despite himself.

Oh good, I say.

What?

That's better. I am glad that you are cheering up.

He sighs and says nothing.

Yes, I think, It is important to look normal. Here we are, a tired man and a tired woman with dull clothes and shadowy faces, going about their plodding early business.

Already there are people about. Cleaners with their shawls pulled over their heads. Cattle-drovers on their way to Smithfield and of course the shoremen, though mercifully they rarely raise their heads from the mud.

All the same, I am glad that we look so regular. I am glad that Billy can manage to yawn and sigh a little. I am glad that not one of our three bags could possibly contain something as big and unwieldy as a surgeon.

Christ, Laura! Billy exclaims rather irritably.

What?

What is it now? What're you laughing at?

Nothing, I tell him, It's just – things just come into my head, that's all.

What things?

Oh well, I suppose – this – you know. All this that we are doing –

You find it amusing? It makes you laugh?

Oh. Well, all right, not really –

Then what, Laura?

Nothing. It is nothing. I can't explain.

Billy gasps a little as he shifts his leaden load to the other shoulder.

Oh, God, I say.

What?

There is a little blood. On your shoulder. It must be – there must be a bit of a leak –

Oh, hell!

Billy stops and puts down the bag and pulls the stuff of his worn coat around to better see and feel his shoulder.

It is my only coat, he says.

I can get it out, I tell him, Or I can lend you something, later, I mean.

He looks at me.

Something of his? Oh yeah, what a great idea – that won't look at all strange, will it?

It is only a spot, I say.

Bloody frigging hell, he says.

We wedged a great deal of newspaper into the bag which is a large, soft leather one of Ewan's.

It can't be much, I tell him, It doesn't show. I wouldn't worry, my love, I really wouldn't.

Let's go, Billy says, Let's go and get this bloody well over.

I gesture to him to pick up the bag and we move forward. I have the basket slung over one arm so I can still grip and balance on my crutches. Though the latter takes some of the weight, still the heaviness of it is killing my arm and cutting off the blood. Now and then I change it over –

oh, Ewan, why did you have to have such a big brainy head!

All right, I tell him as I feel a sick lump come back in my throat, I will tell you. I am bloody frightened if you want to know. I am bloody frightened just like you and I feel sick with thinking of it – and I am afraid I will never stop –

I wait to see if he believes me.

Laura, he says.

It is going round and round in my head, I begin to say, The idea of –

But as I speak, the half-darkness is ripped by a scream. Now Billy jumps and I hear his teeth clack together in his head.

– of what we have done, I say.

What was that? he whispers.

I don't know –

Christ!

Nothing, I tell him, It was on the other side, across the river, towards the City –

He puts down his bags and looks around, straining into the grey.

Billy, I tell him, Relax. You are incredibly jumpy and it does no one any good. It was nothing. There is no one around. It was far away –

He looks at me and seems to take in what I say.

I need to rest a moment, he says.

Well, that is what he says, but when I glance at his eyes they are black and fearful. I am sad for the look on him, it really grieves me. I think it will never go away now. I think that these last dark hours have changed him – well, especially the very last hour.

*

It took us longer than we'd expected to divide him up, even though we were extremely fortunate in having a full set of his own best surgical knives to help us.

And I knew one or two things, picked up from himself. I knew that the curvy one with the French name and the evil-looking blade was for the quick chop – though it must be harder than it looks, for I tried with the full force of my strength and got stuck almost immediately, getting the blade lodged in the bone and finding myself with blood spilling everywhere and quite unable to pull it out.

Stoppit! cried Bill, shoving rags and whatnot under the blood flow, For heaven's sake, Laura, stop!

Leave me alone! I hissed, trying my best to elbow him away, I can't stop now – what in God's name are you saying?

But – Laura! – you don't know what you are doing –

I do, it is all fine, I will manage! I told him firmly.

And I went on yanking at the stupid knife, for it is my experience that once you have set out on a particularly horrible route it is best to keep going and achieve the end rather than get stuck in the middle of it just as I was stuck in the hard mass of Ewan's neckbone.

It was a good job B. had thought to get the big tarpaulin from the tacking shed and spread it on the parlour floor where already one rug – the one I beat him on – would have to be burned.

And it was a good job too that I had had the foresight to put on the operating coat that Ewan had left on the back of the cloakroom door. I had it back to front like a butcher boy's apron. It was heavy and stinking and its dried pus weight dragged me down. I consoled myself with the idea of setting fire to it later, along with the rug and everything else that was splashed with his blood.

And Billy? Well, he was crying. He was crying and he was saying – I'm sorry, I'm sorry, I'm sorry – over and over and to no imaginable purpose.

Please, I panted, dragging at the knife, Please stop saying that –

But I'm no good at this, he wailed, I cannot, I cannot –

Oh, for goodness' sake, I told him quite reasonably as – oh joy – the knife came away with a sucky sound, No one is good at this, there isn't a single person that likes blood. I bet you anything even Ewan, who was seven years learning it at the Royal College of Surgeons, found it a hard thing to do –

I spoke these words as confidently and forthrightly as if I myself had had the training. Perhaps I was beginning to think I had, for I confess that, unlike Billy, I found myself exhilarated by the whole business.

My heart banged and my body felt whizzy and wild – well, it was cracking along. I was spellbound. I could not believe I was doing it. Oh, it may sound funny but I would have loved Ewan to see me now. Just the thought of his amazement and – possibly – his praise made me blush.

But no such praise would be forthcoming. His body was very cold and didn't I know it? Cold and wrenched inwards and without the supple weight and springiness it'd had earlier. Also, though it still looked like a lot, there was less blood. It was seeping rather than pumping, more like a cake where the jam is squished out a little at the edges.

I could manage the body but I could not easily look at his damaged face. I could not look at where the poker had gone in and severed something stringy at the edge of his eye. Nor the tarry black stuff that seemed to come in lumps from his nose.

And even I, the expert cutter-upper, had looked away as

the knife slid into the fine bones under his chin and snapped them like barley sugar.

And yet, I was doing it. Here was I, Laura, doing what the men do.

I should have been a surgeon, I told Billy as – with less and less to hold it in place – Ewan's head began to loll dramatically to the side.

He did not reply. He made a little squiffy choking noise.

Are you all right? I asked him, with my eyes still on the bloody hole that was Ewan's neck.

Get some more rags, I said urgently, for I felt I must keep him busy, Look in the pantry, there is a drawer, second from the left –

He went and I smiled. I went all around the big bone with the knife, and then I stood up and had a quick, furtive stab at the thigh because that was where I was intending on going next.

What are you doing? cried Billy, who had come back in with a couple of rags and was staring at me with open horror.

Just starting it off, I explained, I'm doing the legs next, in a minute when I've done the head. Whoa! Put a cloth there, quick!

Encouraged by the easy way the knife slipped in, I gave it a few more slicing movements. Then I hit the thigh bone. But it was a lot easier going through clothes – far better when you could not see the inside of him. I should have laid a cloth over the head, I thought. Or maybe not messed up his face with the poker in the first place.

I bet Ewan's never done this, you know, I remarked to Billy as I returned to the head, I bet he's never cut right the way through a neck – why would he, for no one ever has their head took off in the hospital. That's why the knife's not really any good for this, don't you think –?

Oh God, Laura, Billy said, I don't know, please – just get on with it –

The head was almost off, but you needed to be a woodcutter to do the big bone. I was sweating all over, into my hair and down in my drawers. Everything moist – all my creases slippery with it.

I wiped my head on the sleeve of Ewan's coat and instantly regretted it, for the smell – far worse than any that was coming out of Ewan – made my stomach swivel and lurch.

I heard the clock in the hall strike the four and I tried to keep calm.

I asked my assistant to hand me the saw, but as he turned and saw the progress that had been made in the last minutes of cutting, he clutched his belly and began to vomit.

Oh, not on the rug, I managed to shout, It's still clean that one is – look, grab the pot over there – you can take the plant out –

And he pulled the large palm out of its container and mercifully got most of it in the repulsive purplish planter that had belonged to Eve. Gave me immense gruesome satisfaction to see it had at last found its proper function.

He shuddered and heaved again then passed me the saw.

Open your eyes, I told him, Or else you will most certainly fall over.

I set in, working it with all my muscle back and forth through the hardest part of him. This, I thought, this is what he did to me. I felt quite excited and quite sad for Ewan. With this rare glimpse of his working life, I found I could see the world from his point of view and it was a strange one and no mistake.

Every day when he came home he had blood on him, I sighed to Billy, Even though he washed at the hospital, scrubbed himself with carbolic, there was always some still on him –

I was being cheery expressly to keep Billy going, but actually I was about to lose it myself now. Blood was falling into his open mouth and I could feel the raw, swinging weight of him against my knees, for I had instinctively opened my legs to take him as he came loose.

Every time the room began to swim in front of my eyes – and it did, again and again – I put my head down and went down on hands and my one knee on the floor like a cat. It was just like how I had my baby. Like a skinny wild cat clinging to the world. It was harder now, with a leg gone and I had to take care to balance myself. But it gave me a breath and some respite and allowed me to go on.

Oddly, now, at the worst part, Billy had calmed himself down and come to help me. As the head came off the body, as the saw hit the tarpaulin underneath, I cried out, I could not help it.

Oh Jesus, I don't believe it, shouted Billy and I pretended not to hear him.

Get the basket, I hissed at him, for we had prepared Verity's market basket in readiness. He got it and I prepared to lift the head, but found I could not do it.

Billy began to cry again.

Don't, I told him.

I was inclined to try and pick it up by the hair, but could tell the moment I grasped a tuft of Ewan's fine, bright locks, that they would not support the weight of it. I did not want it thunking on the ground and God knows what coming out.

So I put both my shaking hands around and laid it in

the basket like a fresh-baked pie that is still delicate and crumbly. It was only as I removed my hands that I panicked.

I pulled the cloth quickly over the top.

Then I vomited.

Once the head was gone – once his face was out of the picture – it was so much easier to manage the rest.

At almost half past four I sent Billy upstairs to fetch Ewan's leather bags – the large one for the torso and a smaller one that I believed he kept in his dressing room and which I meant to use for the legs. It was nowhere near long enough of course – well, what bag would be? – but I was intending to cut them in several places.

And some more rags, I told him and I explained which drawers he might find some in. We could never have enough cloth to stop the blood and bind the cutting places that we did not want to see.

He was a long time gone up there and soon I began to fret about what he could possibly be doing. Had he hurt himself? Had he fallen asleep? I thought I would kill him if he had forgot what he was doing.

Just as I was about to lay down my tools and go up after him, I heard his slow tread down the stairs and in he came.

Where've you –? I began and then I stared.

For in one hand he had the bags – one of them was not the one I meant him to fetch, but it would do very well – and in the other he had a handful of dusting rags as I had instructed.

And my precious blanket.

I gasped.

What are you doing? I cried, Where did you get that? Give it to me – !

What? he said, looking down at his hands.

I reached out a hand to take it, then realised just in time that both my hands were smeared in drying blood.

B.'s face was white, his hair wild. I saw that he had been crying and then I remembered when and why. Last time he had been in the room seemed like ten years ago.

What is it? he asked me with exaggerated calmness, You sent me for rags and I have got –

Not that one, I cried, That's –

He looked at it. He was waiting for me to go on. I said nothing.

This? he said, holding it out.

Put it down, I told him, holding my filthy hands out helplessly in front of me like a sleepwalker, for I wanted very badly to touch it and I could not.

Why? he said in a cold voice, What is it?

It is mine, I said, Put it down. Really, Billy, please – I swear it is not for anyone to touch –

Billy still held it in his hands.

I hope your hands are clean, I said.

He said nothing.

Ignoring him – or trying to – I began to wrap Ewan's shins and feet in newspaper, curling his toes inwards to fit them in better. He had narrow feet like a girl's, with prominent blue veins and high insteps. His boots had to be specially made by a man in Pimlico. I wrapped the two lower legs into one neat parcel and stuffed them in the small bag which they fitted perfectly.

We will need another bag, I said.

But we have two –

No, I said, For the thighs. They are much bigger than I had thought, they'll never go in there –

Billy did not seem very interested in what would go in

what. He still held the blanket. Now that I had drawn his attention to it, he seemed fascinated by it.

Put it down, I said.

I don't see what's so special about it, he said slowly as if all thoughts of Ewan were forgotten, But I do know it used to be a different colour. Am I right?

I looked at him and flushed.

Well, it's old. Obviously. It's faded —

No, he said, It was more of a purply pink. How did it get to be so washed-out?

I looked at him and he looked at me and vague feelings that I could not decipher washed over me. I did not know what they were but they had the effect of fear. I felt as if the hair at the nape of my neck was being pulled and released, pulled and released.

How do you know that?

I don't know, he said.

Have you seen one like it? It's very old and it came from my father's house originally. He only had the best —

Yes, he said, It was definitely violet —

I don't want to talk about it, I said.

I can see that, he said.

It is mine, I said again. I said it firmly, angrily even. But as I met his eyes, I felt only uncertainty and upset.

Why are you doing this? I asked him.

He dropped the blanket on the floor. It landed in the dust by the coal bucket.

Have it, he said, It's a faded rag, that's all it seems to be. It's not even the right colour. What I would like to know is why do you keep a rag, Laura? You with all your decent bloody clothes and fine things?

I said nothing.

Funny thing to dote on, he said, Isn't it?

I looked at him and I refused to cry which is what he wanted me to do.

Give me a hand with this, will you? I said, We have to leave the house before dawn –

He clapped his hands together energetically. Together we wrapped the torso in newspaper but it was not enough so we undid it again and bound it in an old linen table-cloth – bound it tightly so the veins were thoroughly stopped.

Feeling better? I asked him, because he seemed able to look at the sections of Ewan's body quite easily now without vomiting.

He nodded.

I had cut him off at the tops of the thighs and that had gone so well that I had been sorely tempted to lop off the penis too – or at least make a small slit so I could see what was inside. Only the thought that Billy was watching had stopped me. If I had been alone, I should have had a right old snoop, a proper picnic.

Realising this, it was hard not to think of my own poor leg at the mercy of some student on a rough kitchen table somewhere. I winced. And then I laughed despite myself at how eerily the world had been turned around.

But I worried about the blanket. I could not remember where I had left it. Was it on the bed? The back of the armchair? Had he found the rags and then gone through my cupboards?

Often – very often – I slept with it, though not always. Sometimes holding it calmed me and other times it stirred me up and gave me dreams that made me wake crying, the pillow wet and my whole body alive with grief.

Where did you find it? I asked him, for I was resigned now to trouble.

He shrugged.

I don't know. I just saw it –

Well, it's mine, I said again.

As I said it, he came up to me where I stood among the blood and scrunched-up newspaper and bags and he took me by the shoulders and he kissed me.

It was a straight-in-the-mouth kiss, and I held my hands out – powerless to stop him – for it was not in my interest to cover him in blood. He gripped my shoulders and he did not spare me. He used his tongue to feel his way around in my mouth. He touched my teeth and he touched the spaces of gum where I had lost teeth too. He sucked at my saliva and he drained me dry. As he came out, he bit my lip a little – not too hard, but hard enough to hurt – like lovers do.

Don't ever lie to me, Laura, he said, I mean it, you know. Don't frig me around –

I stood there like a circus clown, my red hands still out to the side. I did not know what to say. Tears freely ran down my cheeks.

It's mine, I said again, but he made sure, the little devil, not to hear me.

Bird

From the moment he put his hand on my empty skirt on that rainy afternoon that I was sent hobbling from the hospital, Ewan, I suppose, was my intended.

Yes really, I believe he was. A professional man and a man of steady living and held, I gathered, in the greatest respect by many I had never met. And he liked me. I was shocked and amazed – it was natural to be so. I was in a fog of misunderstanding – I could not even begin to see how these things had come about.

What? I had gone under a cab and lost my leg and all at once my fortunes had changed and I had a kind, intelligent gentleman as my escort?

I, who with the full load of limbs, had never managed to obtain steady or decent company of any sort! For once, the world was treating me kindly – so kindly that I now occasionally woke at night, sweating at the baffling responsibility this seemed to put on me.

Well, I knew I would marry him, for he was very flush with money and his way of looking at the world made me smile. And that was enough, for the only love that had ever properly pinched my heart was the one I still suffered for my baby boy.

But Ewan was kind. He fixed me up with lodgings close to his own place and he got me a job making artificial flowers for weddings and so on. At first I worked all hours and I was grateful, but soon I got bored.

I would much rather work with kids, I said, for – though I did not put it this way – it was easier to slack when you looked after babies and anyway I was hankering after the touch and smell of them.

But Ewan had a better idea. He said I should stop the work altogether and he would pay me an allowance.

Not like that! he cried when he saw my cynical face, for I had been quite properly reticent in that department, As a friend, Laura, I would like to help you out – though it's true that I'm very fond of you – but please let me.

I could be a proper nanny, I said as persuasively as I could, I could push one of them big black prams in the park and have a bonnet tied under my chin and –

But I broke off, crestfallen, as I realised that most proper families who would employ a nanny would not want a person who was missing a leg.

But Ewan laughed anyway and then he stopped me.

We will get you a job after the summer, he said, If you still want one by then. Though you might not, you know – you might just get used to the easy life. But for the moment, please, just give me the pleasure of taking you out –

Just go out? I said, You mean that is all I'll do?

I could not believe this was what he was suggesting.

He laughed again.

Yes, why not? he said, When I am working you can do what you like. And when I am off, we can have fun. Don't we both deserve a little fun, you and me? We deserve it, don't you think?

I said yes – though I had no idea what he meant by fun.

Well, what it was was taking me out and buying me

clothes — not quite as many as I would have liked, but enough to make me look like a very comfortable and well-behaved person. And having a very thin lady come over specially to show me how to put my hair up in the posh way, with pins — and how to fix a hat on top of the whole lot.

Oh, you look adorable, Ewan said, when he saw the effect of the long, tight, dark mauve skirt and the feathered hat bought that morning from Aldridge's, How does it make you feel? Does it make you feel, you know, elegant and girly?

Girly enough, I said — and I stared at the glass and nodded the hat up and down in a peekaboo way so the brim hid and unhid my face.

Ewan stood behind me. I quite enjoyed him looking at my bum in the skirt and he was very good and did not try to touch which was just as well for I would not have let him.

All the same he was getting a whole lot fresher with me in every way — using words and giving me looks that made it clear he would some day like to take me to bed. I put up with it all for, along with all the cheek and banter, there was a gross awkwardness about him — a surprisingly pungent odour of a man who had never in his life touched a normal woman and thought the only way was to tease and cajole and jostle her along.

I am not experienced, he told me once, gloomy after beef and cigars and sherry, The only thing I know is cutting off limbs.

I told him he was quite wrong. I told him he was really very good at having fun.

He took me to the Eel and Pie Shop and the Fried Fish Shop and to the music hall and to Stanley's Cocoa Rooms, where he squeezed my poor aching ankle under the table.

These are all run-of-the-mill establishments, he advised me with endearing self-consciousness, Just you wait and see the grand things we'll do at a later date –

I told him this was quite enough for me as I had never been to any of these so-called establishments before. I added that I was very grateful to him and hoped he knew what a fun time I was having.

Fun? he said, laughing, for he seemed so bloody intent on the idea of it, Are you really having fun?

Yes, I said – because it was God's truth and because I had softened considerably towards this hopelessly inept and furiously well-off, red-haired gentleman – Thank you, Ewan, I'm having fun.

And then sometimes, his mind would flick off the question of courting and I would see his face go dark and sad.

I don't understand, he used to say, Where've you lived all this time, Laura? I just don't get it. Your life is a blank to me – there are so many gaps. What have you been doing and where have you been?

I told him the best truth I could afford.

I told him that after my father died and my aunt's mischievous Will put me out on the streets, I had been a crawler. I told him I had lived rough along the edges of the river with the dossers and tramps and sometimes with the miserable old women on the steps of St Giles, actively choosing and preferring that to the abject despair of the workhouse that rose grimly at the top of them.

I did not mention the child.

At least there was fellowship there, I told him stoutly, Among those old women. You shared what you got – I was often given bread and a mug of tea by some wretched person I barely knew. And when it rained, you huddled together under the one oilskin, stinking though it was –

Ewan shuddered at the thought.

I was a favourite to huddle against actually, I told him, enjoying his face, For they said that young, hot flesh warmed them up like nothing else –

Ewan smiled.

I would like some young, hot flesh, he said and he flashed a winning smile at me as though it was the normal thing for any young man to say.

I ignored him.

Though actually, I continued, Now I come to think of it, a young girl died against me once. Just fell asleep in my arms and did not wake up –

Now Ewan put away his smile and looked startled. He fixed his gaze on me.

That was what happened on the ward, he reminded me, With the boy –

I was about to say: What boy? – but I didn't. I stopped myself just in time – and felt the hot rapidly fill up my face.

Mmm, I said, The little poorly boy, I had not thought of that – I mean I had not put the two together – but you are right, it is absolutely true.

Poor Laura, Ewan said.

Well, poor child, I exclaimed and then, making a show of laughing it off, I added, Though hardly my fault, I think, Ewan, if folk keep on choosing to die on me!

He laughed and then he moved over and, with somewhat rigid fingers, stroked my arm which had got covered in gooseflesh.

I told him how I looked after the babies belonging to others. How I minded them during the working hours in exchange for twopence or a piece of old bread, whatever they could find. I did not tell him about little Margaret or what happened after.

Ewan looked at me hard. He took my hand and he squeezed it, but only gently as if I were a delicate thing to be appreciated and valued and not taken for granted.

Well now, I have never seen any dosser on the street as young and pretty as you, he said.

Ah, I told him, They are all much younger than you'd think. They may look like old women – and often it is true that they reach the ends of their lives right there on the steps – but many of them are barely out of their twenties and yet to look at them you would think they were a bunch of old arse-faced crones –

Ewan frowned.

That is not a very nice expression, Laura, he said.

What? Crones? I said.

No, I mean the other.

Oh, I am sorry, Ewan, I said, relishing his discomfort, I had forgot for a moment that I am nice now.

The blanket used to be a pinky violet colour.

It was the best and softest wool from Argyllshire for my father believed you got what you paid for. Everything in his house was the best quality and lasted longer than the lives of any of the people in it. When I was a child it went on my bed and I sniffed a corner of it when I went to sleep. But I was a careful child and it lasted well. It did not have to be laundered very often and was always returned to me soft and springy as new.

I took it from the house after he died and the bailiffs came and took all the lovely old things. I don't know what happened to them. I took the blanket off my bed without thinking, probably because I could not imagine a night without it, but the truth is I never knew how much I was going to need it. It was the last thing I had of my father and the first thing I gave to my baby. It went with him, clutched in his tight fist when I let him go – and was returned to me by the men after he died.

I kept it with me in Tatum Fields and it was there in the fumigating ovens that it finally lost its lush colour and became grotty and sad.

My baby had probably sucked it – and he had certainly picked some of the edging off it – but he had not lived long enough to wear it out. Now I held it against my breast and tried to give it enough flesh and bone and breath. Tried to make it into my baby.

It was easy to be mad in there, for they were all mad to some degree. The dark, the damp, the crying out at night, all made you forget where you came from and what exactly you were.

Prison fever, it was called. If you were unlucky, it turned your brain for ever.

I was a good girl, very good. What else was there to be? So they removed the veil – sudden, painful, overwhelming light – and sent me to work in the laundry which was underground and therefore did not hurt the eyes so much.

Down there the women were matter-of-fact and foul-mouthed and good-natured due to the pint of beer you were allowed as payment for the work.

Because of the close atmosphere and the booze there was some palling-in. I had never been touched in that way by a woman before and at first I did not like the thought of it, but the one called Dorcas had a nice way of looking at me as she stroked my cheek and squeezed my hands and it was pretty clear to me she meant no harm.

You had your pint in the afternoon then it was back on the mangles for another hour and then a longer chance to walk around the yard where all of us stomped and stretched and squinted in the weak sunshine.

Dorcas walked very close to me and twined her fingers in my belt. I could not stop her and I did not try – it was what she wanted to do so I let her.

Once during our fun days, because I would not go to church, Ewan took me to the Sunday morning birdfair at Epping Forest.

It is a kind of a tradition, he said stiffly, I have done it on and off for years. Well, anyway, in my opinion it is quite a fun thing to do –

I had never heard of it and I said so. Actually I was pleased to be going. Any outing was good in my books. I had on my hat with two brown curled feathers on it. I asked him if we would buy a bird and he looked suddenly bashful and serious.

I am not sure I think birds should be kept in cages, he said, In fact, Laura, I think it's jolly cruel – what about you?

I said truthfully I had never given it any thought at all. I mean, they were only birds, weren't they?

He half closed his eyes at me and rubbed his chin where already the hair was coming through scorching red.

They are living creatures, he said, All of them are God's creatures –

I laughed at the word God – for I had already told him that God gives not a toss for me or anyone else I know – and I spat on the cobbles as I stumbled along on my crutches.

Laura! he exclaimed, but he was laughing too, You can't be a lady in a hat and spit on the street like that!

I played the game. I stuck my hands on my hips and pouted at him.

Why're you laughing then? I demanded to know, I don't see what's funny about it if it's so very bad.

I am laughing as I would laugh at a child, he said firmly, For a child does not know any better –

And neither do I know any better, I told him – and then I laughed and so did he because we both knew it was a stupid conversation to be having.

At the fair there was such a noise of singing and men shouting out prices and holding cages up above their heads. I got so excited, swooping from table to table and looking at the sweetest, tiniest wickerwork containers that hung from the hawkers' caravans and so on.

Ewan put his arm around me and I was glad that my waist was so slender that his fingers came round and rested where my belly button was. Normally I didn't like to be touched in that place, but today I decided not to mind for he seemed so relaxed and happy and he was much better-looking when he was relaxed. I liked him when his face didn't have the pinched, uncertain look that he seemed to get when he did too much thinking.

I smiled at him and he smiled back. What had begun as a dreary old day laden with clouds was now clearing to be hot and open and blue.

I want one! I told him suddenly, Please, Ewan –

What? he asked me sternly, You want a bird? In a cage?

A little songbird, I said, Yes. One of them dear little brown ones with the upset faces –

Ewan paused and considered.

Well, I would gladly buy you one, he said, It isn't that. But I don't think I could ever be happy at the thought of you keeping it in a cage –

You would not have to see it, I told him firmly, It would be shut away in my lodgings –

Ewan winced. Then he had an idea. He kissed my cheek as if it was already settled.

What if I buy you one, he said, And we let it go? We could give it the best gift of all – its freedom! We could release it and watch it soar and fly –

What if it did not want to? I said quickly.

All birds want to, Laura – of course they do. All birds are designed to fly away –

Oh, I said, but in a deliberately lacklustre way.

He frowned.

Think of the pleasure of seeing it go, he said, I mean, seriously now, would you like to be kept in a cage?

I hesitated. The temptation to tell him I had indeed been detained in conditions far worse than any caged bird was very strong. At least the birds had light and company. At least they could make a noise. After the Margaret episode, I had been kept in dark so long that even a dull day hurt my eyes and the sound of my own voice made me jump right out of my skin.

You have to put yourself in their position, Laura, he said with a stern moral confidence that really narked me, It is blind ignorance otherwise – and selfish too.

It is only a ruddy bird, I said.

But, Laura – !

All right, I said, But let me keep it just a little bit first. Two days, yeah?

One day should be enough, Ewan said.

A whole day and a whole night, I forced him to agree.

He got out his wallet.

I like the teeny tiny cages, I told him eagerly, guiding him swiftly by the elbow to where my favourites were.

Oh, Laura, he said despairingly, his voice lightened by my touch on his arm, Those ones are the very worst –

But I have a small room, I told him in a wheedling voice, I haven't space for one of the large ones –

Well, we walked around a bit and I chose the smallest, drabbest bird I could find that was making the shoutiest noise. It had a beady eye and its tail feathers were all poorly and frayed, but when it opened its yellow beak something pure and glorious as honey trickled out.

Give it to me! I told Ewan, putting out my hand for it as soon as he had paid.

The man whose bird it was winked at Ewan. He probably thought he was in for some good spooning later.

Poor bird, Ewan murmured and he made a kissy, chir-ruppy noise with his lips, Poor songbird in a cage –

Maybe it likes its cage, I suggested again, though I knew it was the wrong thing to say.

All the same, maybe it did, for you could not avoid the fact that the little round breast throbbed with happiness as it sang.

How do you know it's happiness? Ewan asked me when I pointed it out, It is only human beings who equate the act of singing with happiness –

Well, it certainly looks like happiness, I muttered – and I blew a soft, fat kiss to my bird who was hopping madly from perch to perch as if he couldn't see there was nothing whatever to be gained from such frenzied activity.

As we reached the end of the fair there was a person selling coffee and another with sugared apples and another with clams and fried potatoes and the like. And benches had been set up with tables in front for people to eat and drink. Ewan bought lemonade but I said I did not want any.

I once had my palm read here, Ewan remarked to me, Just here by the gate there is sometimes a woman who does it —

Oh, really, I replied, though my eyes and ears were all totally taken up with my bird, And did it come true? What did she say?

Too soon to tell, said Ewan, laughing, All I remember, you see — because I must say I do not really take much notice of such things — was that I will live to be very old. Yes, I will with luck be a very old man indeed —

Goodness, I said, trying to imagine Ewan all crumped up and white-haired. I could not.

Yes, he said, That's what I thought.

You're a scientist, I told him after I'd thought about it a moment, Why should you believe it?

Oh, he said vaguely, Scientists believe in some things —

But not in fairground quackery! I protested.

Probably not, he agreed. But I caught him looking at me as if what I'd just said somehow changed me forever in his eyes.

Well, we walked a little more around the fair and I carried my bird around and I must say just holding it gave me the greatest pleasure. And I thanked Ewan quite effusively for bringing me and told him I wanted to come again.

It is a funny place, Ewan said, as if he did not really know what he thought or what to say about anything since the moment we had the bird.

Dorcas had hair that was bushy and reddish in the light. Like me she was seventeen and tired of being under-ground. She said the darkness gave her special powers. She said she could see into the future and she said she loved me.

I did not say I loved her because it would have been a lie, but neither did I brush her off. The attention and touch of her — soft and footling and far different from a man's touch — was both welcome and unsettling.

I asked her what she saw.

Well, you're going to have an accident, she told me smiling all the while.

What? I said, alarmed, What, in here? What sort of an accident?

No, no, she said sadly, Not in here, you'll go from here, Laura, you know you will. It will be somewhere else —

Will I die? I asked her with a little leap in my heart.

She thought about it. She looked at my face.

Not the first time, she said at last, But the second time, possibly, yes I think you may.

Good, I said, Then I can join my boy in heaven —

I had told her about my baby.

How do you know he's in heaven?

Well, I don't, but, well, I don't know —

She smiled in a knowing way.

God's a joke, yeah?

I shrugged.

I don't believe in Him, but I want Him to take good care of my boy.

Well, yes, she said with a sigh, When you leave this world, you'll be with him —

I looked at her.

You're just saying that —

No, she said, I think you will. I have a strong feeling, here (she touched her heart) and here (now her forehead) that you'll find your baby —

Oh, Dorcas! I said.

But not in the way you think —

Any way will do for me, I told her and then she touched my neck and asked me if I would forget her when I was let out of that place and I answered her truthfully that I probably would.

Dusk was coming.

What about you? I asked her.

Oh, I'll be hanged.

We stood still in the yard for the turnkey had gone in and only we two were left. On the wall was a creeping ivy, its leaves curled like fingers in the shadows.

Dorcas ripped off a leaf and chewed and swallowed it before I could stop her. She thought it might be a poison that would kill her, but she was still alive and well the next day so I guess it didn't do anything.

I told her she ought not to eat ivy, but I did not make out that I was shocked or impressed. Dorcas was the sort to give herself airs. She was in for murder just like me but unlike me she had really done it.

She had chopped a man to bits and hid the parts of him in a flock mattress. She would have got away with it had not the mattress turned scarlet with his blood or so she said though I don't know if I believed that part of it.

Billy and me come finally to the odd and desolate place beyond the sack-makers and the hoop-benders where the wharf turns bleak and empty and the river is fairly choppy and high.

Now the tar-paved road we are on gives way to sad weeds and broken glass and bread and mess and all manner of dismal rubble and rubbish. A building on the corner is totally black, its wiry innards spilling out like guts.

Gas explosion, Billy informs me, for he knows the place very well. It was his idea.

It is a place where stuff you chuck in just disappears, he said.

The early-morning air is slippery and grey and the mist does a good job of cloaking the bank on the other side, though vague factory shapes stand out. I shiver. It is cold, but not that cold – just more or less normal for the time of year.

It is a funny district and not a place I would ever go – there are so many peculiar smells in the air, I have never smelled such a cunning mix: jam, glue, leather and sweets – or burning sugar anyway. There is a bone boiler's down Perseverance Street, I do know that, but the treacle whiff of confectionery is a mystery to me.

Well, dawn is breaking, that's the trouble. Billy is shining with sweat. His fingers are lined with black dirt that seems to have come out of nowhere and there is still blood – but only thank God a rough, darkening stain of it – on his shoulder.

It is with relief that I put my basket down on the ground and jiggle my arms which are tight and sorely strung up from about an hour of carrying.

If I get stones, says Billy, Will you put them in? Can you? Each bag is going to need as many as we can get in –

I tell him to get some bricks too, pointing out a half-ruined wall I had already noticed that is loosely and conveniently crumbling.

They may be too big, he says doubtfully, Will you get them in –?

I look at the bags where Ewan's sticky limbs and torso are all wadded in paper.

All right, I say, Maybe try stones first.

He dashes off. He is breathing hard. He is just a slip of

a boy really and I feel very sorry for him to be involved in all of this, I really do.

I sink myself down in front of the bags and pull up my skirts to try and scratch my stump which is tingling with an itch I can never quite get to. It always eludes me. If I scratch one place, it resurfaces somewhere else. It crawls all over and can never be relieved and is most aggravating. It is like a part of your body turning around and laughing at you – maddening and shameful both at the same time.

In the end I am driven to grasp the rough nub of flesh tight and spit on it. But even my saliva is not cool enough.

Determined to fix on something else, I turn to watch Billy instead.

Stones. Bricks. The weight that will do it – the solid mass that will make a person go down. And then I am thinking of the day I drowned myself: the river beckoning, the heavy rubble plucked panickily from anywhere, the unreal texture and shape of that long-ago morning.

Well, not so long ago.

How long then, since my skirts dragged me under? How long since the daylight dissolved over my head and I felt the streams of silver velvet bubbles tickling my eyes, neck and nose? How long since I died and went to join my baby?

This is heaven for me.

Everything is gone out of kilter since then, I think. How much time has passed? It is anyone's guess, since the world has turned into something quite different since I put an end to myself.

Likewise Ewan's death: flimsy and unreal. Nothing happening at all as it used to and us taking it very much to heart, even though the heart as I know it is dead.

Thinking these sombre thoughts to myself, I help Billy

stuff as much weight as we can into the bags. Thinking that the basket is easy – I just cram the stones in around the head like packing a picnic. But the bags must be undone and then patiently done up again for they must stay weighted down.

Not a soul is in sight. The water is very grey – very dark and thick. I could never put myself in there now. B. goes to have one quick look over the edge – I don't know why – then returns and without speaking takes the basket and throws it in.

I did not think he would do it yet.

I push myself up and get over there to see.

The basket with Ewan's head in sails through the air and the splash when it lands is enormous.

Sprays of water, waves, circles of disturbance.

We watch as it goes down and then it bobs back up again and floats. We take a breath as it see-saws back and forth like a merry little boat and then we see the cloth starting to come adrift.

Oh no, I don't believe it, says Billy.

No – I say, touching his arm, Look, it's going – and before I have finished saying it, the whole thing is gone down out of sight, water closing over it.

Over your head as it went over mine.

Bye, Ewan.

Over our own heads is a different story: the sky is lightening and the gulls are shouting.

Quick, says Billy, The others –

He has to put the big one in as I could barely lift it, but I have some pleasure in swinging the other with my stronger arm – whoosh! – and chucking it. These both go down immediately, with plops that are quick and leaden and sudden.

We stand in silence a moment – only the gulls – then he sits and pulls out a cigarette.

Thank Christ, he says, Thank frigging Christ –

I am standing behind him and leaning on just one crutch. I try to breathe in the morning air. There is weak, shallow sun catching the tops of the factory buildings which you can clearly see now on the other side.

So, says Billy, What now?

Well, I have a fat stomach, I tell him, You ought to know I am putting on a little weight on my stomach.

Good, he says, That's good. You need it. You are too thin all over –

No, I say, I mean it. Billy, look –

He barely glances up, he is busy enjoying his cigarette, the puff and suck of it.

Oh, you're not, he says, Come off it.

I am.

Well, I must say I haven't noticed –

I smooth my skirts down, but there is still something there.

Ah, I say, But you wouldn't. But I assure you I am. It is not the first time I have thought it – it just did not seem the right moment to say it until now.

There's a pause. Billy offers me a cigarette but I say no I don't fancy it.

So what are you saying? he says at last.

I don't know, I say, suddenly unsure, I don't know that I'm saying anything.

That's all right then, he says.

So forget it.

I will.

Behind his head, so he cannot see me, I put my tongue out at him. I put my tongue out till my jaw muscles ache and I cross my eyes till the pain snags my temples. Then I smile at the great crowd of buildings across the river – and I fancy they smile back.

Oh well, says Billy after a moment.

Oh well what? I say quickly.

This is a bad place.

Mmm. Why?

Don't know really, he says disconsolately, Just is.

I put my free hand on my belly. I feel a flutter. It is not possible that something is fluttering, for I had blood just this night – last night – when I began to hurt Ewan.

Where are you going? Billy says.

Nowhere, I tell him, Stay there, I will be back in a minute –

Behind the largest brick pile, I squat and put down my crutches. It is too hard and complicated to get my drawers undone, so I do the simplest thing which is to go in sideways and stick a finger in.

It comes out slimy-clean with nothing on it. It smells of cheese and salt and good things cooking.

I go back to Billy.

I hope they stay down, I tell him as I look at the water, What if they don't?

They will, he says coolly, For long enough –

How long is that?

He looks up at me and puts a sudden happy arm around my knee, as if he has forgiven me for all I seem to know.

One hundred years, Laura – is that enough time for you?

He smiles. I haven't seen him smile in ages – in all these hours of problems.

Oh, I don't need a hundred, I say truthfully.

He laughs, then glances up at me again.

You're not – in difficulties – are you, Laura?

I sigh.

I am in no difficulty at all, Billy, I say, Now that he is gone and it is just us together here, I am in heaven.

At first, when I got my new bird back to my lodgings, I thought again and again how happy it looked, hopping back and forth merrily between the two perches and singing fit to make its little heart burst.

What a sweetie you are, but what a drab fellow too! I told it teasingly – for isn't that how ordinary folk talk to their friends and loved ones, with mock criticism but thin enough to let the affection show through?

The bird eyed me beadily but did not stop for a second.

And busy too! I added.

I watched my bird as it jumped, turned and jumped again, always the same rhythm – jump, turn, jump, jump, turn, jump.

Bird, you're getting boring, I said, If you're going to be my companion, you've got to think of something else to do.

Ewan had got me a small brown paper bag of seed and I opened it carefully and tried one myself, but it was that bitter I spat it straight out.

Then I carefully prised open the little door and scattered seed on the floor of the cage where there was already a substantial pile of empty husks from previous meals. As I did so, the bird carried on with the jumping, but fluttered as well in a panicky way.

Shall I clear up? I said, trying to scoop up the husks with my big hand.

Then I realised the bird needed peace and quiet more than it needed housekeeping, so I came out and shut the cage and made some kissy noises with my mouth.

Eat, I said.

But my ungrateful bird did not even look at the seed.

Instead, it kept on hopping back and forth and singing like a mad thing which, now I came to think of it, was getting to be all I had ever seen it do.

I began to wonder whether Ewan was right – whether being in a cage was driving it mad, for it seemed to have turned into a mechanical bird and I admit that made it somewhat less attractive to me as a pet.

So I lifted the cage by the little loop handle and placed it on the table by the small window. I hoped the stench and muck from the street wouldn't put it off – Epping had been so fresh and clean – but at least there was some brightness there and the sun would go on it.

But it made no difference at all. My bird did not preen or sunbathe. It barely seemed to notice the sunshine. It barely noticed anything – and finally the singing and hopping began to drive me crazy.

Is that all you ever do? I asked it, Sing and hop? Sing and hop?

I went right up to the cage and I spat on it. The spit landed on the floor of the cage on the husks, but a little splashed the perch.

Good, I thought, Maybe you will slip off and I can at least have a laugh.

But the bird carried on. Jump, turn, jump, jump, turn, jump.

I struck the floor with my crutch to frighten it. I lay on the bed and put the bolster over my ears. My stomach was turning to ice with the repetition of it. I tried not to cry.

Oh, I cannot live with such a repetitive bird, I thought, I was wrong to think I ever could.

I wondered whether if I picked the cage up and shook it, the bird would either stop or die.

I never thought I would want silence again but I did. In the prison they put brick all around us and a cloth over our heads. Blackness and silence led to penitence, especially for women, they said. Loneliness was supposed to make you good again, but it didn't – it made the evil bits rise to the surface of you. It made you see the point of the error of your ways.

Darkness and stillness crackling in my head. I was thirsty for it. I laid myself wide open and waited.

Bird! I yelled at last, Shut up or I will kill you!

Then, just as I was about to rush and dash it against the wall, I remembered what Ewan had said about letting it free.

Of course! That was it – the perfect solution for it was both kind and also what Ewan wanted.

Sweating a little, I went over to the cage where the damn thing was still bobbing and tweeting.

I prised open the door and turned it towards the open window. But it did not come. I waited a little longer, but it seemed that the small feathered dullard could not see life beyond the two perches.

Come on, I said, Get out.

I tried tipping the cage a little to get it to perhaps fall out the door. But when I tipped, it just flapped and fluttered – a soft, flippy-floppy sound which brought sick into my throat and turned my hair on end.

Then, just as I was about to give up and kill the thing, it jumped from the perch to the edge where the door was open. And flew.

I stepped back, keen to watch its progress over the roof-tops of London, but instead the stupid thing panicked and lost its bearings and cracked its head against the opposite wall.

It fell and died where it landed – with a visibly broken neck and a rim of scarlet round its stupid yellow beak.

After the bird episode, Ewan made me take some small white pills. He shook them from a vial that was all dusty and thin and made me swallow two of them. Two immediately and two more at suppertime, he said.

To calm you down, he told me in his best daddy-doctor voice.

But I am perfectly calm! I protested as I gulped the delicious sweet lime juice he proffered, I am not upset at all. As you know, I did not especially want to give the bloody bird its bloody freedom –

Ewan looked a little bothered by my cursing, but he squeezed my hand and smiled.

That's why you must take the pills, he said, You are hysterical. If you can relax, your responses will soon get back to normal –

Back to normal! I exclaimed, But I tell you, Ewan, I am normal –

He thought for a moment.

Women are often upset at the death of a small animal, a pet –

I laughed and he looked at me.

But you, he said, continuing, Don't even seem remotely troubled –

I laughed again, I couldn't help it.

Come off it, Ewan, I only had the thing five minutes. It was not a pet –

I knew of course what my mistake had been – and I cursed myself for telling him the truth instead of just wiping up the mess and pretending the wretched thing had flew away.

But the day my bird died, I met Ewan as arranged at Welton's for tea and shrimps.

Well, I was wolfing down the bread and butter when I suddenly remembered and took the package from my purse. I had done it up in paper and string because that was all I had and I did not know what else to do with it. It seemed very much smaller than I remembered – the package that is – all shrunk and flat. It could've been a piece of meat. What also gave that impression was the fact that a corner of the paper was stained an inky red.

What the –? Ewan took the package and held it by the string and stared at me as if I was a witch.

My bird, I told him through a mouthful of buttered bread, It flew right bang into the wall –

Carefully, Ewan placed the package on the table. He could not take his eyes off my face.

It's – what? you mean it's not alive?

I laughed a little.

Not alive! That's right, Ewan – would I wrap it up if it was alive? It banged its head. It was its own fault since it did not look where it was going –

Ewan wiped his fingers on his napkin and looked around him.

And that's the bird in there? he said.

I nodded and took a shrimp with my fork.

It dropped dead –

But he stopped me, put a hand on my wrist.

I don't understand, he said, Why are you – what are you doing bringing a – dead bird in here, Laura?

Well, I struggled to think why, You bought it, didn't

you? It's yours. I didn't know what to do with it. I suppose I thought you'd want –

Want what?

To see it?

I grinned then as an idea occurred to me.

You could cut it up if you wanted, Ewan, I said loudly, Like you cut up my leg, remember –?

He went pale and put the package on the floor under the table. He looked all around him to make sure no one had heard. They had not.

It was not me that did that, Laura, he said and gripped my hand tight as if he could hurt me into shutting up.

I shrugged and slipped my hand out of his grasp.

You or whoever, I said, It's all the same to me.

Ewan settled up and we left the place promptly which was sad for I would have liked some cake. I was getting used to it, the sudden explosion of softness and sweetness, the look of all that unnecessary choice on the one plate.

You need some sorting out, Laura, Ewan said grimly as he hailed a cab and packed me into it.

What?

You are not human, he said, You do not bleed or wince or cry. Nothing can touch you – there is a part of you missing. You scare me – do you know that?

I scare myself sometimes, I admitted, then I laughed.

Maybe you should stop giving me fun? I suggested – though I did not know why I said it for I did not at all want to give up the trips and cake, Maybe I am not the right woman for you to play around with after all –?

Ewan looked shocked again – and then he smiled a funny little smile to himself.

Oh, I don't know about that, he said, Luckily I am not

put off by what I don't understand. I like a challenge. And as a matter of fact I like you more and more –

But – I began in protest, but he held up his hand.

Don't try and understand, he said, For it barely makes any sense. You are not the only one who scares yourself sometimes, Laura –

I shrugged rather rudely then and stared out of the window for I was a little fed up with his ranting.

Don't know what you're on about, I said and he laughed.

I still thought that, because of my misjudgement about the bird, our fun times might actually be over, but I couldn't have been more wrong.

For it was there in that argumentative cab that he suggested the trip to Folkestone where he was to ask me to marry him. And it was in that room in the boarding house by the fat grey windy sea that he crammed the first two pills in my mouth and found that – once I had gone sufficiently fuzzy round the edges – he could stroke me all the way up the thigh and into my drawers without me shouting stop or help or something similar.

Head

By the way, Billy says, as he lights up another cigarette –
his third since we put Ewan in the river – Did you know
that our Pinny thinks you're dead?

He laughs as he says it, but hearing his words makes my
heart tip right over.

I try to speak but I can say nothing. Nothing but his
name – Billy, Billy, over and over like a silly song.

He doesn't notice, he doesn't hear. He laughs some more.
Then he grabs my wrist and pulls me down to sit by him.
I lose my balance and topple slightly so now I am on his
knee. My heart is banging and my head heaving. Our cheeks
touch briefly and he moves my hair from my face and
touches my neck with his fingers.

She thinks what? I whisper.

I push him off, noticing with vague unease that Ewan's
blood still marks his shoulder.

Hey, you've gone all wobbly, he says and offers me a
drag of his cigarette. Which I refuse.

Oh, Jesus, I say, Oh, Jesus Christ – and it comes out as
more of a moan than I mean it to.

No, no, he says lightly, You don't understand – she's
being funny – she doesn't mean really dead, Laura! She just
came across a stone somewhere that had your name on it,
that's all –

Much like a clock that has been stopped a long time and just sprung back into life, a quiet, firm ticking begins in my head.

Where? I demand to know.

Look, he says, It is not such an uncommon name. Is it so surprising that there are other Laura Blundys about –?

Where? I ask him again, the ticking getting louder and meaner and angrier.

He screws up his eyes.

Well, I don't know, he says slowly, Some cemetery up by London Bridge – Moor something or other, I think she said. Look, you are getting vexed for nothing, it's nothing –

Mawbey Place?

He looks at me quickly – so quickly that I know it must be the one.

Could be. I don't know.

What was she doing in Mawbey Place? I ask him as calmly as I can.

Doing? Oh, he says, Pinny gets all over the place – you never know where she'll turn up next. It's her way. Ever since she could walk she's been bucketing around here there and everywhere. We used to call her the beagle, Cally and me, on account of all the travelling she'd manage in the course of a day –

In his fatherly doting, he has not noticed the look on my face. He stops when he does.

Hey, Laura, he says, Don't go bothering about it. Like I said, it's just a funny thing, a joke. I wouldn't've told you it if – I mean, I really thought you'd see the funny side –

Why? I ask him patiently and for want of something better to say, Why in heaven's name would I laugh about such a thing?

He goes all gloomy.

You are right. It isn't funny. It's just one of those spooky coincidences. Or maybe she read it wrong – or perhaps she's making it up. I wouldn't put it past her, the little squit –

Why? Why would she make it up?

He thinks about this and straightaway his face goes even more shadowy and pained.

Well – he hesitates.

Well what?

I think she's jealous, he says finally.

What?

I think she knows that we are – well –

She knows! I exclaim, But how? Why didn't you tell me?

I was going to, he says, stubbing out his cigarette petulantly, But then with all this it didn't seem half so important any more. Anyhow, there you are – I'm telling you now.

But how could she? I say, How could she know anything about us?

She won't tell Cally if that's what you're wondering.

I take a breath, bite the skin of my lip. It's not what I'm wondering of course, not at all. I don't give a fig for his wife. No, I'm thinking of the tock-tock in my head and of his bad-tempered girl with her long rats' tails and dreary knowing little face.

Why not? I ask him rather snippily, Why won't she?

Because she loves me. And because, as you know, she is a spooky girl – she is a one-off, that one. Bright as a button, but weird as all hell.

I begin to tremble.

Right from when she was a tiny girl, Billy goes on as if he thinks I'm interested, She'd hear and see things – voices and so on, things that weren't there –

What, I say, You mean spirits?

If you want to call it that, perhaps. She just – well – she knew things. If you lost something she'd know where to find it, just like that. She wasn't like the other babies. Right from the start she could drink from a cup. She watched out for people in the strangest ways – and for herself. Why, if you gave her pins and needles to play with she'd roll around and test their sharpness and not hurt herself at all –

Well, what with that and the travelling, the child must be truly gifted, I remark acidly – and then I break off to catch my breath and cry out.

What? Billy turns his head sharply to see what I'm looking at.

Oh God, please God don't let it be – I say.

But it is.

Oh sweet Jesus, no please no, says Bill.

For the bad old river has refused our basket and sent it back to us. And there it is, riding the dark, oily water, lodging now and then in clods of weed and muck. Because it has lost its covering of cloth, it stands out a mile for as it bobs along it drags behind it a shock of bright red velvety-wet hair.

Once I knew my baby boy was gone to his grave, I found it very hard to get the proper spirit back for the mush-faking or the beer-making.

You need hope to do these things. You need a big dose of hope to get you up in the morning and more hope to collect the scrag-ends and bits and pieces out of which you can fashion something new. You need dollops of hope and charm to get your livelihood going again – as well as a little dash of grit and luck – and it seems I had none of them.

Nobody likes a mourner just as nobody likes a loser. Loss contaminates. Even the wretchedest, meanest little sparrow hops fast away out of your path, put off by the stark and unappealing scent of pain.

What I had lost was mine and no one else's. I had no one to share my grief with, no one who could bear to watch my tears. I was heading for the darkness – hurtling so fast on my own grim track of hurt that no one would stop me, even if such a person existed who might care to try.

After a matter of days, I was thrown from my lodgings and had to pawn my shawl and boots for something to eat. The only thing I did not pawn was my boy's blanket which I kept tucked against my breast like an extra scraggy woollen heart. No one would part me from that blanket and I knew I would die with it close against me, even though the spitty smell of it that had made my heart ache had already disappeared from its grimy surface.

I lay in an empty boat that was pulled up on the shingle under Lambeth Bridge and sometimes I slept. Later – whether hours, weeks or days I cannot tell – hatless and smarting from the sun and wind on my cheeks and arms, I wandered for several miles and found myself close to the steps of St Giles, where I was mistaken by an old drunken dozing woman for her companion.

When I told her I was not the person she was waiting for, she offered me some bread and tea anyway. I accepted gratefully and as I bolted it down, I saw in a sudden flash of clearness what I had done. I had joined the dossers and the crawlers, hadn't I? I had done the only thing I could and joined them who had always been there on the crabby edges of my life and who were all there was now that I was dreary again and down.

Well, it was hardly new to me, this existence waited out in doorways and on the stinking workhouse steps and under upturned boats and tarpaulins and I sank into it as comfortably as if it had always been true, had always insisted it would wait for me.

Crawling is what you come to if you have no home and no energy and cannot even bring yourself to die.

The crawlers stayed close to the ground for they had not the spirit to raise themselves up very far. They had not the wherewithal even to steal or beg – or at least they begged from other beggars and would be tossed what was not wanted even by them: a halfpenny worth of tea leaves or a mouldy crust or flyblown joint.

Being younger and fitter, I was the one sent to the coffee house to beg the hot water for a bit of tea which I made in a cracked old pot without either handle or spout. It was a fine comedown from the proud, clinking tea sets of my father's house, where the best was kept in a cupboard and rinsed, wiped and put away again the very minute a parlour person had drained their Sunday cup.

I trudged to the coffee house but when I got there I was reduced to sink down on my knees. It was a sad sight, a woman on her knees which were bound with rags – rags which once upon a fairy, far-off time were clothes but which were now no more than limp and greasy bandages wrapped around to preserve a little heat and modesty.

I was a very young woman then, but crawling ages everyone who does it. My face became an old girl's face. My hair coarse and specked with grey. It happened to everyone, brought everyone down who did it. Pretty shrimps of twenty or so shrank into elderly people with dull, lined faces and matted hair, their bodies so hunched over you could no longer make out the youthful spaces between their bones.

After a time of this life, I lost so much of my original

bounce that I ceased to be the one sent for the water. I gave in and relied on others. I learned to be still and to think of nothing and to be grateful when sleep overtook me.

Here on the steps and in the meagre half-shelter of doorways, no one asked me questions, no one bothered me or wondered why. Days passed like dreams – with no beginnings, middles or ends – and all the characters blurred comfortably into one another, so that it did not matter who you spoke to or what you said, for everyone here had misfortune and death and sadness lodged right under their skin. Everyone accepted that there was no way out of where they were, so what was the point in looking, complaining, crying or even commenting?

Then along came the coloured woman Jackie Pringle.

Jackie had got herself organised, hadn't she?

She came along and told me she might have work in the coffee shop and was in need of someone to take care of her infant between the hours of ten and four in return for twopence or a cup of tea and tuft of bread, depending on what she could manage to put together.

Give it to me, I told her greedily, I'll have it, the little monkey –

And I held out my arms and she passed me the wailing child who struggled and harrumphed, grabbing at the air with her startled hands.

She's afraid of you, remarked one of the gin women who had settled herself in the doorway for a good old look, Hark at her humpy little face –

Not a bit, I retorted and, standing up for the first time in ages, I settled the complaining infant on my hip and I lolloped up and down the steps of St Giles, along as far as the water cart and back again. Bumpety bump. Bumpety bump. The child bless her did a laugh like music and her face lost the crumped-up expression and went relaxed and fat.

My legs were that stiff with sitting down that they felt fizzy and I was weaker than I could've imagined. I worried I would faint and topple with the child so I sat back down and dandled her on my knee.

Well, you've got the job, said Jackie bluntly.

She made no attempt to take her babby back – in fact she seemed pretty glad to get the child out of her arms, for she gave a massive, yawning stretch and rubbed at her back and then bent languidly to lace her boots.

What is it, a girl? I asked and Jackie said yes.

And how old?

Born last June, she said, And by the way I am calling her Margaret.

I peered into the face of the infant Margaret. A smeary, dirty face it was, but not as out-and-out sooty as poor Jackie's. She had a glum little mouth and about four teeth, one of which was already going black.

There wasn't a lot of hair but what there was looked as dark and wild as my own, the uncut wisps protruding from the tatted wool cap on her head. It was tied under her chin, this cap, but so permanently wet from her dribblings that the lace had imprinted a sore red line there.

You should undo this, you know, I advised Jackie, I would guess it's the reason she whimpers all the time –

She'll be way too hot in that, added the crone in the doorway in a totally uncalled-for way, Can't you feel the heat banging down on us this bloody morning –?

I gave the woman a pointed look to tell her to mind her own, but Jackie laughed and reached over to tug at the string. The child's fingers immediately flew up to grab at it too.

Well, she can have it off now, she said, Unless you think she needs her head covered?

I put my head on one side and pretended to consider. It was summer now and the start of a hottish morning, but over the river the sky was still gluey with the promise of cloud.

Oh well, I said, I'll see how we go. Sometimes it is prudent to shield them from the hottest rays –

Jackie looked at me, paused, and then threw her head back and laughed. I wondered if she had guessed that I was making it all up, but to be honest, she was pretty thick and giggled all the time and went along with just about anything anyone said to her. This was the problem later in the court. Her head was a sponge, you see, and she just soaked up every little bloody idea they shoved at her.

Like a little lady! she exclaimed when I mentioned about the sun, Why, she'll be wanting a friggin' parasol next –

I smiled.

That's right, I said, chucking her girl-child under the chin, Like a proper little well-kept lady – aren't you, aren't you, aren't you!

Jackie kept on laughing even though the joke was surely over and she still made no move whatever to take the child back. Maybe she liked my attitude, I don't know. I surveyed her coolly, from under a thin guise of friendliness.

Take the babby and run! shrieked the old crone suddenly – though it was not at all clear which one of us she thought she was addressing.

Anyway, both of us ignored her and moved smartly away. The infant smiled a gummy smile at me suddenly as if she had just made up her mind about it all and straightaway a fat string of dribble ran down her chin.

I smiled back. It was not a show, I meant it.

Well, thanks a lot, Jackie said and I could tell she was about to go. She pulled her tatty shawl over her arms and moved a step away.

She was nice enough looking when you saw the whole of her, though she was, I must say, the very blackest person I had ever seen, with wild woolly hair and a gap between her front teeth and fine dark freckles spattered on her face like the mud that carriage wheels send up on a wet November night. Some people were afraid of her complexion but not me. I was not afraid of looking into the darkness – never had been – not yet anyway.

She was born in the workhouse, Jackie added, though I had not asked, Her father was a frigging gas worker, you know.

I asked her where the father was now and she told me he had been carried off by typhus even before he knew about her condition. She said it was a bloody tragedy – that she was left with nothing and the baby fast growing in her and no means whatever of providing for it.

Didn't you think of taking her to the foundling hospital? I asked her, more out of curiosity than concern, as I swayed the child about and heard its brief chuckles of delight.

But when I mentioned that place, Jackie's face fell. She said she had tried all she could, but that the committee had found her undeserving of a place.

It was carnal passion without promise of marriage, you see, she explained flatly – and the formal and judgemental words sounded funny from her big and guileless mouth – I was fond of the infant's father, you see, and I willingly consented to the bit of shagging that we did –

Oh, Jackie, you should never have told them that! I exploded at her. She bit her lip that was the colour of a fat pink dog rose and giggled again.

Oh, but you have never met my poor Stan, she said, He was so – you know –

Whatever wonderful thing he was, I said firmly, However much of a good ride he gave you in the sack, you should've hid it, you know you should –

Oh, don't tell me that, I know it now, she said more soberly, But, you see, they did not tell me the rules at the start of it all.

To get a child in there you must prove you have been forced, I told her and I was surprised to hear my own voice going as stony rigid as I remembered theirs on the committee to have been.

Jackie's mouth went small and sad.

It would've been hard to lie about my Stan, she said softly.

I shrugged and sighed and looked at little Margaret, the sorry product of all their great good fun.

It's hard on the child, I remarked.

Suddenly Jackie's face broke into smiles.

But I would not be without her for all the world! she said, However much trouble and pain she sometimes is –

And with that she went off down the steps and towards the coffee shop and I watched her go and pulled her child closer to me.

I had not said anything about my own baby that had died and because she was not at all interested in anything but her own self, she never thought to ask me how come I was so good at handling a small person like her Margaret.

*

Billy says we must burn the head. We have to. It is the only way.

We are dead meat if it is found, he says.

Well, according to your Pinny I am already in that state, I tell him tartly.

He turns on me, furious.

Chrissakes, Laura! he says, How can you mess around at such a time?

I look at him steadily but my heart is blank. It is like I want to help us but I cannot. He knows, he knows – what? That the joy we had between us is fast dissolving?

I hang my head, stare at the base of my crutch where it scuffs the dry and scrubby ground. Good for a fire.

I am sorry, Billy, I say, I am in a state and I think you know why –

He looks at me sharply.

I don't, he says, I don't know why.

Poor Billy, I think, such a young face, so earnest – and he doesn't know a thing, it's true.

Let's get on with it, I tell him, but he takes my hand.

I love you, he tells me, I want to go on – like this –

He feels in his pocket for a cigarette but I stop him.

You can do all your smoking later, I say, But we must do this before anyone comes.

It is true. We have been lucky so far – the morning is still empty, the air still. In this deserted place we can have our fire and no one will know about it, but soon there will be action on the river. Or kids will come. Or dogs. Or someone.

So we lay the basket down among the rubble in the burning morning sun. The warmth is on my back and neck.

Oh but it's going to be a real blue dazzler of a day, I say.

Billy grunts.

Paraffin, he says, We have no fuel for it —

Do we need it? Won't matches do?

I don't know how it will burn — I'm afraid of half doing it. I don't want to start what we can't finish —

Is this useful?

I show him the half-bottle of brandy I have in my skirt pocket and he grabs it.

Excellent! he says as he pours it on, Well done, Laura! He will crackle like a Christmas pudding!

Billy can be very crass sometimes.

We put the basket in the middle of the sticks. I try not to look. You can't see the face at all, of course you can't, but still I am afraid to glimpse the place where the hair roots — the pores of his pale skin, the oily tinge, the blood.

The hair which was damp is now fast drying in the sun. What upsets me about it is that it is just like Ewan's hair when he comes from doing his toilet — slightly on end and with a perky little wave in it, before he brushes it back with his mother-of-pearl brushes.

But then it is Ewan's hair.

Then Billy puts a match in it and it changes. It is something worse — something human that was alive and is now burning. Then it goes out. In fact it proves very hard to light at all, smoking a little and then fizzing and then petering out again.

Bury it? I suggest, beginning to panic.

No, look —

Billy grabs my arm as there's a fiercer crackle and a blue flame leaps.

A few minutes later, it's crackling harder and there's a smell of cooking. Brown smoke. Burning pork, grease, fat. My eyes sting.

I get myself behind the wall and vomit till my head hurts.

So I gathered young Margaret on to my hip and took her off on a walk.

A lovely walk, I told her, though I discovered as I stood up again that I could barely stagger, what with my head pounding from lack of food and rest, I tell you it's what we both need – some air, some lovely brown river air –

For a moment we both just breathed it all in. The sky was rosy, the wind hot. Gulls flashed and wheeled in the clammy air. It was a good day.

It was a good day and here I was, with my baby. Or not my baby but whatever it was.

Then, after three steps or so, I had to stop for I almost couldn't believe it – the goodness of it all and the luck and everything that I felt.

And I think what I did was I stopped right there and held her up against my face for a kiss. And she waved her small, fat raggedy arms and cooed at me and I smelled her breath that was pink and clean and moist as a kitten's.

And for a second or two, kissing her madly, I got a glimpse of the world from over the soft and chubby land-scape of her cheek and it seemed to be a sweeter and more awesome place for being seen that way.

I wished it could always have been like this. Me and my baby – everything viewed from a soft and curvy place. I wished it could have stayed like that with my little boy.

You are a real bobby-dazzler, I told her, A beauty and a sweetie and a little love –

And she heard me, I know she did. She grinned and showed her clean wet tongue and then she fidgeted and pounded my stomach with her sharp little feet.

There, there, I told her, though I admit I quite liked the

sensation of being kicked, for it made me feel alive and alert and wonderfully in the way, There there, my love, that's Laura you're kicking –

And though I had previously believed I was tired and miserable, now the energy was coming back to me in bumps and strides. Now I was getting my calm back and my purpose and liveliness. Why, for the first time in as long as I could remember, I felt the rawness of my hunger and my stomach began to growl and the juices trickle.

So was that all it took, then? Just a little child – someone else's child, any child. Just any old small beating heart entrusted to me – a fat wet lip, a tiny snub nose, tight curled fists and bright believing eyes.

Feeling so encouraged, I thought I would give Margaret a guided tour of my landscape. I thought that we two would go everywhere and all around and see all the striking and familiar things I'd certainly have shown my boy if he'd been here to see them. I smiled and I sighed. It was a long time since I'd had a decent sort of companion, someone who would listen and be shown.

Now then, my dear, here's the river, I told her, hoiking her up my shoulder to see, You have a good look at it, the bad old river –

I of course was used to it all – the flat, brown sky and the salt-mud smells, the slide of the shingle beneath my boots – but Margaret was not. And she was just the best, having all the most polite and fervent reactions. She listened and she gurgled and pointed.

Da? she said, Da?

Yes, I said, Da! It's the river, my love – watch out now or it will swallow you up – gulp!

And I made a gobbly gulpy noise and she laughed merrily, so I did it again and she laughed even louder.

Oh, my baby! I said, Aren't you a funny one?

And she carried on watching my face and laughing. She was just like her mother – completely undiscerning and guileless and willing to smile and laugh at just about bloody anything.

But now it was high tide almost and I had to watch my step for my boots were almost falling off my feet, weren't they, and the toe was cracked and had sprung a leak.

Mummy's got to be so-o careful, I told her, Mustn't slip and drop her baby –

I sang and I chatted and I trod carefully, carefully, for I promise you I never meant any harm to Jackie's child. In those days I still had all my limbs of course – both legs fully fit and working – and though I had lost my baby, I was still a healthy and complete person.

And I liked nothing better than to roam along the edge of the water and pass the time of day with the shoremen – or else skip and jaunt among the glinty puddles that are left when the rest flows out to sea.

From time to time during the strange, awful period we were married – and especially while his mother was still alive – Ewan liked to play the doctor with me.

Though he was careful with me during our courtship, hanging back, being sweet, retaining a sense of delicacy and humour, once I had the ring on my finger it all changed. He lost the need to cajole and impress and swiftly became the man/doctor/expert and I the child/patient/receiver of his wisdom.

And with my obvious, drastic disability I was just about the perfect patient too. For, though I was a perfectly game cripple – leaping and hurrying about undaunted on my crutches which were now as ordinary and familiar to me as the bedpost – still in his view there was always difficulty, disability, a series of problems to be tamed and managed, eased and cured.

It began – and ended, I suppose – with the peg. It was the peg that finally drove itself quite literally between us.

To my intense chagrin and frustration, he would insist that every day I strap it on and hobble up and down the dark and shady gravel path in the garden while he watched and shouted stupid, patronising words of encouragement.

Eve, who was too blind to witness my discomfort, would still provide an irksome and sightless audience from an upstairs window where the sinister black shape of her infuriated me just for being there.

And of course she knew it. And of course she carried on doing it for that reason.

Right from the start, I protested. I told Ewan I would rather not do it. I told him I was managing perfectly fine with my crutches.

He told me that this was not a good enough reason to choose not to progress.

Maybe I am progressing in my own way, I told him.

He laughed.

Your way, Laura, it's always your way. Your way would've been to remain on the steps of the workhouse until the next cold winter killed you –

You are a most unfair man, I told him finally when he all but forced me, I should like to see you walk up and down with a leather buckle strapped to the sorest, keenest part of you.

He remained calm and doctorly. He sighed and put his two hands in his pockets and then looked at me in a careful, assessing way, as if he might at any moment take his big, curved surgeon's knife and try and prune another piece off me.

Laura, he said, Believe me, trust me, the pain will lessen as you get used to it. You will have a far happier life if you can accept a prosthesis –

A happy life! I cried – and then I stopped for I could not think what to say next.

That was always the trouble. Ewan never listened and so he always had the power to silence me. However much I moaned and cried at the terrible pain and soreness of it, he remained intent and insistent, never ever paying any attention to my objections and basically playing the bully to perfection.

I swore at him. I cried and cried. I told him I did not want a so-called happy life and I did not want to be a peg leg and I was entirely happy with my crutches.

Finally I refused. Like a horse or a dog, I simply stopped, braced myself.

And for a moment it seemed to be the answer, for he could do nothing. There I sat on the path with my skirts spread around me and I refused to go any further.

He stood there under the swooping shade of the yew and let his hands fall to his sides. He was exasperated but he wasn't going to let me see.

Laura, he murmured, much as if I were indeed a sullen Labrador or wayward colt, Laura, don't be silly, come on –

No, I said and I wrapped my hands protectively around my stump and stuck out my bottom lip and glowered at him like the best bad child, I will be silly. I am silly, Ewan –

Don't let me down now –

I smiled at him, baring my teeth puppy-style.

No, Ewan, I said, I'm not doing it any more. I would rather die. I would rather stay in one place, lie on my back like a beetle and never move again –

When he did not say anything, I pulled up my skirt exposing all my drawers and I unbuckled the stupid thing and chucked it across the path where it fell hard against the brick edging and drove a couple of woodlice from their home.

Then Ewan became angry. His cheeks went white and he chewed the inside of his mouth.

Look, you silly woman, he said, If you employed half as much energy in using the leg as you do in rejecting it, you'd be skipping from here to –

He did not finish his sentence but, in a rush of anger, went to pick up the leg and turned towards me with it and for a nice long moment I thought he was going to hit me. Well, maybe he was – for Ewan could certainly flare up unexpectedly when things did not go his way – but anyway he didn't. He just turned around and headed back to the house.

From here to where? I called after him, From here to the workhouse? Cause that's where I reckon I'll have to go to get away from this bloody torture!

He did not reply or look at me but kept on walking up the path, glancing upwards as he went.

Upwards. Of course. And I followed his glance.

She was there as usual, unseeing, but listening no doubt with her sharp ears. I could not see her face, but there was no escaping the satisfied black shape of her, the total ill-will that was generated by the stiff set of her shoulders and the unmoving long-sufferingness of her puny frame.

I picked up a handful of gravel and flung it as hard as I could at the window, but from where I was sitting I could not ever have thrown it very far. Instead, it hit the foxgloves, whose leaves and blooms it rattled, before thudding with annoying decorum into the silent soil.

Belly

Billy said he was handed in at the foundling hospital at five months old with just the grubby little shirt on his back and some kind of a token but he never knew what.

But what, you mean a token left you by your mother? I cried, However could you not know what it was —?

Oh well, he said without much interest, I don't know, it just got lost over the years —

But when you left the place?

They said they had lost my records — sometimes it happened. I can't say I thought much about it — I mean, I had my apprenticeship to go to — I was well fixed up —

But what? I said, Didn't you care?

He shrugged.

I never really gave it much thought, he said again.

I thought about this and I couldn't help it, hot baffled tears sprung to my eyes.

Well, Billy, they should not have lost the only possession you had, I said, sitting bolt upright in the bed where we had just made love, It was wrong of them. I mean, didn't they take care with such things, wasn't everything written down? Weren't receipts issued, for the children —?

Though I did not say so, I guess I was remembering the big dark room and the fat ledger and the men who seemed to know everything. The blanket that was signed for. The shut doors, the tactful looks, the utmost care.

But Billy laughed.

Oh God, Laura, you have such faith in the systems, he said, They lost things, of course they did – I think you have too high an idea of these places. Maybe you are thinking it was a small place or something, but it wasn't. It was like a big factory. You would be amazed how much was mixed up – papers and such like. And what did it matter who you were? Why, all the children was baptised and given a new name the minute they arrived anyway –

But mums came to claim their babies! I cried – and he clocked me as if to say how do you care to know so much? – There must've been a proper system for knowing who belonged to who?

Belonged? Oh well, probably, he said, But I really wouldn't know. I do remember one or two jammy devils that was collected by their mothers. One time we were brought a piece of cake in honour of it. But most of us – well, what did it matter who we were when we belonged to no one that wanted us?

I was silent. I lay back down. I felt sad and remote. He rolled over and kissed my bare shivery nipples which pointed indignantly up at the ceiling as if they agreed with me.

And many kids died before they could be claimed, he added, Little shrouds in all sizes that came in and out all the time with the laundry. I remember thinking they were well off dead, those kids, for nothing would ever disappoint them any more –

Disappoint them? I said as the gooseflesh chased up and down my arms.

Let them down, Billy said – and the way he said it made a fresh, tight lump come in my heart – Call me a killjoy, Laura, but they was better off dead. They was never wanted in the first place, you know that?

I rolled over and clung to him. I kissed the flesh around his belly button that was hairless and smooth as a little bonny baby's.

I cannot bear it when you say this, I told him as honestly as I dared, You have no idea, Billy, whether you were wanted or not, for you only know your own side of things. Maybe your mum was a child herself. Maybe she was forced to give you up and maybe the separation almost killed her –

As I spoke, I felt the muscles in his belly stiffen and tense. I felt his hands then, rough-moving in my hair, pulling, grasping.

And your baby, Laura, he said flatly and suddenly, The one that you tell me died? What happened to that one? Were you forced to give that one up just as I was given up?

I flushed and was silent. He had surprised me and I did not know what I should say.

Why d'you ask that? I said.

You know why.

Hearing his tone and the coldness and knowingness in it made my heart begin to race.

Don't make me, I said halting, begging.

Don't make you what?

Don't make me say about my baby.

I think I whispered it. I think I spoke the words as small and bowed-down and quiet as I could. For I was very afraid. I knew I could not lie to him about this – for the first time in a long time a lie truly did not seem to be an option.

I am ashamed, I said very quietly and realised as I said it that it was the truth.

There was a terrible, spiky silence in the room and then out of this silence, B.'s voice, painful and sad.

So where's it buried?

He, I said, It was a he –

Where?

In a place – a place I have never been to, I said at last.

What? Billy sounded surprised, You mean – not even back then? Not even at the time?

I sighed a long sigh.

No, Billy, not even at the time.

Why not? he demanded to know, Why haven't you been?

I closed my eyes.

Why?

I don't know, don't ask me –

You do – you do know, Laura, don't lie to me –

I'm not lying. There was just no point, all right?

That's not the reason.

Isn't it?

Laura, his voice was cold, You know it isn't.

Billy, I said, You don't understand. You think you do, that you know about these things, but you don't. It isn't like with your Jack – I mean, there is no grave. They were all – he was –

Buried together?

I said nothing. He paused then, a little more softly, he said, Still Laura, I know you. You would go.

Would I? Yes. Well, maybe I was going to go – intending to, you know, and then, well –

Then what? Billy said.

Time went by, I said flatly.

Billy sighed and moved on to me. He pressed himself against me. Right from the start we had marvelled at how we fitted together – we were perfect, one nakedness against another – a simply, uncannily perfect fit, if you disregarded my missing leg that is.

Now I began to speak – at least I tried to, but he stopped me. He put his hand gently on my mouth and then crammed his fingers in so they pressed on my teeth and my tongue. He ran his mouth and nose over my skin, moistening me with his breath and then breathing me in.

I don't mean to give you a hard time, he said, You know that. But I'm not such a noodle, you know. Your mysterious life. I know there are things you aren't telling me –

I tried to speak again but still he pressed his hand there in my mouth so how could I? He ran his other hand down over my belly and inside my thigh, around the place where the flesh was curtailed and folded over the bone.

I think I know the answer, he said at last.

Mmm, I said.

I think you put your baby in the hospital, he said, Just like my mother did, whatever sort of person she was. Am I right?

I nodded, relieved that he would not let me speak. And as he touched me, my body began to relax – for it was a revelation to me, that even though he had this terrible information, he was continuing to touch me, to want me, to have things to do with me.

After a short time of doing this – and asking me no more questions – he came into me and we gave each other a bit of a shag, though it was briefer and sadder and I must say a great deal less worthwhile than usual.

It gave me little pleasure, but I know I felt great waves

of love for him all the same. That is when you know you love someone – when the feelings in your heart outweigh those others down there.

He slid out of me then and wiped me with a rag – for we still took care not to make a mess on Elsie's bed – and then, as he passed me a fag, I told him the rest.

I might've gone to look at the grave later, I told him, For I do know where it is, but I could not. It was impossible. I spent the following year in Tatum Fields, Billy –

He looked at me lazily and without anger or surprise. My words had stopped – trailed off – even though he had not interrupted me.

You were – what? – in the jug –?

I said nothing.

Oh well, he said slowly, That would be difficult, wouldn't it –?

I raised my eyebrows.

Yes, I was inside. And they don't let you out for tending graves, I pointed out, It's a shame, that, isn't it?

He laughed and so did I.

After a moment, he said, What did they put you in that place for?

I flinched.

I cannot say it even to you, I said.

Ewan's head is not cooking well. The grease keeps on drowning the flame and the smell is unbearable and clings to the back of my throat and now my body is in the rhythm of it I cannot stop the vomiting.

What is it? Billy asks me as, with a certain amount of tenderness, he watches me chuck, Are you up the poke? Are you, Laura?

No, I say, gasping, as nothing but bright lurid yellow is

spat out into the sunlit bindweed and rubble, It is – this – the smell –

Finally I stop and get my breath. My face feels cold, my teeth on edge, the spit in my mouth like iron filings.

Grasping each other's hands like little kids, we turn and look at the bonfire.

We will give it a while longer, says Billy, but he does not look hopeful.

The flesh does not burn to ashes as you might think. It stays like charred meat, like pork that is a little overdone. The sockets of his eyes are almost empty but seem to stare all the more for being so. His teeth are coated in shiny brown from the smoke and the fat.

I stand still and try to swallow down the taste of ash and death and river muck.

It still looks like him, I say.

It doesn't.

I mean, don't you think it still looks too much like a head –?

I don't know.

Well, Billy, to me it does.

I shudder and Billy stares at me.

You are, aren't you?

What?

You're up the poke. I know it –

Maybe, I say at last, Maybe I am, yes.

Whose?

Oh, Billy! I cry, However can you ask? Yours of course! Definitely yours.

Well – good then, he says, but he looks very startled and unsure.

There's a funny, shy silence as we listen to the river lapping. I want to give him a good big hug, but I cannot.

I feel thin and sad and insubstantial. I hold my hands up to the yellow sunlight and I can almost see through them – yes, I can. Where are you going, Laura Blundy?

Oh, I know what it is. I am beginning to be sad because the adventure is almost over. Soon all of this will be gone. Whether or not Ewan burns, whether or not I am found out, I think that very soon I will have to leave my dear love all over again. Don't make me, oh please don't make me!

So what'll we do? I say.

About him?

Of course about him. He'll be found. We're buggered now, aren't we – well, aren't we, eh, Billy?

Strong language from you, Laura –

Well, we are, aren't we?

Shh, he says, Shut up a moment, darling, and let me think.

He thinks for a minute – the thoughts all go ticking over his face and oh he is so good when he thinks! I relish the side of his face – frank and shadowy when seen in relief – as he magics up a plan that might be best for us to do.

No plan, I think, can keep us together. Not when there are his precious babbies to think of.

After a moment he lets all his breath out in a rush as if he's done it, he's thought. He fixes his calm black eyes on me.

I guess we'll have to run, he says, You know, to France or somewhere like that?

My heart jumps.

What? Just as I always wanted? Just as I said in the first place?

He looks at me and his eyes are so sad and deep.

Yes, Laura, he says, Just like that.

Stay together?

I reckon so, don't you?

And now he smiles. Just a small one. Just the smallest smile for me.

Oh, Billy! I say, jumping up and down for I can't quite believe it, Oh, Billy, yes! But I thought – what about your kids, your family?

His face darkens for a second as he stares at Ewan's smouldering head.

I can't walk away from you, Laura. I don't know how to do it. I love you in the strangest way. How did you do it? How did you get in here –?

He does not point to his heart but his stomach, the deep hard core of him – the part that shuddered when he took his first breath and that will be still and calm when he takes his last.

I smile even though my face is wet with tears. When I speak my voice comes out soft and faraway.

I don't know what you mean, I say, You know I don't, Billy – all these things you say, they make no sense to me. All I know is – well, the feeling that has kept me going –

He looks at me as if he doesn't believe me. As if he doesn't mind. I get the feeling he has made his choice. None of this matters any more.

I never killed Ewan, I tell him, I never did all that, you know that, don't you?

He nods.

It never happened –

I know it didn't, he says, Ewan is fine, that's for certain, Laura –

He thinks a moment.

Then what have we been –? he says suddenly, running out of words for what we have been doing.

We did what we had to do, I tell him firmly as I stretch

out my wavery small hand and feel for his, We have been in it together – this time has passed with us together – you know that, Billy my love –

We both look at the bonfire which has gone out now. Only grey-white ashes, edged with the deep bright remembered end of a flame.

France, then? he says.

I watch his face closely to see if he means it and he does. I clap my hands together for joy.

We'll be together and you'll continue to haunt me, he says in a voice that is suddenly heavy and sad.

Billy – I begin.

I mean it. I have no power over it – any of this –

But you are choosing –?

Yes, I'm choosing.

You love me?

He shivers and hugs his coat around him.

You are a frigging nuisance but – yes, so much, Laura, so –

Shh, I say, putting my arms right around him, round and around, making them fit for ever, I love you too.

And so we are to have a happy ending, Billy and me.

He is still smiling as I fold him in my arms. Still smiling as, trying to ignore the harsh brown wind off the river that blows the clean crackle of smoke straight in our happy smiling faces, I put my face in his soft and dirty boy's hair.

And it doesn't actually matter any more whose baby is whose and who's burning who, or why or when or how exactly.

No, all that matters, all that is real is this: that pretty soon him and me will be in a tight, rented bed together and smoking into chipped, rented ashtrays and looking out at a cold grey borrowed sea.

And we will be waiting for the boat that will take us to an unlikely place we've never been, never expected to go, and will probably never manage to come back from ever and yet, in this strange, haphazard and largely impermanent world, who cares a fig about that?

So I was sitting on the steps of St Giles in a light mizzling rain and it was the second day of having Margaret and I was getting so used to her – the smell and small weight of her, the mix of sleep and laugh and cry.

This is his blanket, I said, for hadn't I been telling her all about my dear little boy? It is wool as you can see and once upon a time it was a lovely deep pinkish colour. It also used to have ribbon stitched around it, but I imagine he picked it off, the little terror –

Margaret watched my face.

You're not having it, I told her quickly – though, to be fair, she had not asked for it.

After some time I realised she was wet so I took her to the tap where I rinsed the split of her that was hid under her dress and – once I'd soothed her fussing and crying – I hung the rag she wore on her bum out to dry in the wind.

I dried her by wrapping her in my own grimy skirts and I thought what a heartbreaking picture we must make, mother and daughter, even though her skin was a whole notch muskier than mine, but all the same.

After that we occupied ourselves in watching the people go by – most of them children sore-eyed like my baby girl but well-fed and the women hatless. And then when we got bored of that, we turned to watch the chalk dredgers chugging along the river with their funnels painted red and yellow, everything getting better and better.

I tried and tried to make Margaret look but her poor rheumy eyes would keep on shutting in the wind. It was a shame for she missed a great deal and I told her so, but she was having none of it and kept them shut.

All right, I told her, Have it your way.

I thought it was very sad that she wasn't seeing what I could see. From this place you could look out towards the shot tower, the iron foundry, the City Bicycle School. And down below there was always the river, flowing greasy and noiseless and wedged between its two useless banks in the sun.

After a while, she went to sleep on me.

Or at least she let her eyes fall slowly shut and then she opened them again with brief butterfly smoothness, but I could tell she was already slumbering and the eyes were just pretending to look when in fact they were staring blackly at nothing at all which I suppose is why they fell shut again.

Shut and floating back into sleep.

The one terrible thought, the one big bother that has stayed with me all this time like a glove over my heart even now and which kept stopping my breath on that day with Margaret was this: the idea that my boy might have died all alone.

Did he die alone please, sir?

I knew I had asked the question on that day, but I had not remembered the answer. I had been too distraught to listen or to grasp the important facts. Now I was furious at my sloppiness. Was I so uncaring? How could I have been so stupid and had so little of my wits about me? I should've paid attention and listened. I should have known it was a question that could never be asked again.

This gap in my knowledge of my own child's fate vexed me terribly. It ate me up. It was the last thing I thought of as I fell to sleep and the first that wandered uneasily across my mind on waking.

Did he die alone please, sir?

And I watched Margaret's tight-bud mouth – so delicately, placidly shut – and I thought yes, she has the look of her mum, a mix of certainty and stupidity and plain surprise. And then I was shocked at the pure blind jealousy I felt, that my baby boy was gone and here was Margaret. That he was nowhere and she was with me.

Just to see what happened, I tried pressing my two fingers against her perfect nostrils, stopping her breath. I wanted to see if her mouth knew to open again. After a moment of her breath being stopped, it did, so I took my fingers away. She carried on breathing. I was so relieved she knew how to carry on. I hugged her close and kissed her all over her sleeping face. Thank you, Margaret, I said, Thank you, my darling, my precious little one –

And then, just to be certain, I tried it again.

Later, when she was quite cold in my arms, we went for another of our long walks.

She was very quiet now, much easier to carry, just slung over my shoulder any old how. If only, I thought, babies could always be like this. Gone was the struggle and the sudden shifts and gasps that they always do when they fight against sleep.

I sang a song to her, I don't remember what, a happy one I'm sure.

I picked up my skirts and we went wandering down the

shadowy alleys along the river, with their narrow uneven cobbles and damp doorways and falling broken chimney pots. There we saw bright pots of geraniums and a lot of women wandering, like me, without hats – as well as a crowd of dirty children kicking around the street with bare feet and runny noses.

I shouted out for them to mind the glass, for as usual there were great piles of broken bottles everywhere, but none of them took the tiniest bit of notice and they probably cut their feet to shreds. If they did, they deserved to do so, for they should have listened to a stranger's well-meant advice.

And I thought, if only they knew, if only they realised that I am quite used to children and very good with them. I am far more sensible than most of the mothers I know, who would rather stop and gawp at a pretty trimmed hat in a shop window than notice that their child is about to go under a hansom cab in the road.

Many a child I have plucked from under the wheels of a cab, I know I have – in my life, in my dreams and in my time.

And now here's a funny thing: Buckridge's the grocer's had a sign up saying 'Easiest of Easy Terms' and, though I'd seen it a million times before, something about this sign attracted me that day and I went over and sat on the ironwork bench that was underneath it.

And it was right there that I sat and stayed cuddling the dead-cold infant and waiting for Jackie to find me which she did eventually after some searching. Followed, a little time later, by the police.

Baby

What you have to understand is that it is no easy matter to get a young baby into the foundling hospital for you have to provide all manner of proof and evidence and be interviewed over a period of consecutive days by a full-blown committee of men with grey forbidding whiskers who are out to get you basically.

They want to keep you out for places are short and must be kept for the truly deserving. It is only the mothers who really, really care – the mothers of children whose conception can be proved to be entirely unfortunate and blameless – who succeed in giving up their children to it.

At first they laughed. They said that the chances of me getting him in there were frankly remote. But when I convinced them that my good faith had been be-trayed and especially when I had a friend of my aunt's come forward and testify that I had always been of good character and hard-working and blameless and that it was only the misfortune of a mischievous Will that had knocked me into the streets in the first place, then they relented.

They said it was all right to bring him at seven in the morning on the very next day and that if I knocked on the big doors I could hand him over right there and then and they would give me a written receipt for him. As simple as that.

Well, that night I lay on a pallet in the workhouse with my baby boy and held and touched and fed him a little for the last time.

With a tight upset heart, I ran through it all in my mind – what I was going to do and how and why. The why was especially important. Because it was the best thing for him and the best for everyone, I knew that, for I had recited it till I had it lodged like a piece of hardness in my soul. Because it was what I wanted for him, because I loved him madly.

I told myself I was happy for him, but I did wish the tears would stop falling out of my eyes. I wished my teeth did not chatter and I wished the touching of him did not cut me to the heart.

All that night, in all those last hours, I never once took my hands off him. When his lips had finally parted and let go of my breast, I moved my fingers slowly over every bit of his small body, remembering the whole self of him, committing it to memory, learning it by heart.

I felt the slender curve of his back which had ever since his birth been covered in the most delectable fine black hairs like a baby monkey's back. For the very last time I stroked the warm nape of his neck where a fuzz of hair bloomed and where I liked to put my face when I was cold or sad or angry.

I touched his thighs, the small skinny bum that sloped away to nothing, the long slender feet that would one day carry him all over the Earth – or certainly all over London if he lived to be that curious and healthy.

In my own hands I held his two small ones whose perfect

shape I knew better than my own. I ran my finger pads along the soft, bendy rim of his nails, squeezed the warm palms, smelled the clean cheese smell of the inside crook of his littlest finger.

I explained everything carefully to him.

Even though I knew he could not understand or make use of the words, I told him that I had tried my best to keep him, but that I could not afford to work and look after him at the same time. In the workhouse, where we had ended up, he was getting poorlier and poorlier. He knew that, didn't he? He knew that he had nearly died of the diphtheria? Babies died in the workhouse all the time, so many of them and so fast that no one seemed to notice.

But in the hospital he would be well looked after and fed and clothed and taught to read and write. Babies, I was told, entered the hospital all skinny and sad and came out as men with their chins up and their futures rosy and firm.

I told him that all through his life, I would always call for news of him. On every single one of his birthdays I would bless him and cry for him. I would never stop asking after him and in my heart I would be watching out for him –

Wherever you are, I said, I will be with you. And you will grow to a big, strong happy man and then if I'm still alive I'll find you – I will, my darling, it is a promise. I will find you –

My baby did not cry or laugh or make a single noise. He just looked at me as if he would never stop looking. There was a bluish film of my milk still on his lower lip. I did not want to feed him again though I ached to do so, for he must get used to going without. He put his thumb in his mouth and held his wool blanket and looked at me.

He was very calm and quiet. He did not go to sleep, nor

did he fret or cry, but – with his thumb in his mouth and his blanket pressed against his nose – he kept his dark eyes fixed on my face. He checked and studied me as I did him: every curve and wrinkle and tear and frown. And I was glad to smell his breath on me – the cool, milky breath of my baby that would not come my way again.

I had intended not to sleep. I so did not want to waste my final night with him, but I must've. For one moment it was dark and silent and the next there was a soaring blue sky through the topmost panes of the room and I could hear the treadmill starting up.

I watched him sleep for half an hour. His eyes were tight shut and his mouth open, the thumb still wet in the air with a shiny string of saliva still on it and his precious favourite blanket pressed hotly on his cheek.

An hour later, having made our way there, I opened my arms in the stuffy dark room and let them take him from me. He let go easily. I felt him letting go. I did not look at his face though I know he turned to look at me. He made no noise, barely a sigh. He was a good boy. That was the last time.

I did not look.

I thought I killed a little girl, I told Billy as we pulled Elsie's rough coverlet over us, But it turned out well, you see – it turned out I did not –

I waited, but he said nothing, though he did not turn away from me but kept his hands on me, his two hands on the stump of my leg where it had been cut all those many months ago.

I shivered.

Did you hear me? I said sharply, I said it was all well and good in the end –

He looked at me. He looked into my face as if it was a baffling and unreadable thing.

Billy? I cried.

I'm here – he pressed me against him, I'm here –

I think he was weeping. He was looking at me and then he could not look at me and I thought I heard the catch of tears, but maybe it wasn't. Maybe I didn't.

I did not do it! I said again.

Billy looked at my face which was between his two hands. He was not crying, his eyes were just watery, that's all.

You did not do it? he said, So how could you think you did it, Laura? What do you mean?

I could not speak.

What are you saying, my love? That you were put in the prison for murdering a little child?

I stiffened at his words.

Oh no! I said, Not that – I was only in a brief while. After the silent time in the cells, they put me in the laundry to work –

Then, said Billy, You mean you were tried –

It was chucked out –

And they let you out?

That's it, I said and I let rip a plain sigh of relief as he got it, Yes, I thought it was what I did that killed her, but I hadn't. It wasn't. I hadn't done it –

What? said Billy, What hadn't you done, Laura?

I shut my eyes.

What? he said again.

I do not know, I said, None of it.

You don't know? Billy said, You thought you killed someone but you don't know –?

She was such a dear little girl, I told him, And Jackie swore to them it was I who did it, but then they discovered that every single one of her babies had died, one after the other, all dosed up with laudanum –

And you believed her. You thought it was you?

I did, I said, nodding to him and trembling at the memory of Jackie's face, Yes.

But why did they think –?

I told them, Billy, I told them it was me who did it. I told them straightaway, so that Jackie could know precisely who to hate –

Billy touched my cheek where the tear was falling down so fast I couldn't stop it.

But – Laura – why?

I try to think of why, but only the sadness of it comes rolling into my head.

I had killed my boy, I said, And then I reckoned I had killed a girl. Two babies. Why should I not have done both?

Laura, said Billy, My darling girl. You have killed no one, not ever –

I looked at him lying there in Elsie's bed with me and all the sympathy bursting out of his sweet face.

Don't make me think of it, I told him, I can't think of it. I have not thought of it in all these years –

I pushed more heaped-up tears from my eyes and took a breath. I shut my eyes again but straightaway pictures of Margaret came, so I had to open them again.

After Dorcas was hanged, I thought I would go mad in the jail. I could not think or breathe or find any space in the room in my head. But soon it became quite normal to stare into blackness.

I was left alone with my ideas and though at first these thoughts – Margaret, the brown river, the dizzying confusion of the court – terrified me, soon those pictures receded and I found to my joy that the darkness made it easier to be with him.

And then – oh my God – really and truly, he came to me.

At first I held my breath, for the sober part of me knew it was impossible. But slowly, in the darkness, or out of it, he came back to me – at first just a smile or a finger or a memory of some special softness. Occasionally a chuckle, or a sensation of wetness – the salt smell of just before I cleaned him.

But then I woke one night and saw there was light in the room. Soft and grey, a lightness that broke up the dark and should not have been there.

There was no mistaking it this time. Now I felt the quickness of his pulse, his breath on my cheek. I was not afraid.

I called his name, softly and secretly, so as not to rouse the turnkey.

There was a small sob in the darkness. I put out my arms.

Are you there? Are you?

I saw and heard nothing but I felt love all around me. I felt glad and happy and warm. I felt my bones relax and my heart lift.

Where are you? I cried, My love, where are you?

He climbed – yes, climbed, even though he was no more than a babby! – into the bed with me and I felt the fidgety heat of him and straightaway I slept.

And in the morning – gone, nothing.

Yet in the morning was also a whole different story, for everything had miraculously lightened and brightened – as if the veil had lifted, though it remained in fact as thick and dark as ever.

But forget light. Now I longed for the darkness to continue. I begged for night, for black, for silence. For now if I sat very still with my hands folded in my lap and my eyes closed, he would come to me.

Always. Without fail. My baby coming.

And I let him.

Sometimes I wondered how exactly it was happening and who was doing it, God or the Devil? But if it turned out to be the latter, then I would have preferred not to know. Better to stay in the perfect sweet blameless dark and have it carry on.

Better to shut up and hold my breath while my baby came closer. And closer. Better to be able to see and touch and snuggle him.

Better to give in to whatever it was and to enjoy the hot tight fit of my body against his, for hadn't we always fitted together perfectly, and didn't I just know that we always would?

Billy

I did not tell Billy I was going to Goad's Place to look for my baby. I did not tell anyone. I certainly was not going to tell Ewan, who was still intent on burdening me that way himself.

But finally, now, after all these years of thinking I would not do it and avoiding his spirit, I knew I must. Even if my heart burst with the hurt of it, I must claim him. I knew I must sit on a stone and look at the black knitted-up ground and know the full truth: that my baby was buried down in there under all that still, dark earth.

It was a blazing morning, but there had been a storm in the night and the long grass in the churchyard was still soaked and flattened and the smell in the air was of peppery damp and rain. It was a surprisingly peaceful place, and I thought that it would not be so bad to find him there.

I moved slowly up the overgrown path, for my crutches kept catching annoyingly in the bindweed and thick greenery. Under the spreading darkness of the yew, I stopped and looked around me. It may have been peaceful, but some degree of peace came from the air of neglect and silence. No one came here any more. Whoever lay here was long forgotten. Many of the oldest gravestones were clothed in a wilderness of weeds and suckers.

I moved on.

Spiderwebs daubed with wet hung undisturbed between the stalks of a thousand complicated plants and pale fraying petals were eaten up by snails and even the nettles seemed to have lost heart and given themselves up willingly to be crushed and tangled.

You could tell that no one got married or buried here any more for even the church had fallen into disrepair with slates jutting off the roof and the lead stripped from the windows which were smashed in parts where looters had no doubt tried to climb in.

As I moved through the dog rose, lichen and cow-parsley and whatever, the hem of my skirt was already soaking and my heart was beating painfully and hard. At first I thought it was from anxiety – the terrible importance I had put on the finding of him – but then came another wave of sensation that entirely surprised me.

It was disappointment. Disappointment and let-down. Along with the feeling that this was not after all such a bad place – lonely, but calm and safe – came another, more bruising certainty. The certainty that I had come to the wrong place.

Baby, where are you?

I sat down on a piece of granite that had come off a grave and looked around me. I knew he must be here under the ground, so I ignored my heart and struggled to relax and feel his presence. But all I heard was the hum of bees dipping in and out of the weeds and the faraway sound of labourers' carts in the street.

And even though I said some things to him – endearments spoken enticingly into the flimsy air – still my voice trailed off, embarrassed. I almost laughed. He was not here. He was not buried in this place and there must have been some mistake, for nothing had ever been clearer to me or more certain.

I began to cry. They were tears of disappointment. If not here, then where?

I had brought a bunch of black-eyed Susan to lay there – stems clutched so tight that my palms turned green – but now I let them drop in my lap. What was the point?

Well, I sat for a long time. Insects moved furiously through the livid grass and the heat was thick and sullen. In a few minutes the sun would be high and the shadows would diminish and dissolve.

But why should I care? There was no child of mine buried there nor had there ever been.

I wiped my eyes and laid my flowers in the crook of an old fat tree and left.

That night as I lay in bed next to Ewan, something woke me. It wasn't a dream, it was this:

It was that I saw the plot at Goad's Place very clearly – not as it was now, but as it must have once been: dug and planted in a dutiful way, with neat rows of stones and cut grass and even a gravel path that twisted off towards the church.

And in among all this unholy neatness was my boy – yes him, just as sweet and certain as I remember him, skinny and dark-eyed, clutching his blanket to him and calling to me.

My darling.

In a second I was alert, trained on him. My heart dipped and my body tensed, straining to where I thought he was. Come. Get. Have. Need.

Where are you?

Not here, Mumma, he called in a voice that I had never

heard for he had not grown it when I last saw him.

I know that, I whispered back to him, full of pain and panicking so much that he would slip away again, But where? Please, where are you?

He moved his hands.

Here, he said, Me – with you –

Yes, I cried, trying to control my upsetness, But where? Where did they put you, my darling?

With you, he said.

Tears sprang to my eyes, for I did not understand him, not at all and it would not do – such vagueness.

No. Not with me –

Yes. With you.

Oh, tell me where you are, my love, I said again, Don't you see? If I know where you are, then I can come to you –

With you, he whispered and now like me he was beginning to cry, I am with you already – always – with you –

Oh God, I cried, You say that, but what use is it when I can't feel you anywhere at all?

I felt very sad then, for I knew that, despite all my searching, it was no good at all, I would never find him, never know for sure where he lay.

I think I laid my head in my hands and wept.

You have found me, he said – and his eyes were so sad and dark, just as I remembered them, You've already found me, Laura, I'm with you –

It's a lie, I whispered as the sight of him left me and I sat up in the bed with tears on my cheeks, Don't say it, it's a terrible lie.

And I thought how the love you carry in your heart as a mother ought to be enough – it ought to be but it really is not. And they do, they lie to you, that you will be free.

But the truth is you carry a child in you and it seeps into your bones and infects you for ever and you spend the rest of your life trying to get it back: that fierce weight and delicious heat, that sweet, sudden flesh-touch of the life inside.

It is amazing really that Ewan did not wake, for I got right up out of the bed and I threw up the window and for the first time in more years than I could remember I called out his name.

Billy! I cried, Don't go! I am here! I am your mother and I love you, I love you, I love you. Tell me where you are so I can come to you!

I pushed my boy out on hands and knees under an old tarpaulin down by the river. I knew he was coming, for I had a burning in my back and thighs and I could not control myself, I had to let him come.

He slipped out quite easily for he was terribly little – the thinnest and the smallest, certainly not full-grown. He came out with a thick bubble of water all around him. Born in a caul. Supposed to be lucky or so they say but, given how things turned out, I guess it was not so good either for him or for me.

Like a mother cat I bit it open with my teeth and the water spilled all around me over my legs and knees. It shrivelled to a see-through sack as out came my boy. Him. He had the blackest eyes and a startling, shrimpy penis, pale and bloodless. It was the first time I had seen one. I could not help staring.

He looked at me too. He took a breath and he wailed and I laughed with joy and relief because it meant he was alive. I held him against me and straightaway he found my nipple and sucked. I smiled. I could see no milk but he was getting something. It was the strangest feeling, to give a part of my body to someone else.

A few minutes later another thing came out of me, brown and slippery like a chunk of meat. I dug a hole for it in the sand and buried it. I put the caul in, too. When the tide rose the brown water lapped and frothed over the little grave and my boy and I moved away clear of the water and we went to sleep under an old whelker.

At Shanklin Court it is a normal Saturday, with dull skies and a sharpish wind. The early sun, that had looked so pure when Cally wakened to feed the babby and the ex-babby in the early morning, seems to have slid away and muddied itself before the rest of the world was up.

She – your wife – is rubbing lard on Lulu's chest to soothe the troublesome cough that has kept the family awake all night and Pinny – dependable Pinny! – has been set to stringing up some empty red and yellow cocoa tins in the window, to catch the light and give the babbies something to look at.

Pinny knows you haven't slept in your bed, for she went in just now to find Arthur kicking and clamouring in there. Lucky he was tied to the bedpost or he could have done himself some harm. Arthur is strong as a ten-year-old and with the appetite of a horse.

Pinny left Arthur tied, but she rubbed his ankles that were cut and sore. She did not tell her mother that you weren't there. Why should she? She is your friend and anyway, there are plenty of things Pinny knows – plenty that she keeps from plenty of people.

And so life goes on. You won't come today, nor the next day, nor the next. If Cally manages to go out early to the market, there is a chance she will have saved enough to get you a sausage.

Normally you would be well pleased. Life at Shanklin Court is so thin and thrifty that a sausage is a bit of an event. The smell lingers for days – in your hair, in your clothes, even on the street. The neighbours notice.

But you won't be coming home for your tea. They won't pull out your old half-broke chair so you can put your feet up and watch Cally wash the baby in the copper.

In the water, baby Dora might happen to shit herself with the pure pleasure of it and if it is one of those times, then Cally will swear and curse and have to cope with all those mucky bits floating around. But one thing is certain, you won't be around to see it.

At first Cally won't be very vexed with you. She'll curse you for leaving her alone all night, but she'll think you've gone off with one of your mates, for it isn't in her nature to be suspicious. She is ever so good-natured. And besides, she is a busy woman and family life is like this: aggravating and messy and a little unpredictable. Love – and the knowledge that everyone else lucky enough to live beyond babyhood has it just as bad – sees most of us through.

But you aren't with your mates.

You won't watch Cally wrap Dora's bottom in a piece of rag and think for the hundredth time how shrunken and insubstantial she is compared to me, your Laura – how aloof and yet familiar, how prematurely grey-haired.

You'll be in another place with your two hands on my body and a jolt of love in your heart. You are escaping to be with me, your love. You'll have convinced yourself that you aren't needed here at home. The street will rally round. Cally will always find bread to put in the babbies' mouths.

The days, you will tell yourself, will still unravel perfectly well without you.

Well, the sun is up and it's a bright, windy morning. Someone ought to go and get Arthur up. Arthur is easy to forget about. Even his noise is absorbed by the house. Not like little Jack, who would have been at the window right now, watching out for the dustman's horse.

Cally begins to nurse the baby who must come before all of them.

If you were here, Pinny would come over and wrap her arms around your neck and you'd breathe in the faint, exciting dirtiness of her.

She would remind you of what you already know: that your heart has been haunted well and truly, that there are things going on in your head that no one – not God or your boss or fat books or even a policeman – could explain.

If you were here you would laugh at her. But the laugh would be shaky and sad and she would notice that.

Going out later? she'd ask you, looking carefully for your answer.

Might be, you'd say, But not with you, my girl –

Oh but she mightn't take that too kindly. She'd straddle your knee and you'd flinch at the brief, bony hardness of her groin.

Why? you'd say, Where d'you want to go?

Maybe she'd bite her lip and say, Oh, nowhere really, Billy, I just thought we'd go for a blow in the street. You know, just you an' me –

You might hesitate a moment. Touch her hair. God knows why, but you love your girl.

And Cally, pressing her bubby into the wet, gasping mouth of Dora, would look up with pretend impatience and say, Oh, run along the two of you if you want to go –

That's what used to be good about Cally. That she is willing to keep it light – to pretend that life is easy as that. Easy as walking down the stairs.

But you won't go.

You won't take Pinny out to see the dredgers going up and down the river. Nor will you point out to her where the new sewers are going to be, and tell her about the electric lighting and the underground railway.

And that sausage – being got out of its paper and put in the pan even now at this very moment – will not ever be relished by you. You won't watch the skin catching light, the juices spurting – or notice the satisfied sigh of flesh relaxing as it cooks.

All the way.

All the way in the train to Folkestone, Billy holds my hand. Holds it, but. But I am fading fast. Can barely feel his touch.

I look at my hand in his, his hand in mine, and I don't know what to do. I want to touch him and I don't. I don't know how to look at him any more.

Am I gone yet already?

Light flashes at the windows, then a spatter of rain, then light again. My eyes burn. I am trying to see what he sees, trying to remember.

The fields and cottages rush past. Horses. Clouds. Other things I can't name.

Laura –

What?

Nothing.

Billy squeezes my hand. I don't feel it. The child inside turns over quickly in its sleep.

*

It was the strangest thing, to be back in there behind those doors. Everything a bit smaller than I remembered, and lighter. New windows perhaps? Someone bothering these days to put flowers on the table.

All I want, I told the youngish man who came out frowning when I pressed the bell, Is to know where my child was buried – I want to know exactly where, the cemetery, the plot, where I can go and find it after all these years –

He looked at me carefully. He still frowned, but it wasn't out of unfriendliness. I think it was his way of being helpful.

I did not mention Goad's Place. I thought it better not to. I thought I would see what he came up with. Then I would know.

It will be hard to be exact, he said as he tried to work out how much I knew, It will not be a – a single grave –

I know that, I said.

It is a long time ago, he said, sighing heavily when I told him the date.

Please, I said, trying not to let my voice go desperate, Just tell me where.

In another room, a bird – a parakeet or something – was making a terrible noise, squawking and banging in a cage. He kept turning his head towards it.

I'll have to go and cover him, he said, Will you excuse me?

I walked up and down the room. Outside in the street was a lot of noise, a lot of coming and going in the square. So much traffic. It was a long time ago that I had last been there.

Twenty-one years, he said, coming back into the room, I will have to go to a totally different cupboard –

Thank you, I said, Did you cover the bird?

I did. Don't thank me yet. Let's see if we can get any-where first, eh?

What sort is it?

The bird? It is some sort of a parrot, he said, I don't know what it's doing here. It was left outside. We are not a home for birds –

He was very young and guarded. His face kept jumping all over the place out of nerves. I wondered how long he had had the job. He was like one of Ewan's students – trying to please and hating himself at the same time for doing so.

Carefully, he wrote my name and the date and the name of the child on a pad of paper and he disappeared into another room for some time.

I waited and looked at things.

I looked at the door and the wall and the flowers. I saw the laburnum waving its yellow fingers outside the window, and the sycamore. I thought that those trees would have been there on that day that I stood in this room and was told the news, but I did not remember them. It was like something someone else had told me happened. I did not remember much of it for myself.

He came back in, still frowning. The look on his face was not a surprise to me.

I'm sorry, he said, Only I don't quite know how to – well, this is very odd indeed. I think I'd better –

What? I said, though I knew already.

Can I check the names and dates again? he said.

Our bed is high up and the view is mostly of the sea. It is the grey sea and the grey sky with the clouds piled up so high they are about to float off the top of the world.

It would be wonderful, wouldn't it, I said to him, If they could?

You have some odd little fancies, don't you? he said.

This is very unusual and really rather unforgivable, the young man told me with real consternation.

Maybe it was his first such problem. His face was flaming as if it was all his doing.

It's a big place, he said, There are always mix-ups, that much I do know. Think of it. In that period, many files were lost. You'd be surprised how many – but this one is, well, as I say, pretty unforgivable –

I stood silent. In the next room you could still hear the parrot's muffled banging.

Still, he said after a moment, It could be worse after all – I mean, he could be –

Could be dead?

He nodded.

You can find him easily, he said, We still have all the papers. I will have them pulled out for you. A cause for celebration, wouldn't you say?

I gazed at him without surprise or anger. My boy. All those years gone. A celebration. Everything up in smoke. The journey away from here, to France.

They even gave me his blanket, I said dully, How do you think he managed without it?

The young man blinked. You could tell he had used up all his words.

I didn't tell Billy a thing, not a single thing. Why ruin a life when you won't be there to lend help or comfort or see how it all turns out?

If we are to be together we must stay exactly as we are. Lip on lip. Limb on limb.

All our lives have been leading to this – me and him and the sea which could take us anywhere.

And Pinny was right. I lie, just as she guessed, in Mawbey Place.

Ewan chose it, for the obvious proximity to home, because it's pretty and well-tended, because Eve is buried there. I don't mind. I am on the other side from her, under the black spreading yew. It is cool here, dark. My spirit is loose, unguarded – I go anywhere I please.

After they pulled me from the river, Ewan spoke to the police and signed papers to say I was not a suicide. I was lucky. If not for him, I would have gone in unholy ground. Would I have minded? Well, what do you think?

Still it is a peaceful place, the earth dark, the air tawny and cold. Some of the stones are so old and falling over that the names have been wiped, dissolved to nothing.

Others are sad and fresh with bright cut flowers and luminous white gravel – old men's inevitable graves and babies' sudden ones, newly visited and cried over and freshly turned.

I know what will happen next.

One of these days she will come by again on her way to somewhere – or maybe not going anywhere, maybe just running around as you told me she liked to do. And out of habit, she will grab on to the black railings and peer through into the long grass and shadows.

This is the place, she'll think to herself, This is where I saw her name carved clear as anything –

And she'll see the grave – not so fresh and dark any

more – again and it will give her a shivery feeling, a feeling she can't describe or name. And she'll think of how long you've been gone and she'll whisper a little and hum to herself, to keep away the bad spirits.

You never believed her, did you? You thought: what on earth is she talking about? For she's bright as a button, Pinny is, but too fanciful for her own good – so many bunches of ideas all sprawling together in her head, you could never keep up. In fact you didn't bother. Men would sort her out, you knew that. Boys and men courting.

Well, she already has the buds of breasts. And there's even a particular store that she won't run errands to without first tying a scrap of ribbon in her hair. It is happening already and you aren't around to see it.

Pinny will stare through the thick evening air. Stare at my grave. Then she will notice the man who's standing there gazing thoughtfully and soberly into nowhere right there by my stone.

She'll notice him because of his hair. She'll think she's never seen such amazingly bright red hair. She'll think it belongs in a circus, hair like that.

Which will make her think that she saw the circus once with you. You took her there when she was younger and she saw a sea lion – a slippery honking dog-thing with a ruff around its neck. She looked and looked at it till it lumbered back behind the curtain. She has never forgotten its pitiful, going-away noise.

You aren't there any more, to take her places. Sometimes since you went, she cries and cries.

No, I didn't tell you a thing, not a single thing. Why? Why ruin a life that was going along very nicely?

I needed you, Billy. How long do you think I'd been

searching for you? Was I really going to let you go again? I need you, my darling, but you don't need me. That's why it's dangerous – that's the way it always is. How it will always be.

They infect you, children do. They get in your bones. Is love ever enough? Is it? Love. You know the answer to that. For heaven's sake. We all do.

Now I will give you comfort, my baby. I gave you some once and now I will give it again. All our lives have been leading to this. Don't feel sorry for me, I have what I want. Even if it took a hundred years, it was worth it – worth it to hold you again. Worth it to love you madly. Worth it to let you go.

Author's Note

I could not have written *Laura Blundy* without the insights and information provided by several books. They are:

Round About a Pound a Week by Maud Pember Reeves (Virago, 1979)
The Streets of London – The Booth Notebooks (Deptford Forum Publishing Ltd, 1997)
Love in the Time of Victoria by Françoise Barret-Ducrocq (Penguin, 1992)
The Great Stink of London – Sir Joseph Bazalgette and the Cleansing of the London Metropolis by Stephen Halliday (Sutton, 1999)
Coping with Limb Loss by Ellen Winchell (Avery, 1995)

I hope the authors will forgive me for plundering their work for facts which I then ruthlessly distorted to suit my own needs.

Finally I want to thank Felicity Horada at The Old Operating Theatre in the Herb Garret of St Thomas' Church in Southwark. One memorable wintry afternoon as the light drained away, she vividly re-enacted a Victorian amputation. It inspired me more than I can say.

About the Author

Julie Myerson was born in Nottingham, England, in 1960. She is the author of three previous novels, *Sleepwalking, The Touch,* and *Me and the Fat Man.* Her work has been translated into many languages. She lives in London.